Grounds for Murder

BETTY TERNIER DANIELS

Grounds FOR Murder

A JEANNIE WOLFERT-LANG MYSTERY

Published by ECW Press
665 Gerrard Street East
Toronto, Ontario, Canada M4M 1Y2
416-694-3348 / info@ecwpress.com

Cover artwork and design: Ashley Santoro

LIBRARY AND ARCHIVES CANADA CATALOGUING IN PUBLICATION

Title: Grounds for murder : a Jeannie Wolfert-Lang mystery / Betty Ternier Daniels.

Names: Daniels, Betty Ternier, author.

Description: Series statement: The Jeannie Wolfert-Lang mysteries ; 1

Identifiers: Canadiana (print) 20240399196 | Canadiana (ebook) 20240399226

ISBN 978-1-77041-780-9 (softcover)
ISBN 978-1-77852-332-8 (ePub)
ISBN 978-1-77852-333-5 (PDF)

Subjects: LCGFT: Novels. | LCGFT: Detective and mystery fiction.

Classification: LCC PS8607.A55668 G76 2024 | DDC C813/.6—dc23

This book is funded in part by the Government of Canada. *Ce livre est financé en partie par le gouvernement du Canada.* We acknowledge the support of the Canada Council for the Arts. *Nous remercions le Conseil des arts du Canada de son soutien.* We would like to acknowledge the funding support of the Ontario Arts Council (OAC) and the Government of Ontario for their support. We also acknowledge the support of the Government of Ontario through the Ontario Book Publishing Tax Credit, and through Ontario Creates.

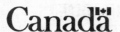

PRINTED AND BOUND IN CANADA   PRINTING: MARQUIS   5   4   3   2   1

Purchase the print edition and receive the ebook free.
For details, go to ecwpress.com/ebook.

For Doug, who's made it possible for me to live here,
and for Diesel, who shares our home.

SATURDAY, JULY 28

My troubles started with a phone call on the afternoon of the storm.

I'd been weeding perennials in the shade garden when my mobile rang. Lulled by birdsong and the trickle of water from a nearby fountain, I would have ignored the intrusion if the caller hadn't been my son.

Jordan cut the social niceties. "Good news, Mom. There's a Saskatoon realtor whose client wants to buy the farm —"

I wiped my hands on my denim shorts and groaned. "If you mean Monica, she's already made me two offers. I told her I'm not interested."

"Her client's willing to pay big money," Jordan said. "You won't get another opportunity like this one."

"Fine, since I don't plan to sell."

"The gardens are getting too much for you." He enunciated his words carefully, as if he were speaking to an old woman.

"I know it's going to be hard to give up this place, but Dad would have wanted you to take life easier."

"Neither of us has any idea what he would have wanted. Besides, it doesn't matter. He's not here. I am."

Jordan sighed. "Tanya and I are worried. How will you manage come winter?"

I yanked out a thistle seedling that was crowding my favourite hosta. My daughter was a worrywart like her mom. "Why the sudden concern for my well-being? Dad's been gone almost six months."

"If we hadn't spent five days with you after the funeral, you couldn't have coped. We were happy to be there, but what happens the next time a blizzard dumps two feet of snow? Neither of us can quit our jobs in Saskatoon."

A peal of thunder caused me to look up at the darkening sky. The light was vanishing, the air suddenly still. I didn't want to think about blizzards or the coming winter.

"You've got to be sensible," Jordan said.

Was I only imagining the note of desperation in his voice? "Sweetheart, has something happened? You don't need money, do you?"

"Jeez, Mom . . ."

"Then what's the problem?"

"Monica can be very persuasive," he said.

"How do you know?"

"We've . . . had dealings."

A gale-force wind sprang up out of nowhere, and I had to yell to make myself heard over the sudden din. "I hope there's no conflict of interest here."

"Why would there be?"

"That's what I'm starting to wonder," I said, before ducking out of the way as a tree branch flew over my head.

"There's a storm brewing, and I'm in danger of decapitation by a flying missile. I'll call you back from the kitchen once I've made a cup of tea."

I picked up my hand weeder and trowel and started for the house. Preoccupied by Jordan's call, I didn't notice Monica until she materialized in front of me.

"Jeannie, my dear, it's lovely to see you."

I didn't return her smile. "You've wasted your trip. Better go home before the storm hits."

"It already has," Monica said, dodging an air-borne shingle as she followed me up the stairs and onto the deck.

Diesel, my fluffy orange Maine Coon, yowled as he waited beside the back door. A good-natured fellow, he usually greets me with a friendly meow. This time he was pissed off by the storm and didn't care who knew it.

I picked him up and snuggled him against my chest. "Don't grumble about the weather, buddy — we need the rain."

Thunder rumbled and a flash of lightning speared the sky. The temperature had fallen, and I was unexpectedly cold. What I wanted was to curl up on the sofa with a hot drink, a mystery novel, and my cat. Instead, I had to cope with an unwelcome visitor.

"I'll give you shelter until the storm's over," I said to Monica as we entered the house, "but we have nothing to discuss."

Although the kitchen clock said five thirty, the sky was getting dark. A sudden spatter of rain, driven by the pounding wind, slammed against my windows. Outside, something heavy crashed to the ground. I turned on the kitchen lights, plugged in the kettle, and spooned decaf Earl Grey into my favourite teapot.

Monica perched on a stool at the counter. "I can't stay long because I'm meeting someone in Saskatoon for drinks at eight." Her cheeks glowed a delicate pink. If it were anybody but Monica, I'd have sworn she was blushing. "He hates me being late."

For a moment, I felt almost kindly toward her. "Then you'd better not linger — it's a two-hour drive."

Although she must have been pushing fifty, Monica looked like a runway model. Her short blond hair was fashionably tousled, her face lightly tanned, and her make-up perfect. She wore a double-breasted suit the colour of ripe mango and high-heeled navy sandals that shrieked Parisian couture.

While I looked okay for a woman of sixty, I wasn't in Monica's sartorial league. My T-shirt was grubby from gardening, the hem of my shorts needed mending, and the wind had tied my hair in knots. In well-cut clothes and with my shoulder-length bob freshly cut and coloured, most days I could pass muster in a room full of younger women. That afternoon was not one of those days.

My house, on the other hand, looked beautiful — at least, I thought it did. Home decorating magazines gushed over the "olde farmhouse" look, but my kitchen was the real thing — a wood-propane cookstove, walls and ceiling of tongue-and-groove pine, handmade wooden cupboards, rustic ceramic tiles, and lots of artwork. Most of the paintings were mine, brightly coloured pictures of my flower gardens and the local prairie landscape. Sophistication be damned — I liked cheerful folk art and the beauty of Nature with a capital N.

Monica got straight to business. "You might want to reconsider, Jeannie. My client has increased their offer by two hundred thousand."

The kindly feelings vanished. "Tell them to forget it."

"Think about it," she said. "You could buy a luxury condo on the riverbank in Saskatoon and still have spare change. No more slogging in the garden —"

"Beats working out in a gym."

Monica ignored my retort. "Your children don't want to farm. Isn't it time to start planning for old age?"

I spooned cat food into a bowl and placed it in front of Diesel. "Leave my kids out of this."

"They're concerned about you living here alone. What if you had an accident and couldn't get to the hospital? These roads must be murder in winter."

Iron hands clutched my chest. Could Monica be aware of the circumstances surrounding my husband's death? I took a deep breath and exhaled slowly.

"Wouldn't it be better to live near your kids?" she continued, her smile exuding a nauseating sweetness. "Think of family dinners every Sunday, weekly shopping with your daughter, morning coffee with friends —"

"You've got fifteen minutes to drink your tea if you want to be in Saskatoon by eight," I said.

"They want you to sell."

"Clairvoyant, are you?"

"I took Tanya for lunch before she went on holiday," Monica said. "She's been eying an exquisite cottage at Turtle Lake. Unfortunately, it's expensive."

"You talked to my daughter?"

"That's why I'm a successful realtor."

"Of all the underhand —"

"It's good business practice," Monica said. "Don't you want what's best for your children?"

"Tanya and her partner earn more than her father and I ever did. Darned if I'll sacrifice my farm because of their extravagance."

"Would you sacrifice it to protect your son's reputation?" she asked.

I looked at her in surprise. "There's no need to do that."

Monica laughed. "Mothers are always the last people to hear about their children's . . . misadventures."

Jordan's phone call half an hour ago was starting to make terrible sense. "If you've got something to tell me," I said, "say it. Otherwise, finish your tea and get out."

"A little bird told me that Jordan's having personal issues at work."

"Personal issues?" Although he's almost forty, Jordan's still my baby. I felt a sudden shiver of fear. As soon as Monica left, I'd talk to him again.

"Of a romantic nature."

"I don't believe it."

Monica shrugged. "The lady in question has a chequered financial history. I can't be more specific without betraying confidences. Still, you know what these venerable institutions are like — they can't afford scandal that would frighten off prospective donors."

My son supervised publicity and fundraising for a major hospital in Saskatoon. He'd been divorced for almost a year now. I wasn't aware of a new woman in his life, but, hey, I was his mom.

"It would be a shame if the hospital fired Jordan." She put her cup on the counter and stood up. "You might want to talk to him before you make your decision."

I picked up Diesel and gave him a hug. He licked my cheek appreciatively. "People who bully me come to regret their mistake." When it comes to fight or flight, I favour the latter. But Jordan's my son — and nobody gets away with threatening my kids.

"You're playing out of your league, Jeannie." Monica crossed to the window that overlooked the parking area east of the house. "Thanks for the tea— Oh God, my car!"

I rushed to the window. "What's wrong?"

The rain had stopped and the wind died down, but not before they'd created havoc. My own problem wasn't serious. Although the gravelled parking area was ankle-deep in debris, it wouldn't take more than a few hours to clear away the mess. My guest wasn't so lucky. Festooned with branches, its roof caved in and windshield smashed by the top of my prized silver maple, was Monica's red Lexus SUV.

"Oh, no!" I wasn't sure which was worse: the loss of my tree or the prospect of an unwelcome overnight guest.

Monica's face was ashen, but she hadn't made it to the top of her field without stamina. Without a word she pulled out her cell phone and started punching in numbers.

"A tow truck won't help," I said, putting Diesel on his favourite chair. "And the nearest place to rent a vehicle is in Saskatoon."

"Damn." She slammed her phone on the table. "I'll have to borrow your car."

"You're joking."

"Can you think of another way of getting to the city by eight?"

"No, but —"

"I'll pay you five hundred dollars and return the car first thing tomorrow," she said. "The alternative is that I sleep on your couch tonight. Neither of us wants that."

I grabbed my car keys. "Let's go."

Tangled branches made the sidewalk almost impassable, but Monica in her high-heeled shoes navigated like a pro. When we reached the garage, I handed her the keys.

"Bring it back in one piece."

Monica frowned. "This old Prius is your car?"

The windshield was cracked, and a dented bumper needed replacing. "It's not what you're used to driving," I said, "but it is road worthy."

"It's fine." She smiled hesitantly. "Thanks, Jeannie."

The brief storm was over, and the sun was shining. Monica got into my car. I watched as she drove carefully down the driveway and onto the grid road. It was the last time I saw her alive.

—\\\\/—

My son was a good-natured man, intensely loyal to his friends even when they did something stupid. He wasn't happy when I called to ask about Monica's vague allegations. It took a lot of digging to find out that he had a new girlfriend named Brandy and that she worked with him at the hospital in the accounting department. Apparently, she'd met Monica at a party, and the two women had struck up an unlikely friendship. One night the realtor had taken her out for cocktails to celebrate a house sale, and drink had loosened Brandy's tongue. The upshot was her confession that, a few years earlier, she had "borrowed" money from the hospital foundation in her hometown.

"Brandy was only twenty at the time," Jordan said. "She'd just got a part-time job as a junior CA, and her boss suggested that she join a non-profit board to gain experience. That's why she was the treasurer."

"How much did she take?" I asked.

"Only a few thousand. It was a dumb thing to do, but she had to make a payment on her student loan, and —"

"Jordan," I said, "it wasn't just dumb, it was dishonest."

"I know that. Do you want to discuss ethics or hear the rest of the story?"

"Go on."

Jordan sighed. "One of the other board members got suspicious and started asking questions before Brandy could pay it back. The foundation didn't lay charges, but she was asked to leave the board."

"No surprise there," I said.

"She returned the money. Unless Monica's a real bitch, there's no reason for anyone at work to find out what happened."

"Monica wants my farm," I said. "And she's willing to use blackmail to get it."

"Brandy could lose her job."

"Are you suggesting I cave in to blackmail?"

"Not exactly . . ."

"Then what *are* you suggesting?" I asked.

After circling round the issue, Jordan finally admitted that he wanted me to accept Monica's terms — my farm in exchange for her silence. When I pointed out the wisdom of looking for a new girlfriend, he exploded.

"You've got nerve, I'll give you that. After all your whining about Grams and Gramps putting principles before people —"

"Since when is it a moral duty to shield theft?"

"Brandy returned the money," he said. "You used to tell Tanya and me it's okay to make mistakes because that's how people learn."

"And if I sell my farm in order to protect her from the usual consequences of stealing, what do you suppose she's learned?"

The conversation didn't improve after that. Jordan made allegations of hypocrisy and said I was just like my mother. I questioned his judgement and suggested he figure out where his priorities lie. Then, after more accusations that went nowhere, my son slammed down his phone.

My own priorities were clear — or so I'd thought. As long as the farm was in my name, I could protect the lakeshore from development. Brandy's problem paled in comparison to what would happen if the bulldozers moved in. But, of course, *her* problem wasn't the issue. Jordan felt betrayed by his mother, and I cared about my son. He and Tanya were the most important people in my world. How could I meet their needs without violating my own values? There seemed no good way to solve that dilemma.

Our call had left me restless. I didn't want to dwell on Jordan's accusations. Nor did I feel like making supper, painting, or doing any of the other things I usually enjoy. Diesel was no help — he'd gone upstairs for a late afternoon nap. It was time to implement one of my rules of adulthood — if you can't think of anything you *want* to do, do something useful. I'd start by checking my gardens for storm damage.

The farmyard was divided into a number of distinct areas. My house, surrounded by an acre or so of landscaped grounds, sat at the top of a low hill. Below, on three sides, were a vegetable garden, an orchard, a mixed planting of deciduous and coniferous trees, and several sloughs ringed by native poplars.

The rest of my land spread out beyond them — 1,120 acres of fields and pastures dotted by poplar bluffs and stone piles. To the south, edged by rolling hills and woodland, lay Crystal Lake. I didn't blame Monica's client for wanting my land, but no way was I letting them have it.

The temperature had dropped at least five degrees, so I changed into jeans and a long-sleeved shirt. Then I headed out on a tour of inspection.

The path down to the vegetable garden and orchard was criss-crossed with fallen poplars, some of them too heavy for me to move by myself. The orchard itself had escaped with minor damage — it wouldn't take more than ten minutes to pick up the five or six branches that lay on the ground. The vegetable garden had likewise emerged relatively unscathed. Corn and squash plants had been blown over, but as long as their branches weren't broken, they'd spring up again. Silently thanking the horticultural gods, I started back to the house.

I was halfway up the hill when a pale young man appeared at the top of the path. With his white shorts and T-shirt, slight build, and longish ash blond hair, he looked as if a strong wind could pick him up and whisk him away. When he saw me, he stopped, turned around, and disappeared over the hilltop.

"Hello," I called, raising my voice so that it would carry the distance between us. "Are you looking for someone?"

There was no answer. I crested the top of the path in time to see the man hop onto a small motorbike and ride off down the road.

The incident left me spooked. Strangers who wandered onto my land normally stopped and talked to me. This young man hadn't. However unlikely, could his appearance have had anything to do with Monica's nefarious scheme?

Baffled, I returned to assessing the storm damage. Most of it had resulted from the conflict between wind and trees; my flowers, unfazed, bloomed as exuberantly as ever. The parking area, however, was a mess. Frank and I had planted ash, elm, and maples behind the garage the year we got married. The wind had played with them, tearing off leaves and tossing branches to the ground like toddlers bored with their toys. I pulled on my gloves and started piling up the debris. The silver maple that had crushed the roof of Monica's Lexus was heavy; I'd need help to move it.

However unreasonable, I resented Frank's abandonment. Until six months ago, we had shared the work. Then he died. A neighbour rented the cropland and pasture, but I was left responsible for our fifteen-acre homestead. Responsible — and on my own.

One gigantic pile of branches later, I was ready to quit for the day. I took off my gloves and was about to head for the house when a small van turned off the road and onto my driveway. Moments later it pulled up in front of the garage. A man got out and walked over to Monica's SUV.

"What the hell —"

"Casualty of the storm," I said. "It's a good thing the owner wasn't in it."

He held out his hand. "I'm Derek Tanner, and you must be Jeannie. What's Monica's precious Lexus doing here?"

"You just missed her," I said. "Right now, she's in my car and driving to Saskatoon."

"Nothing surprises me where Monica's concerned," he said. "But you're the person I want to see."

The man standing in my parking lot was small, dark, and wiry, with startlingly blue eyes, a dazzling smile, and hair that was going grey at the temples. He looked good in faded jeans and black T-shirt. Conscious of my scruffy clothes for the second time that day, I returned the smile as we shook hands.

"Forgive the question," I said, "but how do you know Monica? And why are you here?"

Derek grinned. "I'm a freelance journalist writing about the transfer of farmland. Heard that Monica had been making inquiries and figured I'd follow up that lead."

"You could have phoned or emailed first."

"No contact info — all I had was the rumour that she was sniffing around a lakeshore farm north of town. Now that I'm here, I can see why she's interested."

"It's not for sale," I said.

"And Monica won't take no for an answer?"

I nodded. "The lady's persistent. But then, so am I."

"A battle between titans?"

"More like two stubborn donkeys," I said.

He laughed. "Tell me about it."

"I need some tea. Want to join me on my deck for a cup?"

The sidewalk was still strewn with fallen tree limbs, and I was tired. Halfway to the house I stumbled over a particularly large branch. Derek reached out a hand to steady me.

"I hope you've got someone to help clean up this mess," he said.

"Don't worry about it." I climbed the three steps up to the deck and looked out over my flower garden. The sight of it always revived my sagging spirits. Broad paths linked beds of perennials and small shrubs that were interspersed with huge pots of bright-coloured annuals. I turned to Derek. "Some women have grandkids. I tend my garden."

"Nice," he said, taking a seat at the patio table. "But a lot of work."

"You should see it when it's not a drought year," I said. "Tea okay, or do you prefer coffee?"

I made another pot of Earl Grey, put together a plate of sandwiches, and carried them both outside.

"Cream cheese and cucumber or tomato and cheddar? Don't know about you, but I haven't had supper yet."

While we ate, I told Derek the story of my relationship with Monica.

"She turned up when I was transplanting peppers a couple months ago. The crazy woman followed me around the garden getting her elegant shoes dirty and promising me everything but eternal salvation if I'd accept her offer."

"Did she threaten negative consequences if you refused?" Derek asked.

"Not at first. But on her second call she hinted I'd regret it if I didn't sell. No concrete threat — just a few references to people who'd experienced misfortunes after they'd hung on to their land too long. I would have complained to her boss if she'd had one."

"What kind of misfortunes?"

"Someone had died by suicide," I said, "but I couldn't make out if he'd done so because he'd gone bankrupt or because he was consumed with regret over lost opportunity."

"Suicide, eh? Either there is more than one such incident, or you got the story wrong."

"You mean another person also lost their life to suicide after rejecting her offer?"

"That's not exactly what happened," Derek said.

"No?"

He finished his tea and put the mug on his empty plate. "Good sandwiches. Thanks."

"How did this person die?"

"I shouldn't have said anything. Monica's threatened my boss with a libel suit if I talk."

"What boss? I thought you were freelance."

Derek laughed. "I'm supposed to be interviewing you, not the other way round. Let's get back to your story. What happened next time she called?"

"That was today. She suggested that my son's girlfriend might suffer financial consequences if my stubbornness persisted."

"Is this woman . . . vulnerable?"

Common sense dictated discretion when talking to a man whom I'd known for less than an hour, but I was still fuming after my conversation with Jordan. "This is off the record, right?"

"Of course."

"She stole cash as the treasurer of a non-profit," I said. "Now she works in accounting for a big hospital."

"So, gossip and rumour could be deadly." Derek looked thoughtful. "Must be tough for you."

"My son wants me to sell." I pushed my empty plate aside. "Could you be sued for libel if you published a story about Monica's shady business practices?"

"Yes, I could. She's careful. It would be your word against hers."

A grey catbird taunted me from a thicket of shrubs west of the deck, its raspy mew a parody of Diesel's voice.

"Then how can I put an end to the blackmail?"

"Only thing that would stop Monica would land you in jail with no chance of parole for twenty years," Derek said. "But I expect she made you a lucrative offer. Why not sell and buy a smaller property? It must be hard to maintain a place this size."

I admitted it had been rough since my husband died. "But I'm keeping the farm. My kids don't want it, and I won't sell to a developer."

"And Monica's client is a developer?"

"She wouldn't say who they are, and I'm not taking chances. No way I'm letting anyone clearcut my land or eradicate every slough, pothole, and fence-line on the property."

"I knew someone else who felt like that, poor devil."

"What happened to him?"

He shrugged. "You're what — the third generation on this farm?"

"My husband was. His grandparents settled here back in the thirties. My folks owned an adjoining quarter section."

"And they farmed too?"

"After a fashion," I said. "They were hippie back-to-the-landers ahead of their time. Came here back in the fifties and stayed. End of story."

"Oh?" Derek raised an eyebrow. "What happened to them?"

"They died fifteen years ago. Left the land to my sister and me, and I bought out her share. Some people from Saskatoon are renting it. They're living in my parents' old house and trying to farm."

"Yeah? Tell me about it."

"Look, I've been up since five this morning. I've coped with the aftermath of a storm and the machinations of an unscrupulous realtor. I don't want to talk about my neighbours. I want to move the poplar that's blocking my path to the garden and clear away the branches cluttering up my sidewalk."

He laughed. "I might not be able to rid you of Monica, but I can give you a day's help with the yard work."

"You're joking, right?"

"We journalists will do anything for a good story." Derek stretched and lazily got to his feet. "Thanks for the tea and sandwiches. I'll camp overnight at the provincial park and be back in the morning."

"I haven't accepted your offer yet."

"See you tomorrow around eight."

Whistling softly, Derek sauntered down the sidewalk. I stood watching him until he jumped into his van and was gone.

When you live in rural Saskatchewan, you don't often meet new people. The men I socialized with were either relatives or the husbands of friends, most of whom I'd known for at least forty years. Derek offered the possibility of fresh companionship and good conversation. Chances are he was married, but that would be okay. With any luck, the next few days would be . . . interesting.

As it turned out, I was right — although not in the way I'd anticipated.

SUNDAY, JULY 29

The sound of my phone woke me at six. My friend Liz was an early riser, but she didn't usually call before eight. Alarmed, I picked up my cell.

"Liz, why are you —"

"Thank God, you're home." She sounded as if she'd been crying.

"What's wrong?"

"I thought it was you in the car."

"Me? What car?"

"Your Prius," she said. "It's at the bottom of the ravine, and there's a body inside."

For one frightening moment, I couldn't breathe. "It can't be mine. That realtor who's been hassling me borrowed it last night. She's going to return it this morning."

"The car's a wreck," Liz said. "But I can see the National Farmers Union sticker on the back window."

Heart pounding, I got out of bed. "Are you still at the ravine?"

"The nine-one-one operator told me to stay here until the police arrive."

"I'll see you in twenty minutes," I said.

Ten minutes later I was dressed and numbly scrambling across the field that separates Liz's homestead from mine. The ravine ran from the municipal road to the lake and straddled the line between our two properties. Not only was it home to a family of great horned owls that Liz liked to photograph, but it was also the site of the accident that had cost Frank his life.

Sirens screamed in the distance as I arrived at the ravine. Liz was standing near its mouth at the lower edge of my hayfield. Beside her, tail wagging, was Goliath, her Bernese mountain dog.

"Jeannie," she said, running to meet me, "are you okay?" She threw her arms around me and pulled me into a tight hug. "For a while there, I thought I'd lost my best friend."

"Can't get rid of me that easily," I said, trying to keep my voice from shaking. I closed my eyes and took a deep breath, comforted by the sweet scent of clover blossoms and the feel of homespun wool against my face.

Goliath whined softly.

"He wants to help," Liz said.

I stepped back from her and dropped to the ground beside him. "Thanks, buddy."

Goliath nudged me, and I scratched his head. That's one of the things I like about dogs and cats — their affection never comes with a price tag.

"The body's so badly mangled, I couldn't even tell if it was a woman," Liz said. "But it must be your friendly realtor."

"That doesn't make sense." Monica had been a vibrant woman. I couldn't imagine her dead. "Travel conditions were good last night. She can't have totalled my car."

The ravine cut to the bottom of a steep hill. Even though the municipality kept it well gravelled, more than one vehicle has ended up in the ditch when the road was slippery. Yesterday's rain had been insignificant, though, and visibility had been fine when she'd left my farm. There was no reason for an accident.

"A person's running late and floors it," Liz said. "The car hits gravel, and next thing you know it's on its roof."

Liz was my closest neighbour, and — despite twenty years between us — one of my dearest friends. A short, stocky woman with close-cut dark hair and an infectious grin, she was one of a growing number of city kids who fell in love with rural life and chose to make their living raising food. Four years ago, her mom inherited a quarter section next to my farm, and Liz has lived there ever since. She ran a small flock of sheep, pastured chickens for egg sales, and raised endangered Tamworth pigs.

"I need to see the car," I said, getting up from the ground. "The NFU sticker doesn't prove anything. Maybe it's not Monica's body."

Liz touched my shoulder. "Jeannie, get real."

"I'm going down to see for myself."

"You can't —"

"Try to stop me."

"Then I'm coming with you."

Liz put Goliath on a leash and the three of us headed into the ravine. It was thickly wooded with poplars and a dense underbrush of saskatoons, chokecherries, and rose bushes that scratched your face, legs, and arms as you pushed through them. The difficulty was compounded by the steep slope and by rough ground that threatened to trip you up at every step. I was breathing hard by the time we reached bottom, but the problem wasn't just challenging terrain; the ravine was only a few hundred metres from where Frank had died six months earlier.

My heart was pounding as we approached the crumpled Prius. It had collided with a huge rock and looked as if a giant had smashed it with a hammer. I shooed away a couple ravens and peered through what was left of the back window. A body lay inside, still held in place by the seatbelt. It was drenched in blood and crushed beyond recognition. Only a single navy sandal had escaped unscathed. Monica had been wearing those shoes when she'd left my house the previous night. If I'd been the person driving, would it have been me lying there cold and lifeless?

I grasped a poplar branch to steady myself and pointed at the car. "It's Monica alright. That's her sandal."

We bowed our heads and stood quietly for a moment, contemplating the fate of the woman who'd wanted to buy my farm. Relief at my escape from blackmail warred with horror over her violent death. Much as I'd disliked her, I was sorry that she was dead.

Liz broke the silence. "Ready to go back?"

Saying a silent prayer, I trudged behind my friend and her dog as they fought their way through the underbrush. Visions of Frank's bloodied body smashed inside his car battled in my head with images of Monica. Despite the sunshine, I shivered.

"It's the shock," Liz said as she handed me her grey wool sweater.

I pulled it on over my shirt. "Thanks."

We'd almost reached the top when a man's voice alerted us to the arrival of the police. "Ms. Nolan?"

"Right here," Liz said as we crested the rim. "I'm the person who called nine-one-one. And this is my neighbour, Jeannie Wolfert-Lang. She owns the car that's at the bottom of the gully."

Two young men in RCMP uniform stood in front of us. "I'm Constable Ironbow," the tall, dark one said. "And this is my partner, Constable Dawson."

He gestured to the ambulance attendants who had just arrived. "Is there an easy way for these guys to get down to the accident site?"

"I wish there were," Liz said. "But the victim's beyond needing medical help. And it's going to take a hydraulic cutter to pry her out of the car."

"We'll deal with that," Ironbow said as the emergency medical technicians started to descend our rough trail marked by crushed and broken branches. "In the meantime, what can you tell us about the accident?"

"I was going to photograph the great horned owls that nest down there," Liz said, "when I saw my neighbour's Prius. I phoned for help and then I called Jeannie."

Dawson turned to me. "Do you know who was driving it?"

"Monica Ashton," I said, my stomach roiling as I unsuccessfully tried to block out memories of Frank's blood spattered across the snow. "She owns Ashton Realty in Saskatoon." I told him about my relationship with Monica and her interest in buying my land. "Her SUV's still parked by my house, so you can verify my story."

"And you're sure it's this person who's inside your car?" Ironbow asked.

"Absolutely."

Liz put an arm around my shoulders. "Can't we finish this interview tomorrow? My friend's had a tough morning. She needs to sit down with a cup of tea."

"Give me another five minutes," Ironbow said.

I took a deep breath. "Okay."

After a few more questions and the confirmation of my car registration, he said we could go. "Constable Dawson will give you a ride home." He smiled sympathetically. "It's tough, eh, first time you see a dead body?"

I wasn't about to tell him that I'd already seen one accident victim earlier that year. Instead, I nodded politely and said that I'd be fine.

"You can spend the rest of the day with me," Liz said.

I felt strangely reluctant to tell her that I was expecting Derek later that morning. "How about a rain check? Diesel hasn't had breakfast yet, and I have potted plants to water . . ."

She wrinkled her brow, but for once didn't argue. "Make sure to call if you need me, eh?"

Ironbow headed for the bottom of the ravine as I shakily followed my friend, her dog, and Constable Dawson to the cop car parked just off the road. Much as I liked walking, I was grateful for the prospect of a ride home.

Dawson dropped off Liz and Goliath at her door, then drove to my place. Monica's SUV was where she'd left it, the massive length of silver maple still straddling its roof.

"Did she leave the keys with you?" Dawson asked.

"They're probably in her purse. She expected to be back this morning."

"We'll need to rule out the possibility of foul play before the vehicle's turned over to the estate," he said. "One of our guys will pick it up later this morning and take it to the detachment's compound."

It was almost nine when Dawson left. Monica's violent death had destroyed my appetite for breakfast and left me unsettled. Diesel, a reliable source of comfort, was nowhere in sight. It was a good time for me to make peace with my son.

My mobile rang as I was about to key in Jordan's number.

"Mom, I shouldn't have asked you to give in to Monica's blackmail. Brandy had been asking me to move in with her, and I was feeling a lot of pressure. But that's no reason for you to sell the farm."

"Move in with her? I thought the two of you had just started dating."

"We'd been going out for almost five months," Jordan said. "Brandy was keen about settling down and . . ."

"Is that what you want?" I asked, curious about his use of the past tense.

He hesitated. "She's awfully clingy."

"Maybe time to call it quits then."

"I tried a couple days ago, but she started crying."

My son's always been a soft touch. "So, what are you going to do?"

"Last night I told her it was over."

"That must have been tough," I said.

"Yeah, it was." He laughed unconvincingly. "There goes Monica's power to blackmail."

I took a deep breath. "She died in a car accident last night."

"Jesus! What happened?"

I told him about Liz's phone call and our trip to the ravine.

"That must have been a nightmare. Are you okay?"

"Just thankful it wasn't me in the Prius." Jordan was already coping with a relationship breakup; I didn't want to add to his burden.

"When Dad died, the doctor said you might experience post-traumatic stress —"

"Don't worry about me," I said. "I'm fine."

29

Although our call had eased the tension between us, I still felt restless and out of sorts. And despite my good intentions, I felt guilty about lying to my son. Monica's accident *had* revived painful memories. Maybe a walk would help banish the haunting image of Frank's mangled body. I'd hike along the lakeshore to visit my tenants at Thickwood Farm.

The locals knew it as the Wolfert place. Back in 1948, Dad had bought the quarter section from his uncle, Peter Wolfert. My sister, Mandi, and I had inherited it from Mom and Dad when they died in a train wreck sixty years later. Frank and I had bought out her share, and he had farmed it until six months ago, when I'd leased it to three young people from Saskatoon. Renaming it Thickwood Farm was my attempt to mark its transition to a new identity.

I'm not sure what possessed me to rent the place to city kids. Ava and Thor were wannabe farmers I'd met at a permaculture workshop in Saskatoon. A short time later, they met Jade at a climate change rally in front of city hall. Three months later, the unlikely trio was co-operatively farming part of my quarter section. Maybe my willingness to play landlord was a nod to the idealism of my parents. They'd believed in self-sufficiency, small-scale agriculture, and all the other good things that became fashionable in the late sixties. As a child, I'd rebelled against their primitive way of life. Was it karma that had led me to accept as tenants these young folks who would follow in their footsteps?

The morning, however, was too lovely to indulge in such abstract speculation. I walked east along the lakeshore, my feet familiar with every inch of the path we'd made when, during my final year of high school, Frank and I had been a courting couple. In the bright sunshine, with gulls flying overhead and a light breeze skimming the water, I could almost forget the horror of his death. Even so, I wasn't sorry when I reached Thickwood Farm. My young tenants would provide a welcome distraction.

Most people would have called the lakeshore farmstead picturesque. The summer before he died, Frank had given the shabby house a coat of pale blue paint, replaced the cracked windows, and hauled away a load of broken-down machinery. My tenants had pruned the half-wild apple trees and planted a shelterbelt of tiny spruce and pine. Their efforts hadn't eradicated decades of neglect. Grass needed cutting, ramshackle outbuildings needed to be repaired or torn down, weeds needed hoeing — I told myself it was unreasonable to expect Ava, Thor, and Jade to perform miracles, but the ill-kept grounds still made me cranky.

Jade was in the vegetable garden, down on her hands and knees thinning carrots that should have been thinned three weeks earlier. She stood up when I approached. A tiny, dark-haired woman dressed in a cotton print blouse and long twill skirt dirty and ragged around the hem, she looked like a child costumed as a prairie homesteader.

"Hi, Jeannie. Have you come for a visit? I'll put the kettle on for tea."

"Thanks, but I want to get home before the day gets any hotter. Is Thor around? I'd like to borrow the truck."

Jade's smile vanished, and I felt mean. Her previous experience with growing vegetables had been limited to time spent in her mother's backyard garden. It couldn't be easy for an unskilled person like her to transition from middle-class urbanite to peasant farmer.

"Oh dear," she said. "He and Ava just left for a load of mulch. They won't be home for at least an hour. If you'd called last night, they could have done something else this morning."

"I didn't need the truck last night," I said. For a moment I debated the wisdom of telling this fragile youngster about the accident, then decided that she might as well hear the story from me.

Jade had tears in her eyes when I'd finished. "The poor woman. What a horrible way to die."

I nodded, glad that at least one person was saddened by her death.

"It must be awful for you," she said. "Shall I go to your place and stay for a day or two?"

"I'm fine, thanks." Jade was a sweetheart, but I liked her in small doses.

"Or you can come and stay with us. My dad is coming to visit — we can have a party."

"Great," I said. "When are you expecting him?"

"In a few days. We've got lots to do to get ready. Dad hates a messy house, and he's really fussy about his food."

I looked in dismay at the weedy garden. "I'll let you get back to work then. And don't worry about the truck. If I need to go somewhere, I'll call Liz."

As I walked home, I thought about Jade. From what I'd heard, her father wasn't much better in the parenting department than mine had been. Aside from my first year of high school, Dad had been home for most of our childhood, but he wasn't one to play crazy eights with us or take us on picnics the way parents did in the children's books we used to read. Dad was too busy organizing meetings and writing political exposés. While Jade's dad had been equally unavailable, at least he'd had an excuse. Jade's parents, Ben and Lana, divorced when she was twelve, leaving Jade, an only child, to live with her mother, an emergency room nurse. Her dad owned a sporting goods store; his idea of paternal responsibility had been taking her out to dinner on Sundays and sending her to summer camp. Jade had grown up longing for a close-knit family — and now her absentee father was coming to visit.

The sight of Derek in my front garden woke me from contemplating the upcoming disaster.

"Where were you?" he asked as he came to meet me.

I looked at him in surprise. "Are journalists always this inquisitive?"

"People who hang around with Monica tend to have unexpected bad luck," he said. "I was getting worried."

"She's the one with bad luck this time. Monica hit a giant rock when she drove my car into a nearby ravine last night. The car is totaled."

He stared at me for a moment. "Was she badly hurt?"

"The police said she probably died instantly."

"Jesus." Perhaps I only imagined the fleeting sadness in his eyes. "I saw an emergency vehicle and two RCMP cars a couple kilometres back. What happened?"

"She must have been driving too fast, got distracted, and lost control of the wheel."

"Not Monica," Derek said. "She was a good driver."

"You know a lot about this woman?"

He shrugged. "Word gets around. How did you hear about the accident?"

"My neighbour Liz found the car and phoned me. I met her at the ravine. Even though I knew it couldn't be anyone except Monica, I had to see the body for myself." I cleared my throat and fought back an impulse to burst into tears. "It was horrible."

Derek reached over and squeezed my hands. "I'm sorry you went through that."

"I'm getting too old for such escapades," I said.

"Next time, leave it to the cops, eh?" he said. "Why didn't they give you a ride home?"

"They did. But when I got back, I went for a walk along the lakeshore." The morning had been stressful; I didn't feel like telling him about my visit to Thickwood Farm.

"Want me to make you coffee?"

"Tea," I said. "And toast with raspberry jam."

Over breakfast, Derek asked if I'd told the police he'd been talking to me about Monica.

"There was no reason to do that." I looked at him suspiciously. "Why do you ask?"

He grinned. "Handsome stranger enters your life around the same time a woman is killed driving your car. Some people might wonder if there's a connection."

"Is there?"

"I was joking."

"You haven't told me much about yourself."

He put down his mug and got up from the table. "My story's boring."

"It's all in the telling. Aren't journalists masters in the art of wresting romance from the mundane?"

Derek laughed. "Do you want to sit here talking, or should we get at that yard work I promised to help you with?"

By the time we removed the silver maple from the top of Monica's car and picked up the tree branches piled nearby, it was almost twelve. I cooked new potatoes and made a stir-fry with leftover chicken and vegetables from the garden. Although it was pleasantly cool in my well-insulated house, we carried our plates of food outside to the table on my deck.

"I could get used to this," Derek said. "My condo only has a balcony. It's hot as Hades up there in summer."

The small fountain Frank had given me for my fiftieth birthday gurgled merrily. Robins and goldfinches twittered in the trees, and a ruby-throated hummingbird sipped nectar from a hanging basket of red impatiens. Nearby, Stargazer lilies perfumed the air with their exotic, spicy scent. Monica's death had ensured my continued possession of this prairie oasis. It was lucky for me that her death had been an accident. Otherwise, the cops might have noticed that I had a strong motive for murder.

—\/\/—

After lunch, I stretched out on a lounge chair for a short nap. When I woke, Derek was splitting wood from the pile stacked against the house.

"Got anything else for me to do? I'll accept payment in the form of dinner."

"Help me finish clearing away debris from the storm," I said, "and I'll make pizza."

Four hours later, the paths were free of broken branches, several toppled trees had been cut into stove lengths, and a trellis blown over by the wind had been repositioned north of the garage.

"You've been a big help," I said. "It would have taken me all day to tidy the garden alone."

Derek grinned, teeth white against the dark streaks of dirt on his face. "Now that order's been restored, do I have to leave?"

Although I'm normally reserved, his warmth and friendliness were disarming. I returned his smile. "A place this size, there's no end of work. If I tried really hard, I expect I'd find something for you to do. But don't you have commitments at home in Saskatoon?"

"Nothing that won't keep," he said. "How about I deal with those scraggly trees behind the garage and you start on the pizza?"

While Derek pruned the Manitoba maples, I topped the sourdough crust I'd made earlier with my favourite seasonal ingredients: grilled tomatoes, peppers, onions, and zucchini with basil and lots of freshly grated cheese. Then I popped it in the toaster oven and went to call Derek for supper.

He had finished piling the cut branches against the garage and was cleaning the pruning saw when his mobile rang.

"Kat," he said into his phone, "I told you I'd be on holiday —"

On holiday? Wasn't he a freelance writer researching an assignment? The tone of his voice suggested that the caller was someone close to him; why didn't he want to talk to her? Vaguely embarrassed by my unintentional eavesdropping, I was about to turn away when Derek looked up and saw me.

"How about I give you a call when I'm back in the city?" he said, his cheeks turning red as he quickly concluded the conversation. "We can get together then."

I raised an eyebrow as he holstered his phone. "Problems?"

"Nothing important. Just an acquaintance who wants to meet for lunch."

I looked at him, perplexed. Having raised two kids, I'm familiar with the guilty look of someone telling only half the truth.

"Does this person have anything to do with Monica's accident?"

"Maybe I'll talk to someone from her office. Find out why she was so determined to buy your piece of land." Derek pointed to the pile of branches. "Want me to haul these away somewhere?"

I shook my head. Supper was getting cold, and Derek didn't appear eager to confide in me. "It's time to eat," I said.

"Good pizza." Derek threw down his napkin and pushed back from the table. "All it needed was a bottle of wine. I should have picked one up in town this morning."

"It would have been wasted on me."

"Oh?"

I ignored the implied question. "Don't feel obligated to come back tomorrow. You've already given me a day's work."

"I'm not finished writing my story." His eyes sparkled. "Need another day to soak in the ambience."

"Of course, I'd be happy to see you —"

"That's settled, then. I'll bring muffins and arrive in time for breakfast."

Our casual relationship hadn't justified an attempt on my part to ask Derek about his recent phone call — but I was still curious. And even though it was none of my business, I hated it when people lied to me. If he was uncomfortable because I'd overheard his conversation, the caller must have been important to him. There was no reason for him to be secretive. Why hadn't he told me about her?

"Breakfast's at eight." I usually finished eating by seven thirty, but not everyone rises that early. Hoping that he'd be more communicative in the morning, I took a final swallow of tea and placed the cup beside my empty plate.

Derek reached across the table and touched my hand. "Thanks for supper, Jeannie. I'll see you in the morning."

I smiled as I watched his figure retreat to the parked van.

Sleep didn't come easily that night; even with the windows open, my bedroom felt stifling. Images of Frank's shattered body imprisoned in his car alternated with pictures of my Prius crushed to the ground with Monica inside. They played in an endless loop that circled round and round inside my head. Equally troubling was Derek's unexpected arrival and offer of help. Surely his presence had nothing to do with Monica's death. Why, then, did he ask whether I'd mentioned him to the police? Why the furtiveness around the phone call? And who the hell *was* this woman named Kat?

Maybe I was getting paranoid. Maybe none of this had anything to do with me. Derek's hand on mine had set my heart racing, but that didn't mean I was romantically interested in him. Frank's death was too recent. I closed my eyes and told myself there was no point in even thinking about a new relationship. Another few days, and I'd never see Derek again.

MONDAY, JULY 30

We were having breakfast on the deck when my mobile rang. I excused myself and went inside to answer it. The caller was a Corporal Semchuk from the North Battleford RCMP detachment. He was in the neighbourhood and wanted to talk to me.

"What happened to Constables Ironbow and Dawson?" I asked. "They investigated the accident."

"Major Crimes is handling the case now," he said. "I can be at your place in twenty minutes. Will you be home?"

"Yes, but —"

"See you then," he said, and ended the call.

I looked at my mobile in bewilderment. Why Major Crimes? Monica's death was an accident — at least, I assumed it was.

Derek was finishing his muffin when I returned to the deck. "What's up?" he asked.

I told him about the phone call. "Nobody knew that she would be driving my car on Saturday night. Whatever the cause of her death, it can't have been murder."

"Major Crimes doesn't make home visits for traffic accidents," he said. "I'll make a few calls to find out what's going on."

"No need for that. The fellow I talked to will be here in a few minutes. We can ask him."

"I've got to do some research at the library in town," he said, getting up from the table. "Want me to pick up Chinese food for lunch?"

I shook my head. "I'm making a casserole. And there's no hurry to leave. The library doesn't open for another two hours."

"Got a few things to do first," Derek said. "See you later, Jeannie. I'll be back by twelve."

Before I could ask for details, he'd leapt down the stairs to the sidewalk and was halfway to the gravelled parking area.

I watched sourly as Derek's van sped down the driveway. Why use the North Battleford library when the Saskatoon system had better resources? Any decent journalist would have done his research before he left home. Derek was lying about something. I wanted to know what it was.

The cause of Monica's accident was another mystery. There was no reason for my Prius to have gone off the road. Could someone else have been involved? But if so, who? And how had they known she'd be driving my car? Although the morning was warm, I shivered. There could be no good answers to my questions.

I made coffee, cleared away breakfast, and set out clean mugs on the patio table. Then the police arrived.

Corporal Semchuk, a beefy man with a ruddy complexion and an iron-grey buzz cut, introduced his colleague, Constable

Pierce. She was a slender, pleasant-faced young woman who smiled at me as she took her place at the table.

"I'm sorry to disrupt your morning," Pierce said as I poured them coffee, "but we have a few questions."

Semchuk got straight to the matter at hand. "When was the last time you drove your Prius?"

"Couple weeks ago. I went to town for a haircut —"

"I need the exact date."

"Why?" I asked.

"Just answer the question."

"It was the Tuesday before last." I checked the calendar on my mobile. "July twenty-second. The appointment was for two in the afternoon."

"Has anyone driven it since then?"

"Not a soul. I assume there's a reason you want this information —"

"Would it surprise you to learn that the brake line had been cut?"

So that was why Major Crimes was involved! "Cut?" I looked at him, gobsmacked. "Who'd do a thing like that?"

"That's what we want to know."

"It certainly wasn't me," I said. "And in case you're wondering, I wasn't expecting a visit from Monica."

"She didn't phone to tell you she was coming?"

"I would have told her not to waste the trip if she had."

"The alternative," Constable Pierce said, "is that someone wanted *you* dead. Any idea who that could be?"

"I can't think of anyone except Monica," I said. "But obviously it wasn't her."

Semchuk was understandably curious about my relationship with the woman in question; it took me a while to convince him that my dislike of her sales tactics hadn't driven me to murder.

"No other enemies?" Pierce asked once we'd settled that matter.

"None."

"Are you sure?" She took a sip of coffee, and then put down her cup. "If someone wants to kill you, we can't provide protection unless we know who they are."

"I'm positive."

Semchuk rubbed his chin, which he clearly hadn't shaved that morning. "Wasn't your late husband involved in an accident at the same place where Monica went off the road?" Pierce frowned, but he ignored her. "Six months ago, wasn't it?"

I nodded and took a deep breath. "Visibility was poor, and the road was icy."

"He'd been drinking." Semchuk took a swig of coffee. "Although the coroner said his blood alcohol level was under point zero eight."

Pierce forestalled my reply. "Mr. Lang's death has nothing to do with the realtor's accident."

"Still a bit of a coincidence, eh?" Semchuk said. "Two fatal accidents on an isolated country road, and both of them connected to Ms. Wolfert-Lang."

I silently counted to ten.

"Jeannie, there's no evidence against you," Pierce said, refilling her cup from the carafe. "Where do you keep the car when you're not using it?"

"In the garage. But I don't keep it locked when I'm home."

"You ought to be more careful," Semchuk said. "A woman of your age —"

Pierce interrupted. "Any strangers around recently? Someone lost and asking for directions, maybe, or someone with car trouble who wanted help."

Derek was a stranger, and he'd asked if I'd told the police he'd been inquiring about Monica. But why would he want her dead? And what conceivable motive could he have for trying to kill me? Yet someone had cut the brake line on my car. Could it have been the young man I'd seen lurking in the garden a few days ago?

"There was someone skulking around my house the day of the storm," I said. "Sometimes people stop here to admire the flowers, but he didn't look the type."

"Can you describe him?" Pierce asked.

"Skinny kid in his early twenties. Medium height. Longish blond hair so pale it was almost white. Big blue eyes. Attractive, if you like the ethereal, poet-starving-in-a-garret look. I almost wanted to invite him in for a home-cooked meal."

"Did you talk to him?"

"He vanished on his motorbike before I had the chance." I shrugged. "Maybe the kid was just embarrassed because he was caught wandering around on private property."

"Anything else you can tell us about him?" Semchuk asked.

"No, but there was another visitor . . ."

If Derek was innocent, there could be no harm in telling the police about his presence. Taking a deep breath, I told them about his arrival and his work on a freelance story about the sale of farmland to developers.

Semchuk raised an eyebrow. "Does this man have a last name?"

"It's Tanner."

"Can you give me a description of his vehicle?"

"All I know is that it's a black minivan," I said. "And before you ask, no —"

"We'll find it."

I made myself a cup of tea while Pierce did a search on her computer.

"Are you sure it was a Saskatchewan plate?" she asked a few minutes later.

"Positive. He also said he's from Saskatoon."

"There are no vehicles registered to a Derek Tanner in Saskatchewan."

"That's odd. Anyway, Derek wouldn't have cut my brake line. He didn't know there'd be a storm that would disable Monica's car, and he hadn't even met me until a few days ago."

"Someone planned that accident," Semchuk said. "If the intended victim wasn't Monica, it was you."

An icy chill shook my body. "I can't think of anyone who hates me that much."

"There could be another motive," Semchuk said. "Like financial gain."

"Maybe the killer is Monica's client," I said. "The person who wants to buy my farm. But why would anyone try to kill me to get their hands on my land when there's other rural property for sale?"

Semchuk shrugged. "Lots of crazy people out there."

"We'll look into it," Pierce said. "What's the name of the client?"

"She wouldn't tell me — said it was confidential. But you should be able to find out from her office records."

Further questions went nowhere. Finally, Semchuk handed me his card.

"Call me if Derek Tanner returns. Or ask him to give me a buzz. We want to talk to the bugger."

"In the meantime," Pierce said, "you'd best not stay here alone. Not until the killer's behind bars."

I assured them I'd look after myself. Pierce didn't appear convinced, but she followed Semchuk down the sidewalk to their car. I contemplated my alternatives as I watched them head down my driveway toward the road. Abandoning Diesel wasn't an option. Nor was leaving my gardens. And I hated the thought of imposing on friends or relatives. Although locking my doors and windows might provide inadequate protection, at the moment it was the best I could do.

My interview with the cops had left me rattled. After fifteen minutes spent deadheading flowers, I picked up my pruning shears and headed back to the house. Maybe a cup of mint tea would calm me.

I was climbing the steps up to the deck when Derek returned.

"Did the cops tell you any more about the accident?" he asked without preamble.

"You have nerve showing up here, Mr. 'Tanner,'" I said, emphasizing his last name. Truth is I was scared. Derek might not be trying to kill me, but someone was.

He frowned. "I should have known you'd find out I was using an alias."

"Then why the fake name? And why are you here when you're supposed to be in North Battleford? I hope you didn't come back to revisit the scene of your crime."

"Good Lord, Jeannie, you don't think I killed Monica, do you?"

"The police said someone cut the brake line." The saleswoman had already driven away when Derek showed up, but I couldn't think of any other possible suspects.

"If you left your garage unlocked," he said, "anyone could have tampered with your car."

"No one could have anticipated the storm or predicted that Monica would borrow my Prius." I swallowed hard and took a few deep breaths before continuing. "The police think I might have been the intended victim."

Derek took my hands and pressed them between his. "That's what I'm afraid of. And it's why I'm still here. I didn't cause the accident, but I feel some . . . responsibility."

"Why?"

"I used to be married to Monica. Whenever she can't get what she wants, there's trouble."

"Jeez . . ." I stared at him, open-mouthed. What kind of man marries a blackmailing real estate agent?

"Until now, the uncooperative parties paid for her tantrums," Derek said. "This time, she wasn't so lucky."

I pulled my hands away from his. "At least we know she didn't cut my brake line."

"Nothing is ever simple when you're dealing with Monica. She may not have caused the accident, but she's involved somehow."

"You still haven't told me why you used an alias."

Derek sighed. "It's a long story."

"Then we'd better move inside," I said. It wasn't yet noon, but already the sun was merciless.

"Monica and I got married ten years ago," Derek said as soon as we were settled in the living room. "Second time around for both of us. She was fourteen years younger than me, bright, ambitious, and gorgeous — I thought I'd won the marriage lottery. Then, a few years ago, things started to sour."

I picked up Diesel, who settled in for a nap. "What happened?"

"A buddy told me he'd been talking to one of her former clients. The fellow claimed she'd bullied him into selling his house at under market value. When I asked her what had happened, she dismissed him as a troublemaker. A few weeks later I heard a similar story from a colleague. Then I overheard part of a phone call from one very unhappy customer. Monica always had an explanation." He walked over to the window and stood silently, staring out at the garden.

"Go on," I said.

"At first, I tried to convince myself that she was guilty of nothing worse than assertive business practices. Then a client threatened legal action for blackmail. Monica settled with him out of court, but I wasn't willing to let her off so lightly. We had a big fight, and I decided to call it quits."

"But that wasn't the end of your relationship, right?"

"I couldn't let the matter go," he said. "Having got away with blackmail once, I was afraid she'd try it again. I had to do something."

"You could have gone to the police."

He laughed. "Jeannie, I'm not a journalist. That was a cover story so I could ask you about your dealings with Monica. I'm a cop." He extracted a wallet from his back pocket, pulled out a card, and handed it to me. The man I knew as Derek Tanner was Staff Sergeant Derek Massey of the Saskatoon Police Service.

Diesel was sleeping comfortably on my lap, oblivious to human misdeeds. I hugged him to me as I tried to digest this new information. Derek had wormed his way into my confidence under false pretences. He'd misled me about his identity and about his reason for spending time with me. Suddenly, I was furious.

"You lied to me."

"People get nervous when they talk to cops. I didn't want to scare you away."

"That doesn't explain why you used an alias. Or why you avoided meeting the police."

Derek sighed. "I launched a criminal investigation into Monica's business. She countered with charges of harassment by a vindictive ex-spouse, and my superiors ordered me to drop the case."

"Didn't you have evidence?"

"Nothing solid," he said. "Just bits and pieces that supported my hunch that something rotten was going on. But I couldn't do anything, at least not officially."

"So you assumed a new identity and proceeded unofficially?"

"I'd heard rumours that Monica was after a certain parcel of farmland. The owner didn't want to sell, but she'd uncovered secrets he didn't want made public. By the time I'd tracked him down, the deal had gone through, and the bulldozers had moved in. Poor bugger hung himself the night before my appointment to meet with him."

Derek's concern for my welfare was starting to make sense. "You were afraid I'd do something similar if she'd bullied me into selling her my land."

"I couldn't live with myself if she did."

The living room suddenly felt oppressive. My beautiful house and the paintings on its walls were no safeguard against the power of the outside world. "You can tell me the rest of what happened later. I'm going to the garden to get vegetables for lunch."

As we picked beans and dug potatoes, I brooded on Derek's story. Frank and I had planted hundreds of trees around our house and gardens and left thousands of native poplars in the fields. Bulldozers could destroy in a few days the work of a lifetime. If I'd sold my land, I might have joined the hapless soul she'd driven to suicide.

"I can see why someone might have wanted to murder your ex-wife," I said to Derek, placing the last handful of beans in my pail. "But whoever cut the brake line on my car was trying to kill me."

"Somehow, there's a connection to Monica," Derek said. "I was trying to track down the client who wants to buy your land. She found out and bitched to my boss. He told me to lay off and said that now would be a good time to take a holiday. That's why I was using an alias — I didn't want anyone to hear that Derek Massey was still investigating." He laughed mirthlessly. "Dumb, wasn't it?"

I wanted to believe Derek, but my mind was still reeling. "How do I know I can trust you?"

"Talk to the desk sergeant at the station in Saskatoon. He'll confirm my story."

"I've a better idea," I said, handing him Semchuk's card. "You call Corporal Semchuk from Major Crimes. He wants to talk to you."

"Corporal Bob Semchuk? Is he the officer who interviewed you?"

"Yes," I said. "Do you know him?"

"Big fellow, built like a brick shithouse?"

"More like a heavyweight boxer," I said.

"We worked together during my early years with the Saskatoon City Police. He and I were partners."

"Until he made a career shift to the RCMP?" I asked.

Derek nodded. "Bob's first post was in Winnipeg. I lost touch with him after that. But it would be good to see the old bastard again."

While he pulled out his mobile and punched in Semchuk's cell number, I went into the house to roast new potatoes and make a green bean casserole. When it was ready, I returned to the deck. Derek had finished his call.

"Lunch is ready," I said, placing a pitcher of iced tea on the table. "If you help me carry out the food and dishes, we can eat."

The day was hot and sunny, but the air felt cool on the shady deck. A bee buzzed lazily as it landed on a pot of chives. Nearby, a catbird sang from a thicket of saskatoons. Even with a murderer on the loose, it felt good to be alive.

Derek's company was a welcome addition to my normally solitary lunch. While we ate, he told me stories about patrolling the streets of Saskatoon with Semchuk back when they were both rookie cops.

"The guy's got the tact of a pit bull, but he's a good man to have on your side. He and I have saved each other's bacon more than once."

"Great," I said. "Does that mean he'll let you work with him?"

"Not officially. But he'll let me tag along when he goes out on a call. In the meantime, we both think it's not safe for you to live here alone. How about I park my van by the house and sleep in it until we catch the killer?"

Although it was scary to realize that someone out there wanted me dead, I couldn't continue to live on the farm if I let myself be ruled by fear. "Thanks, but I don't need a bodyguard."

He grinned. "I want to see what it's like to live in a tiny house."

"You'll have to find out another time," I said, trying to sound brave. "I can manage just fine on my own."

We agreed, however, that Derek would spend the afternoon helping me in the garden. He'd leave after supper, and I'd barricade Diesel and me into the house for the night. In the morning, Derek would be off to town for a confab with Semchuk.

"But for now, there's gardening to be done," he said. "I need to work off lunch."

The sun blazed down from a cloudless sky as we weeded the strawberry patch. By the time we finished, we were both soaked with sweat and on the verge of sunstroke.

"No wonder your kids left the farm," Derek said as he dug up a final dandelion. "What's the point of living at the lake if you never take time off?"

I looked at him in surprise. "I like working in the garden."

"A person can have too much of a good thing."

"Want to go swimming instead?"

He nodded. "My trunks are in the van."

The sun was halfway to the horizon as we walked down to the lake and threw our towels on the beach. I dipped a foot into the water. It felt cold after the afternoon heat.

"Last one in's a monkey's uncle," Derek said.

I'm not used to playing on a workday, but the water was refreshing, and Derek's enthusiasm was infectious. We drifted around on old tractor tubes, built an elaborate castle in the sand, and laughed until my belly hurt. By the time we returned to the house, I'd almost forgotten my chagrin at his refusal to discuss the phone call from a woman named Kat.

The sun was setting when we sat down for supper, an impromptu meal of Caesar salad and the leftovers from lunch. Evening-scented stocks perfumed the air, and western grebes muttered sleepily from the lakeshore. Somewhere in the distance, a great horned owl hooted.

The scene was idyllic, but Derek kept breaking off the conversation.

"Okay, what's the problem?" I asked finally. "Either you can't wait to get away from here or you've got something unpleasant to tell me."

He took a deep breath. "Semchuk told me about your husband's accident."

"It's not a secret," I said. "He was on his way home from a stag in North Battleford. Conditions were icy and there was heavy fog. He went off the road the same place Monica did."

"Semchuk investigated the case. He's concerned about the coincidence."

"They happen." I poured myself another cup of tea. "You know what's so ironic? In almost forty years of marriage, it was the first time I'd known Frank to overindulge. He never had more than a few beers if he had to drive afterward. God knows why he made an exception that night."

"Maybe someone else was involved?"

"How? It was a single vehicle accident. And before you ask, there was no evidence that anyone had tampered with the car."

"Semchuk thinks there was something off about what happened. He doesn't have any evidence, just a few things that don't add up."

"Like what?" I asked.

"According to the other guys at the stag, he hadn't been drinking heavily. There was no reason to think that alcohol was responsible."

"The road conditions and weather were bad," I said. "Isn't that enough?"

"His car had four-wheel drive. And Frank's buddies said he was a good driver who knew every twist and turn between Bunchgrass and the farm."

An icy prickle ran down my spine. "What's Semchuk's theory?"

"One of the regulars told him he'd seen Frank talking to a woman in the hallway by the washrooms. She was yelling at him and said she'd make him sorry. Frank walked away after that, so he didn't hear any more. Mind you, the fellow was three sheets to the wind."

"Who was this woman?"

"He didn't know who she was. And no one else had seen her. Since there was no evidence of foul play, the police had no grounds for further investigation."

"The coroner ruled death by misadventure," I said. "If he was drunk, this witness probably made up the whole story."

Derek shrugged. "Semchuk had almost forgotten about the incident. Then Monica was killed at the same spot."

The evening was warm, but I shivered. "Does he plan to reopen the investigation into Frank's accident?"

"He can't. Even if this woman exists, there's no way to find out who she is or her connection to your husband — if, in fact, there is a connection. Semchuk's pissed off because he has no leads on Monica's accident. Maybe he was just letting off steam."

"But that's not what you think, is it?"

Derek reached across the table and took my hands in his. "He's a good cop, but that doesn't make him right. I shouldn't have told you about his suspicions. Let's forget about Semchuk's theories and concentrate on keeping you safe. Are you sure you don't want me to sleep here overnight?"

I'd been having second thoughts about my rejection of his offer, but pride — or prudence — made me stubborn. "I'll close the windows and lock the doors when you go."

"Call if you need help, eh?" He stood up, took a card from his wallet, and handed it to me. "I'll stay in one of the campgrounds at the provincial park, so I'll be close in case there's trouble."

"Thanks."

"Take care of yourself." He pulled me to him in a fierce hug. It lasted a long time, and I was sorry when it ended.

Coyotes howled in the distance as the van's taillights disappeared around the bend in my driveway. Their cry echoed my sudden loneliness. "Guess it's just the two of us, Diesel," I said, picking up my cat and carrying him with me into the house.

Not for the first time since Frank died, I wondered about getting a dog. Preferably a big dog, like Goliath. It was all very well to say I could manage on my own. In reality, I was terrified. Someone was out to get me, and I didn't even know who they were.

Derek's account of Semchuk's suspicions had made matters worse. There was something sinister about a possible connection between the two accidents. But I couldn't begin to imagine the identity of the hypothetical woman who'd been threatening Frank. Nor could I conceive of any reason for open conflict between them.

Seeking distraction, I went upstairs to check the day's emails.

The subject line of the most recent entry read "urgent." I anticipated a financial appeal to help victims of the latest disaster. Instead, I got an anonymous message:

Meet me at the height of land at nine o'clock tonight. I know who cut the brake line on your car. Come alone. If you tell the police, I won't talk.

I stared at the email. It had been sent almost eight hours ago from the public computers in the North Battleford library. The sender had used every cliché in the mystery writer's arsenal, so my impulse was to treat it as a hoax. Further reflection suggested I should take it seriously.

The police hadn't publicized the information about a cut brake line; clearly the sender knew something about the accident. While I wouldn't go to the height of land to meet a possible killer, at least I could find out the identity of the person who'd sent the message.

The time read eight fifteen — forty-five minutes until the library closed. I keyed in the phone number. The woman who answered informed me that the identity of library patrons was confidential. She suggested I call the police. Before I could do so, Liz pulled up beside the garage. I went downstairs and met her at the back door.

"Jeannie, I brought two cartons of eggs. Can't stop because I've picked up Jade —"

"Can you come up to my office? Someone sent me an anonymous email."

"No kidding!" Liz put the eggs on the kitchen counter and followed me upstairs.

I pointed at my computer. "Read it."

"Ho-lee," she said, staring at the computer screen. "Shades of Agatha Christie! I'd laugh if the message wasn't so creepy." She turned to me. "The murderer wants to lure you to an isolated spot —"

"I'm not taking the bait."

"It's got to be someone local." Liz perched on the edge of my desk. "How else would they know about the height of land?"

"That doesn't narrow it down much."

"Maybe George Villeneuve. He covets your farm."

Our neighbour has the biggest property in the municipality and is always looking for more land. But that doesn't make him a killer. "George loves machines," I said. "He wouldn't destroy my car. I'll ask Derek to find out who sent the anonymous email."

"The man who's been helping you in the garden? Why not talk to the police?"

"That's what I'm going to do."

I told Liz about his connection to Monica and the Saskatoon police service.

"Jeez!" she said. "A renegade cop."

"He offered to park his van here and sleep in it until the Mounties catch the killer."

"Hey, you wanna be careful. He'll start out in his van, move to your spare room, and next thing we know —"

"You needn't worry about my virtue," I said. "Not at my age."

"Forget virtue. A wealthy widow like you attracts aging gold-diggers."

Liz is a dear friend, but a two-year marriage twenty years ago left her cynical about men.

"Small farmers and part-time art teachers don't get rich. The only thing of value I own is the farm."

"Owning a house and almost two sections of land makes you wealthy," Liz said. "At least in the eyes of most people."

I flicked a breadcrumb off my desk. "Then you'll be pleased to learn that I turned down Derek's offer."

"Way to go, girl." Liz grabbed my arm and raised it victoriously. "Move in with me. Goliath and I will keep you safe."

"Goliath is a big softy," I said. "Besides, it wouldn't work. Remember what happened after Frank's funeral?" The week I'd spent with Liz had just about ended our friendship. She hadn't appreciated my efforts to create order from the chaos that engulfed her tiny house.

"You were grieving —"

"It's worse when I'm scared. That's when I really get cleaning." I laughed at the horrified look on her face. "Don't worry, I'll lock my doors and windows."

"You'd better," Liz said. "And I'd better hit the road or Jade will have a hissy fit. I'm teaching her to knit, and we've a long way to go."

As soon as Liz was gone, I looked for my mobile to call the police. It wasn't in its usual spot on my desk. Nor was it on top of the filing cabinet. The anonymous message had said to be at the height of land at nine o'clock. It was almost eight thirty. If I didn't reach them soon, the cops couldn't be there in time. Cursing my decision to get rid of the landline, I checked the bookshelves and the supplies cupboard. No phone in sight.

I was on my way to check downstairs when my mobile rang in the kitchen. Then I remembered — I'd placed it on the counter so I could put the eggs in the fridge.

There wasn't time to dwell on my vexation. Derek was on the phone. I told him about my anonymous email and the visit from Liz.

"How old's Jade?" he asked.

"Around twenty. Why?"

"Is she the sort of woman who'd want to play amateur detective?"

"She's young for her age," I said. "And emotionally needy."

"Damn! Call Liz and tell her not to let the girl out of her sight. Then call the detachment. How long will it take me to get to the height of land?"

"From North Battleford? Half an hour. But you won't find it without my help," I said. "I'll stay in the van —"

"Right. I'm just leaving town. Talk to Liz and call me back if either of them isn't home."

Before I could key in her number, my mobile rang again. "Liz," I said, "I was just going to phone you —"

"Jade disappeared. She took my truck. And Goliath. Left a note saying she was off to the height of land."

"Did you call her cell?"

"I left a voice mail. Jeannie, they'll be sitting ducks. We have to go after them."

"Derek will pick me up in twenty minutes," I said. "I'm showing him the way —"

"I'm coming with you," she said, and hung up.

My call to the police didn't take long. The dispatcher listened to my story, took down my directions, and said that a couple officers would be there shortly.

Then I called Derek's cell and told him about Jade's disappearance. He swore quietly and told me to wait for him in front of the house.

"The cops are on their way," I said.

"One of them better be Semchuk," Derek said. "No one else would let me muscle in on their case."

"The local detachment should be glad of your help."

He laughed. "It doesn't usually work that way."

"Maybe Monica's client wrote the anonymous email. Did the cops find out who he is?"

"My ex has always been good at keeping secrets. Her files show no record of any offer to buy your farm. And her staff claim ignorance. Forensics are going through her phone records and her personal computer. So far, they haven't found anything."

When a bicycle headlight appeared in the driveway, I said goodbye to Derek. Then I picked up a flashlight and went out to meet Liz.

"I shouldn't have told Jade about that crazy message," she said giving me a hug. "That woman read too many Nancy Drew novels as a kid."

"Goliath will protect her," I said, crossing my fingers.

"That's what I'm afraid of. But he'd be no match for someone bent on murder."

Derek's arrival put an end to our speculations. Although he tried to discourage her from joining our expedition, Liz stood her ground. It was eight fifty. There wasn't time to argue. She jumped in the back seat of Derek's van, and we set off for the height of land.

Five minutes later we reached the path that led to the top of the hill. Liz's truck was parked beside a clump of poplars.

"Stay in the van with the doors locked," Derek said. "And lean on the horn if you need help. I'm going up."

Liz didn't say anything until he was gone. Then she unbuckled her seatbelt. "I can't sit by when Jade and Goliath are in danger."

"But I promised to stay in the van."

She opened the door. "I didn't."

I'm a coward when it comes to physical danger, but Liz is my friend. "Wait for me," I said.

The height of land was perfect for an assignation. Not only was it miles away from the nearest dwelling, but it also provided the first person who reached the top with a bird's-eye view of intruders. Three brass plates marked the highest point, from which the murderer could imagine themself a powerful god surveying their kingdom.

A narrow trail led uphill over ground scarred with tracks left by joyriding youngsters. Although the light was dim, Liz was a skilled outdoorswoman who could navigate in the dark. Putting a finger to her lips, she took my arm and we set off after Derek.

Before we were halfway up the steep hill, I was gasping for breath.

"Slow down, girl," I whispered. "This old woman can't keep up with a youngster like you."

Liz wrapped an arm around my shoulders. "Lean on me."

"I've got to stop for a rest. You go ahead."

She tightened her grip. "I'm not leaving you here alone."

I didn't have the energy to point out that she wouldn't be much help against an armed killer. Metaphorically gritting my teeth, I lumbered along at her side. Every fibre of my body ached, and I was wheezing like a geriatric patient with asthma.

If there really was someone lurking nearby, they would have to be deaf not to hear me coming.

A coyote howled from a bluff up ahead. Normally I loved the wild, eerie sound. On that lonely hilltop at night, it pierced me with terror. What if the beast was protecting its young and saw us as invaders?

Liz's breath was warm in my ear. "The coyote won't hurt you."

Knowing she was right didn't help. By the time we reached the top, I was shaking with fear and exhaustion. While she scanned the surroundings for movement, I collapsed on a flat outcropping of granite. Then we heard a bang. It was followed by a thump as something big hit the ground. Liz pulled me to my feet. Dragging me after her, she ran toward the sound. A few yards ahead, Jade sat on a grassy knoll. She was cradling Goliath's head in her lap.

Liz crouched beside them. "Are either of you hurt?"

Jade was crying. "Someone shot at me. Goliath ran toward them and got hit instead. Now he's bleeding. I don't know how bad it is."

"We'll get him to a vet," Liz said, and kissed him on the top of his head. "Jeannie, try to stop the bleeding. I'll get Derek's van. It'll be easier to lift him into than my truck."

I knelt beside the dog and played the beam from my flashlight over him. Blood was oozing from a wound in his upper hind leg. I removed my blouse and tied it as snugly as possible around the injury. "Hang on, old fellow. We'll get you some help."

Goliath whimpered as I settled down beside him, one arm clutching his furry body. "Good, brave boy. You saved Jade's life. Liz and I are proud of you." He leaned against me while I stroked his head and softly crooned words of praise. Could fate be telling me that instead of a human bodyguard, I needed to get myself a dog?

The whimpering had almost stopped when it abruptly turned to low growls. I peered into the darkness. A black shadow by the clump of poplars looked like the upright body of a man. Fear fueled my imagination. Maybe it was Derek. Suppose he had sent the anonymous email that lured us to the height of land. I turned off my flashlight and crouched low to the ground. The shadow moved toward us.

"Jade?"

"Don't answer." I said softly. But my warning came too late.

"We're over here," she said.

Derek emerged from the shadows and crossed the space between us. "Jeannie, what the hell —" He flicked on his flashlight and turned its beam on me. "Is anyone hurt? And where's Liz?"

I crouched behind Goliath, shielding myself from Derek's eyes. The temperature was dropping, and I was in shock. My teeth started to chatter.

"She's g-gone to g-get the v-van."

Derek stripped off his shirt and wrapped it around my shoulders. "Is that your blouse bandaging the dog?"

I nodded.

"He got a bullet in his leg," Jade said, and told Derek about the shooting.

"Damn!" He squatted a few feet away from me. "Jeannie, are you okay?"

"I was scared," I said, shrinking from him.

"My God, you don't imagine I shot Liz's dog, do you?"

"Of course not."

Even if he'd had a motive to kill Monica, Derek had no reason for wanting to kill me. My cheeks burned, and I was grateful for the darkness that covered my blushes. If I wasn't careful, I'd be getting paranoid.

Derek turned back to Jade. "Did you see the shooter?"

"It was too dark. I couldn't even tell if it was a man or a woman."

"This person knows how to hunt," he said. "And they know the area. When I spotted them, they disappeared into the trees without a sound."

Jade was crying again. "I wanted to help catch the killer — I didn't mean for Goliath to get hurt."

My relief had turned to anger. "Tell that to Liz."

—\\//—

Although the view from the height of land is magnificent, none of us were in the mood for contemplating its beauty as we waited for my friend to return. We sat in silence, oblivious to the night-sky thick with stars and to the pale moonlight glimmering on Crystal Lake. It seemed an eternity before Derek's van slowly grumbled its way up the trail and stopped beside us.

Liz jumped out. She rushed over to Goliath.

"How are you doing, buddy?" she asked as she knelt beside him.

Goliath whimpered and nuzzled her hand.

"The bleeding's stopped," I said.

Derek had found a blanket in the back of the van. He and Liz were easing Goliath onto it when headlights appeared on the municipal road. The vehicle slowed and turned onto the trail that led up to the height of land.

"It took them long enough to get here," Liz said as the four of us lifted the dog onto the back seat.

A car emerged from the darkness. It pulled up beside us and two people got out.

"Corporal Semchuk and Constable Pierce, Battlefords RCMP," a man's voice said. "We're investigating —"

"Hi, Bob," Derek said. "Did you get lost?"

"Flat tire," Semchuk said. "Massey, you old bastard, what are these civilians doing here?"

The two men slapped each other on the shoulder in what passed for a hug among macho cops.

"Jeannie and Liz had to rescue their friend," Derek said. "I'm just the chauffeur."

I quickly recounted the tale of our escapade. "Sorry you were called out to apprehend a suspect who got away."

Semchuk grunted. "All in a day's work when you're a cop."

"We'll look around before we go," Pierce said. "And come back to search the area when it's daylight."

The mood was sombre as we set out on our return trip, Jade following behind in Liz's truck. Liz had arranged to meet her vet at the clinic and had accepted Derek's offer to drive her there.

"We don't want to move the old fellow any more than we have to," Derek said. "Jeannie, is there anywhere you can stay for a few days?"

I mentally ran through a list of family and friends. "My sister and her husband are visiting their daughter in Regina, and my kids live too far away —"

"Thickwood Farm," Liz said. "It's close, and they have lots of room."

"What about Diesel? I can't leave him to fend for himself."

"I could look after him," Derek said. "If you don't want me in your house, I'd sleep in my van. You could visit him every day. I'd even provide taxi service."

The proposal was generous, but I hated living in someone else's place. Even if the food and atmosphere were good, I needed my own space. My tenants kept a poor table and an untidy house. I didn't want to expend a lot of energy making it liveable. On the other hand —

"Decide already," Liz said. "We're at the turnoff to Thickwood Farm."

I wasn't one of the feisty young women who peopled crime novels. The situation had me scared, and I didn't care who knew it.

"Thanks," I said to Derek. "You can turn in here."

Ava and Thor were playing Scrabble when Jade and I entered the kitchen.

"Something wrong?" Thor asked, staring at Jade's tear-stained face.

"I need refuge for a few days," I said. "There's been a shooting at the height of land."

Ava jumped up from the table. "What happened? Was anyone hurt?"

She and Thor were a good-looking couple in their twenties. Thor, tall and skinny, was already starting to go bald; he wore wire-rimmed glasses and favoured old tweed jackets worn with jeans. Ava was a slender brunette who looked as if she'd stepped from the pages of an L.L. Bean catalogue. They'd both just graduated from university — Thor with a master's in philosophy and Ava a degree in commerce — when they apprenticed at the same Community Supported Agriculture farm. Their subsequent quest for land ended when they — along with Jade — moved to Thickwood Farm the following spring. Although the verdict was still out on their chances of success, all three of them were determined to become farmers.

"They hit Goliath," I said. "Liz is on her way with him to the vet."

Jade burst into tears. "It's all my fault."

With her help, I told them about our terrifying excursion to the height of land.

"Move in with us," Ava said.

Thor seconded her invitation. "There's plenty of room here."

"I'll lend you a nightie," Jade said.

I smiled at her. "That won't be necessary. But thanks for the offer."

If only it hadn't been in my parents' old house. My family's poverty wasn't the problem. Plenty of people make cozy homes, beautiful gardens, and picturesque farmsteads on very small incomes. Not my folks — life on our farm was spartan. Mom and Dad were more interested in anti-war marches and social reform than making an attractive home or fussing over their two daughters.

To be fair, they managed as well as most of the neighbours. My parents maintained a vegetable garden and orchard that fed us and supplied the local farmers' market. They kept the grass mowed, the roof shingled, and the weeds in check. And they weren't the only rural people who considered flowers and water fountains a frivolous luxury. But to a girl who dreamed of English country gardens, the place was bleak.

With my financial support, Ava, Jade, and Thor had tried to spruce up the house. They'd repainted the interior, put a bay window in the living room, and installed new flooring. The resulting improvement was underwhelming. Perhaps I should have hired a professional, but forty years with Frank had given me unrealistic expectations of other people's do-it-yourself skills.

"I'm glad you're here," Jade said. "You can meet my dad. He's arriving tomorrow, and I'm planning a small dinner party. Won't that be fun?"

There were dishes piled in the sink, and the floor needed sweeping. I'd had a hard day, but that was no excuse — I shouldn't have said it. "If you're having company, you'll have to clean up this place. The kitchen's a mess."

There was a long silence. Finally, Jade spoke. "We worked in the garden all day, Jeannie, and we're tired. I'll wash the dishes after breakfast tomorrow."

Ava looked grim. "You're our guest. Don't tell us what to do."

"Ava's right," Thor said. "There's nothing in our rental agreement about housekeeping standards. Those of us who live here get to make the decisions."

"And if you don't like it," Ava said, "you can stay with Liz."

Jade started crying again. I got up from the table, appalled by my own rudeness. If one of my kids had been so critical of someone else's domestic arrangements, I would have bawled them out but good.

"Sorry, I didn't mean —"

Ava and Thor didn't wait to hear my apology. They stalked from the kitchen, backs rigid with indignation. Jade continued to sob. I ducked my head and, like a coward, fled upstairs to my old room. Above the bed I'd hung a painting of my summer garden. Scarlet poppies and bright yellow sunflowers bloomed together in magnificent profusion. They did nothing to dispel my gloom.

TUESDAY, JULY 31

What with a bad conscience, worry about Goliath, and fear of being murdered, I lay awake half the night. The sun, however, woke me as usual around five. I dressed in the previous day's clothes and went outside. Early morning's my favourite time for gardening, the wind light and the air still cool. I picked up one of the hoes that was leaning against the house and walked over to the garden. It had been abandoned for at least ten years, and there were more weeds than vegetables. I'd warned my tenants it wouldn't be easy to grow food the first year, and I was right. The thought gave me no pleasure. Piles of purslane and pigweed suggested that someone had been at work. I would make amends for my rudeness by continuing their efforts.

By seven, I had finished weeding the lettuce. I was about to phone Liz when my mobile rang. It was Jordan. My son knows I'm an early riser and usually makes his calls before he leaves for work.

"Mom, are you okay? Liz told me there was a shooting at the height of land. She said Goliath was hurt."

"I'm fine," I said. "How's Goliath? I've been worried about him."

"The injury looked worse than it was. The vet said it was just a flesh wound. She cleaned him up and sent him home."

"Thank goodness," I said. "But why were you talking to Liz?"

He ignored my question. "She didn't give many details. What happened?"

I repeated the story I'd told Ava, Jade, and Thor.

"This situation's too dangerous for a woman your age," he said. "Stay with me until it blows over."

"Sweetheart, my age is not pertinent. And I'll be fine at Thickwood Farm. Derek asked Liz not to let anyone know I'm here."

"Are you sure you can trust this Derek?"

I wasn't about to admit that I still had one or two reservations. "He's a cop. If you want to check him out, come for a visit."

Jordan was dithering about deadlines at work when Jade called me for breakfast.

"I have to go now," I said, "but thanks for your concern. You don't have to worry about me — my new housemates will keep me safe."

I should have added that this safety might be contingent upon my tolerance for disorder. Although Jade was cheerful as usual at breakfast, Ava and Thor emanated a wintry chill. My attempt at apology the previous night had been perfunctory; I had to appease them somehow, but the necessary words were stuck in my throat. The house and farm, after all, were mine. Considering the low rent I charged, it didn't seem unreasonable to expect my tenants to look after them.

To make matters worse, the lumpy porridge and leaden toast reminded me of breakfasts from my childhood. That my housemates cooked no better than my mother had was a cruel cosmic joke. If I was going to eat at Thickwood Farm, I'd have to teach these kids how to make decent bread.

Ava, Thor, and Jade made it clear that gardening took priority over cooking classes. So much for my generous — if self-serving — offer. I couldn't even make lunch because it was Jade's turn to cook; in the interest of egalitarianism, my tenants stuck to a roster. Feeling totally out of sync with the others, I was about to return to the garden when someone hammered on the front door.

Before anyone could answer, the door flew open and an agitated young man barged into the room. It was my anonymous garden visitor of four days ago.

"I'm looking for the woman who lives on the farm west of here. The one on the lakeshore."

"That's me," I said. "How can I help you?"

"Monica promised me a piece of land for my healing centre, and now she's dead, and the woman at the rural municipal office said I'd need to get legal title to the property —"

I held out a hand to stop the torrent of words. "Wait a minute — you've lost me."

"I want you to honour our agreement."

"Let's start at the beginning," I said. "Who are you, and what's your connection to Monica?"

"My name's Zayden. I work for her. In her real estate business. She said she was buying your farm. Monica believed in my dream and wanted to help me. That's why she was giving me a small piece of the lakeshore."

"The land wasn't hers to give. Monica *wanted* to buy my farm, but it's not for sale. Whatever agreement she made with you is not binding on me."

"You're trying to cheat me," he said. "Monica said that might happen. She told me your kids wanted to sell, and that your refusal was a temporary obstacle we'd have to overcome."

I stared at him. Could he have attempted to take a short cut in removing that obstacle? If I was out of the way, Monica could buy my land . . .

Ava and Thor had been having a whispered conversation; they'd come to the same conclusion as I had.

"Where were you at nine last night?" Thor asked.

If Zayden's look of surprise wasn't real, he'd missed his calling as an actor. "At home watching a movie. What's it to you?"

I looked him straight in the eyes. "You didn't happen to make a trip to the height of land instead?"

"The height of land?"

"It's a few kilometres from here," Jade said. "The place has this amazing spiritual energy —"

"Someone went up there to kill Jeannie last night," Thor said.

Zayden folded his hands in front of him. "I heal the body; I don't destroy it. You're not going to trick me into giving up my claim on the land."

"You have no claim," Ava said.

"I'm willing to settle out of court."

"There's nothing to settle without an agreement of sale." Ava walked over to Zayden and took his arm. "So, unless you have something more to say . . ."

"I'll get a lawyer."

"Tell her to get in touch with Jeannie," Ava said, propelling him toward the door. "Good-bye, Zayden. There's no need to call again."

Jade looked unhappy. "Wait," she said. "We haven't heard about the healing centre. Maybe it's something we can support."

"We've just started farming," Ava said. "No way we're taking on another project."

"Jeannie?" Jade looked at me hopefully.

"Sorry, Jade . . ."

"But if this real estate woman promised —"

I shrugged. "Life's tough."

Jade didn't give up. "I'd like to hear about your plans," she said to Zayden. "Maybe my dad would help."

"Talk to him first," I said. It wasn't likely he would be interested, but I'd let him tell her that.

"Okay." She smiled at Zayden. "You'll like my dad. He's coming for supper tonight and we're having a party —"

I was about to intervene when Thor cut in. "We agreed that dinner invitations need consensus."

"If Zayden comes for supper tonight, he can talk to Dad."

Ava and Thor spoke with one voice. "No."

"Zayden has things to do," Thor added. "And you need to do the dishes."

Jade pouted but had to admit defeat. "I'll walk Zayden to his car and be back in five."

"Motorbike," he said as Jade led him from the house. "They're more environmentally friendly than cars."

Zayden's sound views on transportation did little to reconcile me to his sense of entitlement. What was Jade thinking, supporting his harebrained scheme? She'd just met the fellow.

Ava shared my concern. "Why the hell did we let her join our collective? She acts more like a twelve-year-old than a woman of twenty."

"Jade's a good person," Thor said. "She just needs to grow up."

"We're a farm, not a social service agency."

Ava was right, but I felt a sneaking sympathy for the kid. Under my tough exterior, I, too, yearned to be part of a warm, supportive community. Jade's heart was in the right place; it was too bad she lacked good judgement.

I was about to urge a tolerance I didn't always feel when Derek arrived.

"You two must be Ava and Thor," he said, smiling at them. "I assume the young woman outside is Jade?"

I nodded and introduced him to my housemates. "Derek's helping track down the killer."

"Unofficially," he said. "Who's the man on the motorbike? He looks familiar."

"He worked for Monica," I said, and told him about Zayden's visit.

Derek stroked his chin. "My ex-wife wasn't generous. If she offered him a piece of your land, she wanted something big from him in exchange."

"Like getting rid of the obstacle that stood in the way of her purchase?"

"Exactly. And if he cut your brake line without telling her what he'd done, she'd have no reason to suspect that anything was wrong with your car."

"He didn't act guilty when we asked if he was at the height of land last night," I said.

"That doesn't mean he wasn't there. Talk to my old buddy. He'll want a word with the kid."

I called Semchuk. He told me he'd already interviewed Monica's staff but assured me he'd talk to Zayden again. "Just don't hold your breath waiting for us to arrest him. There's no evidence linking him to the murder."

Evidence or not, I wasn't about to get cozy with Zayden. Jade was another matter. When she returned to the house, she was scowling.

"You're being unfair," she said. "All Zayden wants to do is help people, but you're prejudiced against him because he worked for Monica."

I'd had enough emotional blackmail for one day. With Ava's help, I pointed out that he had a motivation for wanting me dead. "Better not talk to him until the police have arrested the person who cut my brake line."

Jade refused to consider that her new friend could be dangerous — Zayden was a wronged innocent who wouldn't hurt a soul. I was glad that her father would arrive in the afternoon. He could take responsibility for keeping her safe. In the meantime, Derek and I were going to town to visit the woman who may have sent the anonymous email.

"Town" was North Battleford, a rural community that's grown into a small city. As well as the usual business and professional services, it's home to the regional college where I taught part-time, a performing arts centre, two art galleries, a local newspaper, and the charming library from which the anonymous email had been sent. It's also where Frank and I — and our kids — had gone to high school. While big city urbanites might sneer at its limitations, country folks like me are grateful that we don't have to go to Saskatoon to see a dentist, borrow books, or attend a concert.

"Semchuk talked to the librarian and found out that someone named Joan Lawson used a computer around noon yesterday," Derek said as we headed toward town. "When he told me he was going to interview her this morning, I asked if we could tag along."

"Thanks for including me in the visit."

He laughed. "Self-interest on my part. You'd never forgive me if I left you at home."

"I hope you're not implying I'm difficult to get along with," I said, trying to keep my tone light. Mandi's accusation of self-righteousness was an occasional source of tension between my sister and me.

"Women who are always agreeable get boring. That's one of the things that attracted me to Monica — she had a mind of her own. We might have stayed married if she hadn't sacrificed integrity for money."

"Are you sure the initial attraction had nothing to do with her gorgeous body?"

Derek shrugged. "Good looks aren't everything. Jade's a cute kid, but I bet she drives her housemates crazy."

"She's idealistic and naïve," I said. "Plus, emotionally needy. It's a dangerous combination. Makes her vulnerable to men like Zayden."

"Do you think he cut the brake line on your car?"

"Even if he didn't, he's bad news for Jade. Talk about two babes in the woods!"

"Might be good for her to have someone to mother," Derek said, signalling to turn left onto the highway. "Didn't you tell me she's an only child?"

"The only child of working parents who didn't have much time for her. At least, that's her story."

"Most of us find compensations."

"Is that what you did?" I asked.

"Mom had eleven of us to look after. Twelve if you count my dad. We learned to fend for ourselves."

"My folks had a hard time raising two children. How did your parents manage?"

"The older kids looked after the younger ones. I was in the middle, so I got to play both roles."

"You could have formed your own softball team," I said, feeling a stab of wistfulness. "Mandi and I only had each other."

"Weren't there neighbour kids?"

"None our age," I said. "That's what happens when you live in rural Saskatchewan."

Derek grinned. "I hope you made the best of it. Only fools waste time grumbling about things they can't change."

We spent the rest of the trip disagreeing on the pros and cons of raising children on the farm versus raising them in the city. My husband and I had been equally divided in some of our views, but our debates had often ended in bad feelings. The discussion with Derek, however, was *fun*. He appeared delighted by our conversation and exhilarated by the differences between us. Was that the secret to his charm? Or was his attraction a result of the adage about grass being greener elsewhere?

My musings were cut short by our arrival at Joan Lawson's apartment building, a handsome brick structure adorned with wrought iron balconies and floor-to-ceiling windows overlooking a courtyard garden. Semchuk was waiting for us on a wooden park bench flanked by colourful beds of geraniums.

"You're a civilian along for the ride," he told me. "That means you're not part of the investigation, right?"

"No problem," I said. "I want to meet this woman. Especially if she's the person who sent the anonymous email."

The petite, white-haired woman who buzzed us in was an unlikely candidate for murder suspect. She seemed delighted to see us and — once Semchuk had shown her his credentials and made introductions — invited us to join her for tea and cookies.

"I love to show off my pictures," she said. "But once you get to be my age, you don't have many friends dropping by to visit."

The apartment knocked my socks off. Big windows facing south and east flooded the dining and living rooms with light. They illuminated walls covered with simply framed black and white photographs of farm people and rural landscapes.

"Wow," I said, dazzled by the artistic and technical brilliance. "Is this your work?"

Joan smiled. "I figured if Thelma Pepper could become a great photographer late in life, I could at least give it a try."

"They're magnificent," I said, admiring the photo of a sun-hatted old woman weeding a corn patch. "How long have you been taking photographs?"

"I started twenty-seven years ago. When I retired from teaching. But you didn't come here to talk about my pictures." She turned to look at Semchuk. "How can I help?"

Semchuk explained that he wanted to trace the woman who'd used the library's public internet access shortly after noon the previous day.

"I did go to the library yesterday morning," Joan said as she poured boiling water into a pottery teapot, "but I was home by eleven thirty. And I have my own internet, so I don't use the library computer. Are you sure the librarian didn't make a mistake?"

"It was your name on the sign-up sheet," Semchuk said. "And it corresponded with this address. Maybe someone borrowed your library card?"

"Not to my knowledge. But hang on — I'll check my purse."

She disappeared into another room and returned a moment later carrying a red leather handbag and matching wallet.

"It's not here. I walked out of the library with the card in my hand but don't remember putting it in my wallet. I must have dropped it on the sidewalk."

"And whoever picked it up used your card as ID to gain access to the library internet," I said.

Joan frowned. "I hope it hasn't caused mischief in my absence."

"Nothing that the police can't handle," Derek said.

Joan smiled. "That means I shouldn't ask questions, doesn't it?" She poured tea into porcelain cups with matching saucers and then brought out a plate of homemade shortbread. "It's for the grandkids, but I always eat my share."

The tea and shortbread made up for the wretchedness of breakfast. I would have lingered, but Semchuk was getting restless.

"Thanks for your help," he said to Joan. "Now all we need to do is find a witness who saw someone pick up your library card."

"At least you know we're looking for a woman," I said.

Semchuk shrugged. "Or a man who's working with one." He stood up. "Ladies, I hate to spoil the party —"

"Can you leave Jeannie here and pick her up in an hour or so?" Joan asked Derek. "We haven't finishing visiting."

He looked inquiringly at me, and I nodded. There was nothing I wanted more than a good long talk with Joan.

The next hour flew by. Joan had been a grade one teacher, but she and her late husband had farmed southeast of North Battleford for almost fifty years. Like me, they were National Farmers Union supporters; needless to say, we knew a lot of the same people. We also shared an interest in using art to document the beauty of a vanishing rural culture.

"It's not just the landscape that fascinates me," Joan said, pointing to a photograph of a woman weeding a small bed of marigolds and zinnias. In the background were a sagging outbuilding and a derelict car, both surrounded by a tangle of weeds. "Some of these women have incredibly hard lives. Isn't it wonderful that they still manage to grow flowers?"

I looked closely at the picture. Joan had captured a moment of innocence and . . . hope. Maybe even contentment. The woman was faintly smiling. Beyond the outbuilding and vehicle was a mixed band of poplars and spruce. I recognized some of the weeds as native goldenrod and tall blue asters. Could Joan believe what I thought she was saying?

"This woman's husband may have been a shiftless brute," I said.

"He seemed a fine man to me," Joan said. "Just saw the world differently from most farmers. And his wife loved him."

"You knew these people?"

"Not exactly knew. But women usually invited me to stay for tea after a photography session. Often, they'd tell me about their lives. This woman did. She was happily married, with grown children and grandkids nearby. I've no reason to think people like her were less content than their counterparts in the city."

"Not that that's saying a lot," I said. "Considering the high rates of urban suicide and depression."

"Unhappiness has always been with us," Joan said. "But isn't so much of it caused by unrealistic expectations? The ancient stoics may have been on to a good thing."

I would have argued my point, but Joan was a smart woman with years of life experience. What if she was right? Then her buzzer rang, and the opportunity for discussion passed. Derek was at the door. He hadn't learned much.

"The Mounties are interviewing people who live across the street from the library and appealing for information from anyone in the vicinity yesterday around noon. Chances are nothing will come of their efforts, but you never can tell."

"How about the person who used the internet?" I asked. "Can the librarian describe her?"

"Monday there was a kid's carnival in the park next to the library. Some of the kids came in costume. The person who used Joan's card wore sunglasses, a hat that covered her hair, and a ragged purple track suit. The librarian assumed that she'd costumed herself as a tramp. All she could say about the woman is that she was thin and over fifty. But even that doesn't help. The writer could have got their mom to send the message."

Derek ate a final cookie while Joan and I hugged good-bye. We agreed to keep in touch — not only did we share common interests, but Joan now had a vested interest in the case. Someone had used her library card for illicit purposes, and she wanted to know what would happen next.

It was almost noon when we got back to my farm. Although I'd been staying with my neighbours for less than twenty-four hours, it felt as if I'd been away for days. The flowers, however, were still blooming, the birds still singing, and the mignonette still smelling as sweet as it had when I'd left. Diesel circled round my feet, meowing for attention. I picked up my cat and gave him a hug. He purred loudly in my ear.

After lunch, Derek helped me water my potted plants.

"You don't have to do this," I said as he filled a watering can. "There's only so much responsibility a man needs to take for failure to control his ex-wife's actions."

"Hey, I'm enjoying my farm vacation. Any time you want me to move into your house, just say the word."

"Slow down already," I said. "We've known each other only three days."

His grin would have softened harder hearts than mine. "Want me to provide references?"

I plucked a dead flower from a pot of red begonias and threw it at him. "This isn't a workplace, mister."

Much as I wanted to return home, I wasn't about to share my house with a man I couldn't trust. Even if the garden was looking especially lovely. Asiatic lilies were the current stars, but they'd soon be replaced by daylilies and a bed of annual rudbeckias. While I'm no fan of violence, I could almost imagine committing murder to protect land that nurtured such beauty.

Derek's cell phone jolted me back to reality.

"That was Semchuk," he said when he'd finished the call. "He talked to Zayden. The kid might have a motive for murder, but there's no evidence he tampered with your car or had access to a rifle."

"Did Semchuk find out where Zayden was last night?"

"At Jackfish Lodge. The desk clerk swears he didn't leave his room until morning. He can't have been at the height of land."

"Maybe he has an accomplice."

Derek smiled. "Jeannie, you're grasping at straws."

"Don't patronize me. You're not the person they're using for target practice."

"Why do civilians always think they know better than the professionals?"

I ignored the rhetorical question. "Any leads on the identity of Monica's client?"

"None."

The sun was blisteringly hot. Sweat trickled down my forehead. I impatiently wiped it away. "What are the police going to do next?"

"Monica's funeral is on Thursday. I'm going to it, as will Semchuk and Pierce. If we're lucky, the killer will be there."

"Wearing a nametag that says 'murderer'?"

He laughed. "If only it were that easy. Best we can hope for is something that draws attention to that person. Not that it often happens outside mystery novels."

"You mean, someone could become a suspect because they cried at the funeral?"

He shrugged. "We'd have a chat with that person."

"Then I'm going with you," I said. "Maybe I'll recognize someone who shouldn't be there unless he or she is connected to the crime. I could talk to them —"

"Leave that to the police. All you'd have to do is identify the suspect."

I turned off the water and started to coil up the hose. It was time for an afternoon nap.

"I'm going up to the treehouse for a snooze," I said. "If you want to join me, there's a comfortable hammock underneath it."

"What treehouse?"

"It's in the shelterbelt at the south end of the garden."

Frank had built the treehouse as a hangout for the kids; when they left home, I'd claimed it as my personal space. Attached to stout branches halfway up an enormous hybrid poplar, it boasted a magnificent view of the flower garden and provided a cool, shady place to sleep.

"This is it," I said as we approached the hut half-hidden in the trees.

A rope ladder led up to a single room furnished with a small wooden table, two chairs, and a folding canvas chaise lounge.

"This would be a great place to play cops and robbers," Derek said. "I bet your kids loved it."

"They weren't the only ones," I said. "It's my favourite place for a summer nap."

"Too bad that lounge chair's not bigger."

"It's a small treehouse," I said. "You'll have to use the hammock down below."

A light breeze stirred the branches overhead as I made myself comfortable on the canvas recliner. Below me, the hammock rustled under Derek's weight. Despite my flippant response, his comment had got under my skin. Six months of widowhood had left me starved for male companionship. The thought of lying next to Derek on the narrow lounge chair made my cheeks burn. It was a long time before I fell asleep.

When we woke, the air was cooler. I picked, shelled, and froze peas while Derek watered young spruce trees. Then it was time to return to Thickwood Farm and the prospect of sitting down to dinner with Jade's father.

"He runs a sporting goods store in Saskatoon," I said. "God knows what he'll make of the farm."

"First visit?"

"Jade says he's a busy man."

"Look on the bright side," Derek said. "Chances are they'll cook a good meal in his honour."

There was no gleaming BMW in the driveway when we arrived. Either Jade's dad had parked behind the house, or he was late. I didn't want to consider the third option. If he'd postponed his visit again, Jade would be devastated.

"Okay if I come in and say hi to your friends?" Derek asked.

"Please do."

The empty kitchen looked better than usual. Someone had swept and washed the floor and placed a mug of wildflowers on the counter. The scarred wooden table was covered with a bright red cloth and boasted colourful stoneware from the local thrift store.

"The prospect of guests is a great motivator," I said. "They need to have visitors more often."

"Jeannie?" Ava appeared on the stairway, trailed by Thor.

"Where are Jade and the guest of honour?" I asked.

"The bastard's not coming because an unexpected business meeting took priority," Thor said. "Jade's upstairs bawling her eyes out."

"The poor kid spent all morning cleaning the house," Ava said. "And Thor roasted a chicken —" She stopped and looked speculatively at Derek. "If it's okay with the others, would you stay for dinner? We could use some cheerful company."

I wouldn't have been thrilled by the invitation, but Derek accepted it gracefully. While the two men exchanged pleasantries, Ava went upstairs. She returned moments later with Jade, who looked as if a favourite dog had just died.

I gave Jade a hug while Thor set out the food. As soon as he'd deposited the chicken in front of Derek, we all sat down to eat.

"The chicken's a treat," Jade said, wiping away the tears that were trickling down her cheeks again. "This was supposed to be a special occasion."

Derek smiled at her. "It looks wonderful."

Although the food was better than usual, it didn't deserve high praise. The peas, tossed green salad, and new potatoes were good, but the chicken was tough. Derek brushed aside Thor's apologies.

"It's hard to judge cooking time for free-range birds," he said, helping himself to a second drumstick. "Most recipes assume the chicken was factory-farmed and didn't get any exercise. Good on you for trying your hand at cooking one raised on a real farm."

I looked at him in surprise. He was sitting on the other side of the table, expression bland as he forked a piece of meat into his mouth. Then, for the space of a moment, he winked at me.

Dessert was an apple cake made with too much whole wheat flour. I dutifully washed my piece down with a cup of hot tea. Derek asked for seconds.

As dinner parties go, this one would not have rated five stars. Jade was quieter than usual, and Thor's reticence had been exacerbated by embarrassment. I was still stressed out by the possibility of another murder — with me as the victim. Derek, however, filled the conversational gaps with a string of funny cop stories. While Frank would have silently endured the party, my new companion enjoyed both food and company. I was beginning to like this man.

It was almost eight before we got up from the table. I carried dirty dishes to the sink while Ava and Thor washed and dried. They were leaving the next morning for an organic farm tour south of Saskatoon. Jade was going with them as far as the city. Over the banging of pots and pans, I could hear her telling Derek that her mom was taking her out for lunch. The prospect seemed to have cheered her up considerably.

With my three housemates away, I'd have the place to myself. The forecast was for strong wind from the northwest. Since the weather wouldn't be great for gardening, I'd house-clean. It would be a good way to thank my tenants for their hospitality. Maybe I could persuade Liz to help. She wasn't much good as a cleaner, but I'd enjoy her company. Telling Derek I'd be back in a minute, I went upstairs to text her and to check my emails.

My anonymous correspondent had sent another message. It was short and to the point: *I told you to meet me alone.*

I called downstairs to Derek.

He was grinning as he entered my room, but the smile faded as he read the email. "I'm calling the detachment."

Semchuk was in, and Derek told him what had happened. "It was sent at two this afternoon. Could have been from the same place. We should have asked the librarians to keep an eye out for a woman using Joan's card."

"She's taking a risk," I said when he'd ended the call. "What if someone can give a description of her?"

"Semchuk's going to check it out," Derek said. "But don't count on him learning anything useful. There was no joy from our previous inquiries."

"There was for me," I said. "I met Joan."

"The silver lining, eh? I'm glad someone's happy. But don't underestimate the killer. This person's not stupid. They might know you've moved here. With your housemates planning trips to Saskatoon and beyond, I'd like to spend the entire day with you."

I played it cool. "How are you at housecleaning? I was going to ask Liz, but you can't be any worse than she is."

"Housecleaning?" Derek looked baffled. "Your place is spotless."

I told him about my plan to clean at Thickwood Farm while its inhabitants were away.

"Have you notified these folks?"

"It's going to be a surprise. For letting me stay here."

Derek frowned. "How would you feel if someone cleaned your house without your consent?"

"If they washed the windows, I'd be delighted."

"Jeannie, I'm serious. Your 'surprise' sounds like a bad idea."

I shrugged. "If you don't want to help, you can weed the garden while I tidy up inside."

Derek remained critical, but he didn't get a vote. After a last-ditch effort to dissuade me from my plan, he kissed

85

me on the cheek and left. I considered the option of going downstairs to chat with my housemates, but his opposition had unsettled me. People pay big bucks for decluttering and cleaning services, and I was offering to do both for free. Telling myself that he was mistaken, I read the rest of my emails. Then I went to bed.

But not to sleep. Derek's kiss, casually bestowed, had evoked memories of Frank. Had he really been arguing with an unidentified woman on the night of his accident? While I didn't believe that someone else had played a role in my husband's death, I needed certainty. Stan had been with Frank that night. Although he hadn't mentioned any suspicions, my friend was reticence personified. Maybe he'd seen or heard something important. First thing in the morning, I'd give him a call.

WEDNESDAY, AUGUST 1

S tan has an annoying habit of leaving his mobile at home when he goes out to do chores. I'd called at seven, hoping to catch him before he left for work. Instead, I got his answering machine.

"Darn!" I slammed down my cell phone. Stan would see my number on call display, and he'd get back to me. If I was lucky.

Derek arrived an hour later, just in time to wave goodbye to my housemates as they set off on their day trip. While we ate pancakes with last fall's chokecherry syrup, I asked him about his unexpected knowledge of culinary lore.

"Amazing what you can pick up when you keep your ears open," he said. "I've never roasted a bird, but I know some good cooks. If you're willing to listen, you can find out almost anything."

"Thanks for being there and saving Jade's 'dinner party.'"

"My pleasure," Derek said. "They're good kids."

I stabbed a piece of pancake and forked it into my mouth. "Too bad they're also slovenly."

"The place looks okay to me," he said, eyes surveying the kitchen. "Not everyone has your high standards."

"My parents didn't. They were untidy and disorganized. I hated the chaos."

"So, they weren't neat freaks. Get over it." He reached for the syrup. "Our house was a zoo, but I survived. With eleven kids, Mom had a hard time just keeping food on the table."

"Is that why you ate with such enthusiasm last night?" I asked.

"Thor was embarrassed. I wanted to give him a break."

I smiled at Derek. "I bet you're the guy who plays good cop when you and a colleague are questioning a suspect."

"Someone's got to do it." He pushed away his empty plate and got up from the table. "I still think your plan is dumb, but if we're gonna houseclean, let's get at it."

I stood in the doorway and surveyed the kitchen. Although it had been tidied, the room needed a deep clean.

"Okay," I said to Derek, "you start on the walls and ceiling. "I'll do the cupboards."

If there was an organizing principle behind my housemates' decisions about where to put everything, I couldn't see it. Commandeering a notebook and pencil, I made a plan that identified a place for every item in the kitchen. Dishes went in the cupboard closest to the table, spices in the drawer above the tea towels, pots on the shelves next to the stove. Then I got a pail of hot soapy water and started to clean.

Four hours later, I replaced the last of the baking pans on a pristine shelf and closed the cupboard door.

"At least I'll be able to find the quinoa and measuring cups when it's my turn to cook," I said. "Want to break for lunch now?"

Derek wrung out his washcloth and tossed it on a chair. The walls, ceiling and floor weren't perfect, but they looked better than they had before.

"I know men who'd consider your actions grounds for divorce," he said.

I picked up the cloth and hung it on a nail behind the stove. "Nonsense. Look at all the work we've saved them."

Lunch was old cheddar and whole wheat crackers with carrots dug from the garden. Then it was back to my place for the daily session of tending plants and feeding Diesel.

Derek frowned as we turned onto the driveway. "Fresh tire marks. Were you expecting company?"

My heartbeat speeded up as my body went into flight mode. The double tracks had been made by a car or a half ton. Not Zayden, then. "Could be a neighbour who didn't know I was staying at Thickwood Farm," I said, trying to put a good spin on the situation.

He didn't buy it. "Want to stay in the van while I take a look around?"

"My farm, my responsibility," I said. "I'm coming with you."

We pulled up beside the garage. An overnight wind had brought smoke from northern wildfires, but I'd been so pre-occupied with housecleaning that I hadn't paid attention to the darkening sky. I opened the van door and stepped out into a cloud of acrid smog. Despite the heat, I shivered.

Derek touched my shoulder. "Whoever your visitor was, they're gone. There's a second set of tracks leading back to the road."

I nodded and set off briskly down the sidewalk. What if my caller had been the killer and had seen my cat?

Derek must have sensed my distress. "Diesel didn't ask to go out after I gave him breakfast, so I left him inside."

Feeling marginally better, I climbed the steps up to the deck, Derek close behind me. The front door showed no sign of disturbance. Fingers crossed, I rounded the corner of the house — and stopped. Something lay motionless in front of the back door. It looked almost like a dog. A medium-size dog. Only, the shape and the colouring were wrong.

Derek pushed past me. "Stay back, and don't touch anything. I'm calling Semchuk."

I stared at the dead coyote. It was lying on its side. Flies buzzed around a small circle of matted fur rusty with blood. One paw half-covered a piece of lined paper. On it were two short words. While Derek talked to Semchuk, I inched forward until I was close enough to read them.

You're next.

Stomach roiling, I stood rooted to the ground. Derek holstered his mobile and turned in my direction. Three steps later, he was by my side.

"Jeannie, what's wrong?"

I pointed at the paper. Derek read its message. Then he took my hands and pulled me to him.

"We're going to get this son of a bitch."

I tried to smile. "Better make it soon. Before I succumb to a case of the vapours."

"Semchuk and Pierce will be here in twenty minutes," he said, releasing me. "Want to go in the house while we wait for them?"

I nodded. "I need to feed Diesel."

Derek pulled on a pair of the disposable gloves he carried in his pocket and unlocked the front door. I followed him into the kitchen. There was no sign of an intruder.

Diesel was sitting by his food bowl, asking for lunch.

"Sorry you had to spend the morning inside, old boy," I said, spooning food into the bowl. "Although with a killer on the loose, it's safer in here."

"I could install a cat door into your mudroom," Derek said. "Then, if the shooter came around again, he could hide either inside or out."

"Thanks. I'd like that."

When he finished eating, Diesel followed us outside and into the garden. My hands trembled, but I wasn't about to let the killer keep me from tending my plants. As I carried pails of water to the strawberries, I let the mindless work relax my jangled nerves. With luck, I'd be coherent by the time the police arrived.

Semchuk was no happier to see me than I was to see him.

"The municipality ought to install a toll booth on the road to your farm. The number of trips I've been making, they'd collect a fortune."

Pierce smiled sympathetically. "You've had quite a scare. Are you okay?"

I wasn't, but there was no point in telling her that. Instead, I asked what the librarian had told them about my recent anonymous email. "Did she give you information about who sent it?"

Semchuk snorted. "Whoever contacted you used the same library card as last time. Probably figured if she got away with it once, she'd get away with it again."

"Could the librarian describe her?" Derek asked.

"Of course not. She was new on the job and said she didn't know most of the patrons. Probably thinks every woman over fifty looks alike. Who the hell hires these kids anyway?"

With Derek's help, the two cops examined the dead coyote. It had been shot by the same firearm — a .22-250 rifle — that had injured Goliath. Semchuk's observation that the killer obviously knew what they were doing wasn't much help. Most of the male population of my rural community could use a firearm and at least a few of the local women were crack shots.

The handwritten message was equally useless. It had the same blunt style as the previous emails. But unless the writer had left fingerprints, which Semchuk considered unlikely, it wouldn't help identify them.

"We need to come up with a clearer motive," Semchuk said. "I mean, I could understand someone using threats as a bargaining tool when they're trying to buy land. But how could a landowner sell to a person who remains anonymous? The shooter's gotta be crazy."

I sat down on a deck chair as far away as possible from the dead animal. "Why do you suppose they want my land rather than lakeshore land in general? Maybe we need a psychologist to figure out their motive."

Semchuk scowled. "Psychology's a lot of bunk. If you want results, nothing beats good, old-fashioned police work."

"Fine," I said. "In the meantime, what happens to the coyote?"

"We'll dispose of it. Don't want the lady having nightmares, eh?"

Pierce looked at me and rolled her eyes, but she didn't say anything. It can't have been easy being stuck with a sexist boss. I nodded in acknowledgement and held my tongue. Pierce was young — and bright. With any luck, she'd outrank him one day.

When the Mounties had gone, I hugged Diesel goodbye and set off with Derek on the return trip to Thickwood Farm. An unbroken stretch of at least six hours lay before us — plenty of time to finish the downstairs.

"The mudroom needs major organizing," I said as we walked through the back door, "and the books in the living room need to be reshelved. Otherwise, all we've got to do is clean. If you wash the walls, ceilings, and floors, I'll do the rest."

Sorting and categorizing the books was a welcome diversion from thoughts of murder. A lot of them were discards from my collection, but my tenants had made their own contributions as well. Was it fair to assume that the works of philosophy and the fat tomes by great Russian novelists had belonged to Thor? Who had contributed the dozens of volumes on organic gardening and alternative agriculture? The romance novels and New Age books on spirituality and healing? I would have enjoyed escaping to the pages of their imaginary worlds, but the mudroom called.

Halfway through the piles of mismatched boots and old toys that were an unclaimed legacy of my childhood, I began to have second thoughts. What if Derek was right? What if Ava, Thor, and Jade *liked* living in a messy house and would be royally pissed off because I'd failed to consult them? Surely, they wouldn't evict me.

I plugged in the kettle, spooned a chai blend into individual strainers, and tracked Derek to the living room. "Want to take a short break?"

He was uncharacteristically quiet as we drank our tea. Finally, he reached across the table and took my hand. "You're starting to think this was a bad idea, aren't you?"

I let my hand rest in his for a moment before gently pulling it away. "The house needed cleaning."

"That's not the point, is it?"

I wanted to tell him about the embarrassment I'd suffered as a child whenever visitors arrived, but the thought of spilling my guts made my cheeks tingle. What kind of a person holds on to grudges for forty years?

"Exactly what is the point then, Mister Armchair Analyst?"
I asked.

"Something happened in your past that made you obsessed
with cleanliness and order."

I poured a second cup of tea and drank it in silence.
Frank would have left me to my thoughts, but Derek was
less diffident.

"Come on, Jeannie, give. They say confession's good for
the soul."

A fly buzzed around the kitchen, and I swatted it away
from me. "I don't like being humiliated."

"Yeah?"

"We don't have time to talk about this now. There's cleaning to be done —"

He crossed his arms and raised an eyebrow.

"Jeez, Derek, it happened a long time ago."

"Still bugs you, eh?"

I sighed. "There's not much to tell. I met a man in art class
my first year of university. One Saturday in November he
came with me out to the farm. When we arrived, my parents
were cutting up a pig they'd butchered."

"So?"

"I'd told them we were coming, but the place was a mess.
The kitchen table was covered with raw meat, the floor was
filthy, and the place smelled like an abattoir. As for the living
room, I don't suppose anyone had dusted for at least a month."

"Fall's a busy time. They'd been working —"

"Derek, I'd brought a guest. You don't entertain guests
in a messy house."

"My parents did. Not that we often had company."

I ran a hand through my hair in exasperation. "Alastair's
parents' place was immaculate."

"Chances are they didn't need to cut and wrap a pig the day you called."

"He never asked me out again."

Derek snorted. "If the bugger was put off that easily, he was no loss. Besides, weren't you already dating the man you later married?"

"We weren't engaged then, and we hadn't agreed to go steady. And in case you're wondering, I wasn't sleeping with Alastair."

"What if it had been Frank who'd been with you that day?"

"That would have been different."

"I'd say you had a lucky escape and should count your blessings."

The kitchen was oppressively hot and smelled like wood smoke from the forest fires. I rose from the table and used the nearby notebook as a fan to cool my cheeks. Maybe Derek was right — not just about Alastair, but also about my compulsive need for order. For the first time since we'd started cleaning, I considered the possibility that my efforts could have dire consequences. Where would I go if my housemates threw me out?

But as a former Saskatchewan premier famously once said, "Never say whoa in a mudhole." It was too late to undo my decision. I'd carry on with my plan — and hope for the best.

It was dark by the time we ate dinner, but we'd finished what I'd set out to do. The downstairs, though still shabby, was clean. I'd picked marigolds from the garden to brighten the living room and distract the eye from an old burn mark on the sofa table. The next day I'd wash all the curtains and pick up a landscape painting from my studio. It would look good behind the wooden rocking chair.

We were eating leftover apple cake when headlights appeared in the driveway. Tires crunched on gravel, and a truck door slammed.

Derek got up from the table, the muscles in his face tense. "Want me to stay with you, or would you rather face the mob alone?"

I didn't have time to answer before the back door opened and my housemates entered. Ava took a quick look around and then blew up.

"What the hell happened to our kitchen?"

It was a rhetorical question, but I answered. "I cleaned it."

Ava brushed off Thor's restraining arm. "Who told you to do that?"

"She just wanted to help," Jade said.

I tried to smile. "It was a thank-you for letting me stay."

"Bullshit. You wanted to impose your middle-class values on us."

I looked at Derek for support, but he shrugged and threw up his hands. Jade started to cry. Ava ignored her and pulled open a couple of drawers.

"What the fu—"

"I put all the herbs and spices in one place."

Ava stormed past me into the living room. Moments later she returned carrying the jar of marigolds. "Damn it, you didn't even ask if you could pick the flowers."

"I didn't mean —"

"Get out," Ava said. "Now."

Thor put his arm around her shoulders. "Sweetie, it's okay."

Ava dumped the marigolds in the compost pail. "If you're not out of here in five minutes, the contents of your overnight bag will be next." She turned to Derek and jabbed a finger in his face. "Last night you pretended to be on our side. I thought I could trust you."

Derek moved a few steps back and took my hand. "Let's go."

She grabbed the front of his shirt. "Fucking cops, they're all alike —"

"Enough," Thor said, pulling her toward him. There was a ripping sound, and Ava stood in front of Thor with a strip of blue plaid broadcloth in her hand.

Thor broke the silence. "Sorry, dude —"

"It's an old shirt," Derek said.

Although the kitchen was warm, I was shaking as we walked toward the door.

"This is my place, too," Jade said, "and I don't want Jeannie to go."

Thor looked at Ava. "It's not safe for her at home, and it's too late to find another place for the night."

"I don't like control freaks," Ava said.

Derek leaned over and spoke quietly in my ear. "These folks are both your tenants and your neighbours. You'll have to make peace with them at some point. May as well be now."

Knowing he was right didn't make it easy to apologize, but it had to be done.

"Ava, I'm sorry I cleaned the house without asking your permission. I should have consulted all three of you before I even considered it."

Jade beamed. "Now she can stay, right Ava?"

"At least for the night?" Thor said, looking at his partner.

Ava's face remained stony. "One night, and then I'll think about it."

I wanted to point out the lack of wisdom in alienating the person who owns the land you're renting, especially when that person rents to you at half the market price. But I was tired, and the next day was Monica's funeral. This was clearly a case when discretion was the better part of valour.

"Thanks," I said. "I'll call Mandi tomorrow. If she's home, I'll stay there until the killer's arrested."

Jade gave me a hug. She and Thor wished me goodnight, and the three of them headed upstairs to bed.

I smiled at Derek. "Thanks for not saying 'I told you so.'"

"Live and learn, eh?" He put his arms around my shoulders and enveloped me in a close hug. "Are you okay, Jeannie?"

The stoic resolve that had carried me through the day suddenly vanished, and I wanted to weep tears of — what? Rage? Disappointment? Grief? Instead, I lifted my face to his and kissed him on the cheek. "You're a good friend."

"Is that all I am to you?"

I looked into his clear blue eyes. "We haven't known each other long."

He laughed softly. "When you're a cop, you have to make quick decisions."

Next thing I knew, his mouth was on mine, and he was kissing me, hard. I pressed my body against his and returned the kiss with enthusiasm. Then, in the darkness behind my eyelids, I saw Frank's face. He looked like an abandoned child. I pulled away from Derek and tried to erase the image of my late husband.

"Sorry, I — can you pick me up at seven tomorrow morning? I'll need time at my place to shower and get ready for Monica's funeral."

He nodded. I couldn't tell from his expression whether he was angry, hurt, or bewildered. All I knew for sure was that I was both grateful for his companionship and scared like hell of what lay ahead.

Despite my ambivalence, I slept soundly that night, the memory of our kiss wrapping me in its embrace.

THURSDAY, AUGUST 2

I woke early and called Mandi. A trained recreation director, my sister decided early in her career that she would sooner be at home with her kids than organizing crafts and bingo for care home residents. Since then, she's reserved July and August for holidays and worked part-time the rest of the year.

Mandi and her husband, John, had got back from Regina the previous night, and she was bubbling over with news of her daughter and grandkids.

"But you can see my little darlings for yourself," she said. "Melissa and Ty came home with us. They're visiting for two weeks. How about you join us for supper tonight?"

"That's why I called. I need a place to sleep for the next few days."

"Jeannie, what's wrong?"

I recounted the saga of my dealings with Monica and its deadly aftermath.

"My goodness," Mandi said. "Of course you can stay here. You'll have to share with Melissa, but the bed's queen-size so that's okay."

"Thanks." I desperately wanted my own room, but that wasn't an option. "Expect me just in time for dinner. It will be late afternoon when we get back from Monica's funeral."

"We?"

"I'm going with a . . . friend."

"She's welcome to join us," Mandi said.

"Thanks, but he has other plans."

Even from a mile away, I could sense Mandi's social antennae quivering. She restrained her curiosity, however, and returned to a subject we'd talked about earlier.

"You barely knew this real estate woman. There's no need for you to be at her funeral. You'd be better off spending the day at the lake with the grandkids and me."

I told myself it would be ungenerous to desert Derek, but in truth I was curious. Would I recognize the murderer if they showed up at Monica's funeral?

"Just doing my social duty," I said, and signed off the call.

I dressed quickly in the shorts and T-shirt I'd worn the day before, ran a comb through my hair, and went outside to wait for my ride. Derek arrived a few minutes later, hair still wet from the shower and wearing the spiffy suit he'd bought for the funeral.

He opened the van door, and I slid in beside him. "You look great. Is that the mandatory dress for ex-husbands?"

"We had a few good years together," he said. "I owe her some respect."

I nodded. "If I had an ex-husband, I hope he'd do the same for me."

During our short drive to my farm, neither of us spoke about the previous evening. Derek looked preoccupied and I was stricken with an unexpected case of self-consciousness. Had our enthusiastic kisses changed the dynamics of our relationship, or was I hopelessly old-fashioned in my expectations? The uncertainty was compounded by my own lack of clarity: did I trust Derek enough to get involved with him, and only six months after Frank's death?

Diesel was stretched out on a lounge chair basking in a patch of sunshine when we arrived at the farm. The smoke of the previous day had dissipated and left the sky a clear robin's-egg blue. Pleased that travel conditions would be good, I scooped up my cat and carried him with me into the house.

"I've missed my buddy," I said, stroking his silky fur. "That stalker owes us big-time compensation."

Derek turned on the coffee maker. "I've fed the old boy. Want me to make breakfast for us while you get ready?"

Ten minutes later I returned to the kitchen wearing my funereal best. The short-sleeved black linen dress flattered me, and I was unreasonably pleased by Derek's approval. No way I wanted to look dowdy at Monica's last hurrah.

We took our coffee and toast onto the deck, which was blessedly free of dead animals. A patch of red salvias sparkled in the sunshine, their brilliant colour contrasting with the green of trees and shrubs. Goldfinches twittered as they darted around the bird feeder, and two Baltimore orioles sang in a nearby tree.

"Wish I could come back here after the funeral," I said. "Mandi and John brought their grandkids home from Regina, and tonight I'll be sharing my bed with a rambunctious five-year-old."

Derek laughed. "Didn't your kids ever sleep with you when they were young?"

"Of course they did. But they were better behaved. And they were *my* kids."

—W—

Aside from her dodgy business practices, Derek had told me little about his ex-wife. He'd neatly evaded my questions and put on his stoic cop-face when anyone mentioned her name. The two-hour drive to Saskatoon, however, evoked a flood of memories.

"One of my buddies dragged me to a Latin American singles dance," Derek said as we cruised down the highway in his van. "That's where I met Monica. And, my God, the woman could move. Tango, cha cha, rumba — she was dynamite in my arms. Two months later, we were married."

I bit back a snarky comment about middle-aged men and their mid-life crises.

His face softened. "She was so alive. So passionate. She threw herself into everything with such reckless abandon."

"Including business success?"

"That didn't come until later. Until she felt the approach of old age."

"Monica wasn't old," I said.

"That's what I told her. But when she discovered her first grey hairs, she panicked. I guess she decided that if she couldn't be young, she'd be rich."

I nodded. "A dubious trade-off at best."

"My working-class wife had middle-class aspirations. For the first eight years or so. Then her aim ratcheted up a notch. That's when the trouble started."

"What about her first husband, was he wealthy?"

Derek snorted. "The guy was a deadbeat. She married him at eighteen. They divorced two years later."

Outside, the sky was blue, and the sun shone brightly. Much as I wanted rain, most people would have said it was a beautiful day. A good day to be alive. Only, Monica was dead. I reached out and touched Derek's hand. "This must be tough for you."

He signalled to pass a car in the lane ahead. "Our marriage was essentially over a couple years ago."

"I'm sorry."

"Don't be."

"Was your first marriage better than the last?" I asked. "You haven't told me anything about it."

"What is this, twenty questions?"

"Just making conversation."

Derek patted my shoulder. "Jeannie, you are one nosy woman."

"Interested is a better word," I said. "Tell me about your first wife."

"She was a sweet, conventional woman who wasn't cut out to marry a cop."

"Didn't like the odd hours and the overtime?"

"Amongst other things," he said. "Her name was Fiona, and she was my first girlfriend. Strange that I married her, eh?"

"I was Frank's first girlfriend," I said. "His only girlfriend, for that matter. He's never had another woman in his life."

Derek grinned. "How do you know?"

"Small community," I said. "If there had been someone else, I'd have heard about her."

"You'd be amazed by what happens behind closed doors in these small prairie towns," he said, and deftly changed the subject.

For the rest of the trip, we kept the conversation light. I talked about my children and my life as an artist; Derek told cop stories that were in turn heart-rending and hilarious.

By the time we reached the outskirts of the city, we were both laughing.

Monica's last rites took place on the west bank of the South Saskatchewan River in one of Saskatoon's most magnificent churches. Sunlight through stained-glass windows cast jewel-toned patterns on oak pews, and masses of exotically scented oriental lilies covered the altar. As we entered the sanctuary, a tuxedo-clad string quartet played Bach and Elgar. The setting was breathtakingly beautiful, but I churlishly wondered how well it reflected the life of the sharp business-woman who'd tried to buy my farm.

Frank's funeral in the overcrowded Bunchgrass hall had suited the unassuming man I'd married forty years earlier. A Life Cycle Celebrant had led a secular service that focused on his roles as brother, husband, father, neighbour, and friend. People had told stories about his kindness, generosity, and community spirit. Then a local trio had played bluegrass music, and afterward we all gathered around long tables for sandwiches, pickles, and homemade "dainties." It may not have been the height of fashion, but six months later memories of the homey service still comforted me.

The entry of the funeral procession recalled me to the present. Monica's mother, a stone-faced woman in black, limped down the aisle supported by her only son. They were followed by a dozen or so soberly dressed people whom Derek identified as relatives. If Monica had had a lover, her family hadn't publicly recognized his special status.

The church was too big for the several hundred people who filled the pews, but the ushers had seated them so that the space looked full. No one, as far as I could see, made use of the small packs of tissues placed around the sanctuary. Hadn't Monica's death caused anyone even a modicum of grief?

The service itself, however, paid tribute to this woman who had caused me so much trouble. Colleagues praised her financial acumen. The minister, in vestments of purple and gold, quoted Donne and prayed for her soul. As he spoke the words about no one being an island "entire of itself," I thought of the human need for connection and vowed that I would do better in the future.

It felt strange being at a funeral in which I knew no one but Derek. Not surprisingly, Monica and I hadn't had friends and acquaintances in common. Still, this was Saskatchewan — her cleaning woman easily could have been my neighbour's aunt. As the soloist, a soprano in black chiffon, sang an aria from Mozart's *Requiem*, I looked around for a familiar face. To my dismay, Zayden was seated four rows behind us. Beside him, smiling prettily, sat Jade.

I should have known he'd be there. Even Jade's presence wasn't entirely surprising. While short on analytical ability, she was big on feelings. Sensitive young men like Zayden aroused her maternal instincts; she'd do her darnedest to rescue him. Not for the first time, I wished she'd adopt a kitten or a puppy instead.

Finally, the service came to an end. The string quartet played Pachelbel's exquisite *Canon in D* as the rest of us followed the immediate family out of the sanctuary and into a spacious foyer. Derek quietly greeted acquaintances, while I searched the crowd for suspicious behaviour. However unlikely, the killer may have come to say goodbye to Monica.

We were climbing down the steps to the church basement, when I spotted ahead of me a woman who looked familiar. Although she appeared to be pushing seventy, her long grey hair hung down her back in schoolgirl braids. It contrasted sharply with the lines etched on her face and the cheap pink dress that she wore. The woman looked bone weary, as if she hadn't slept for a week. Try as I might, I couldn't think where I'd seen her.

I soon lost sight of the woman in the teeming mass of funeral guests waiting in line at the elaborate buffet. Monica would have loved its opulence: open-faced Danish sandwiches, miniature quiches, wheels of brie on thinly sliced sourdough, pickles and olives and raw vegetables carved in the shape of flowers. Nearby, elegantly coiffed women poured tea and coffee into thin porcelain cups placed next to platters of croissants. People filled their plates, picked up their beverage of choice, and settled themselves at small tables scattered around the room.

While Derek talked to Monica's relatives, I looked around until I saw the older woman. She had piled a plate with sandwiches and pastries and was standing near a door marked "exit." In front of her stood a burly younger man, his long dark hair tied back with a strip of rawhide. They appeared to be arguing. By the time I had made my way through the crowded basement, however, they had both disappeared. I opened the door and surveyed a sun-baked parking lot. There was no one in sight.

Back in the hall, Derek was chatting with a tall, skinny man in a pale grey suit. When I joined them, he introduced his friend Tony, a Saskatoon architect.

"He told me that he was drawing up blueprints for Monica," Derek said.

Tony nodded. "Very hush-hush, but I don't suppose that matters now. The question is, what do I do with them? And who pays for the work I've done?"

"Blueprints for what?" I asked.

"A palatial five thousand square foot log house — indoor swimming pool, six bedrooms, five bathrooms, living room with floor-to-ceiling windows overlooking Crystal Lake —"

"Crystal Lake?" I asked.

"Yeah. It's one hundred and seventy klicks northwest of here."

"What side of the lake?"

"The north side. There's a house there already, but Monica planned to replace it with something grander."

I thought of my resolution, made during the tranquility of the funeral service, to honour the need for human connection.

"That house is mine," I said, forcing myself to speak calmly.

"Really?" Tony rubbed his hand over his jaw. "I assumed she owned it."

"She wanted to buy, but I wouldn't sell."

"Was the new house intended for her?" Derek asked.

"A client, I think." Tony looked thoughtful. "She didn't say who, but I got the impression he was a lover. It sounded to me as if she planned to move in with this guy — I can't remember his name . . ."

"It could be important," Derek said.

"Maybe it started with an H."

Derek frowned. "That doesn't narrow the field much."

"Sorry," Tony said. "I'll let you know if it comes back to me."

The lineups around the food tables had thinned. I tapped Derek on the shoulder. "It's been a long time since breakfast."

He nodded. "Do you want to join us, Tony?"

I filled my plate and found a table for the three of us. While we ate, I told Derek about seeing a woman who looked familiar.

"I know who you mean," he said. "She was alone and stood out from the rest of the crowd. I wondered about her."

"The woman with the grey hair in braids?" Tony said, as he picked up a round of rye bread topped with cream cheese and smoked salmon. "I saw her talking to a younger man.

Come to think of it, his hair was long, too, only it was black and tied back with a leather cord. They weren't together more than a few minutes; the dude kept glancing around as if he didn't want to be seen with her."

"Was he a big man?" Derek asked. "Tall and heavy-set, and wearing a western-style suit?"

Tony nodded.

"He and Monica were having coffee at Prairie Ink last week," Derek said. "I stopped and said hi to her, but she didn't introduce us."

"Did they appear to be on friendly terms?" I asked.

"They could have been lovers who'd quarreled," Derek said. "I got the impression that he was ticked off with her and that she was trying to placate him — which was not typical behaviour on Monica's part."

I bit into the best cherry-filled croissant I'd ever tasted. "Can you ask around about this man's identity?"

"Not officially, but I'll talk to a couple guys who are familiar with the real estate scene. Once we've found him, I'll invite the fellow for coffee. If Semchuk and Pierce haven't already done so, they'll want to have a word with him too."

"Even if he's the client," I said slowly, "he wouldn't have a reason for wanting to kill me. Not when there's other lake-shore land for sale."

"If I had a couple million to spend on a new house," Tony said, "I wouldn't build out in the boonies. For that kind of money, you can buy a place in Cathedral Bluffs or Riverside Estates."

Derek frowned. "Maybe we've got the wrong end of the stick. Maybe the murder has nothing to do with Monica's client. Maybe there's something else at stake."

"Like Zayden's dream of building a healing centre?" I brushed the crumbs from my lap and looked covetously at the remaining croissants adorning the pastry table. "I saw him and Jade in the church, but they didn't stay for lunch."

"Probably didn't want to face your ire," Derek said with a grin. "Can't say I blame them either."

I ignored the barbed remark. "He's short-tempered, wants part of my farm, and has been hanging around my place."

"That's not evidence that will stand up in court," Derek said. "God, I wish I were on the case. Semchuk and Pierce are capable, but they didn't know Monica and they don't know any of the other key players."

"Aren't you an interested party?" Tony asked. "I thought cops weren't supposed to be personally involved in their investigations."

"They're not. But I have a stronger motivation than anyone else for wanting the murderer caught."

Tony looked at me and smiled knowingly. "Good luck, buddy."

By the time we finished eating, there were few guests left in the hall, and the caterers were waiting behind the serving tables.

I folded my napkin and placed it on my plate. "These folks probably want to pack up and go home. What do you say we hit the road?"

We said our goodbyes to Tony and walked outside into the blazing sunshine. The nearby river was a cool oasis of blue water lined by leafy trees, but it couldn't compete with the heat that radiated from concrete and asphalt. The prospect of my shady deck and flower-filled garden had never been more inviting.

I was not, however, going home, but to Mandi's. Instead of a purring cat as bedmate, I'd share close quarters with a lively five-year-old. The very thought made me tired — as did the prospect of untangling my feelings about Derek. The drive back to Bunchgrass, however, presented an opportunity. Frank and I had drifted along with a reasonable degree of comfort, neither of us asking a great deal of the other. But if Derek and I were to continue seeing each other, I wanted more than casual friendship. It was time to be proactive.

I should have known better.

"Jeannie, we're good together," he said when I awkwardly broached the subject of our relationship. "Let's leave it at that. Why risk spoiling everything?"

We'd just taken our seats in the van — which felt like an oven. Maybe the heat had made him grouchy. Or maybe he felt as drained as I did after the emotionally charged day.

"Bad timing?" I asked.

"God knows why women always want to talk everything to death."

I stared out the window at the car parked beside us. "That's exactly what Frank would have said."

"Smart man," Derek said, and turned on the radio.

Merle Haggard was singing about a marriage that had hit the rocks. Telling myself to relax, I closed my eyes and breathed slowly and deeply. Then the air conditioner kicked in. Derek eased into the traffic, and we were on our way. The next thing I knew, I was rubbing the sleep from my eyes as we approached Bunchgrass.

"Good nap?" Derek asked.

"It was fine."

"Sorry to have been a jerk," he said. "Monica's funeral took more out of me than I thought it would."

"It's okay. We can talk later."

The day had been stressful, and it wasn't over yet. Mandi served dinner at six; the dashboard clock read ten to four.

I couldn't face two hyperactive pre-schoolers. Drinking bad coffee at the local café suddenly became an attractive alternative.

"Drive straight ahead instead of turning right when you reach the village," I said to Derek. "I'm treating you to the bottomless cup at Shady Nook."

Bunchgrass would have been indistinguishable from hundreds of other small prairie communities if it weren't for one important feature. Its location on tiny Crystal Lake made it a magnet for vacationers and snowbirds. My hometown included a wide band of lakefront cottages and other dwellings, some of them occupied year around. Otherwise, it was much like its rural counterparts elsewhere in the province: a broad main street housed the village office and post office (once the local elementary school), the town hall, a fire department, a general store, a place that rented everything from rototillers to portable toilets, a fast-food restaurant and ice cream shop, and two churches. Behind them sprawled the homes of retired farmers, local business owners, and the handful of other people I'd known most of my life.

The Shady Nook Café kept an eye on the community from atop a sunny knoll just off the highway. While its sixties-diner décor left much to be desired, no one could fault it on hospitality. Wednesday to Sunday, The Nook catered to hungry travellers and to folks who sought congenial company. A combination of local newspaper and kitchen table therapist, it was the hub of village life.

Nancy, a cheerful youngish woman with purple streaks in her hair, led us to a table overlooking the parking lot. She managed the café dining room while her partner, Dan, cooked and washed dishes. "Haven't seen you for a while, Jeannie," she said, pouring two cups of coffee. "This murder business is keeping you close to home, eh? Can't say I blame you — goodness knows what I'd do if someone was trying to kill me. Is this your cop friend, Sergeant Massey? I hear he's been out to visit you at Thickwood Farm."

"How are those kids making out, anyway?" Joyce Zalenski asked. She and her husband, Al, were sitting at the next table. Neighbours of mine, they operated a big grain farm with the help of several million dollars' worth of machinery. "It must be an uphill battle trying to raise vegetables on land that hasn't been gardened in a donkey's years."

Al grinned as he forked apple pie into his mouth. "Word is their house was a mess, and they gave you your walking papers when you cleaned it for them. Ungrateful little brutes, eh? But that's kids today."

I was about to defend my tenants when Derek entered the fray. "It was an invasion of space. We should have got their permission first."

"They're not gonna stay on the farm," Al said. "Not in the long term. Can't make a living on a quarter section unless you live close to a big city and grow organic vegetables for people who got more money than brains."

Joyce frowned. "Al, it's none of our business —"

"Not that that's ever stopped him giving his opinion," I said.

Too late, I remembered my earlier resolution. I was about to retract my snide words when the café door opened and Stan Hanson walked in. At the same moment, Derek reached across the table and touched my hand. "You'll have to forgive Jeannie. She's had a long day."

Stan was a neighbour who'd spent three years studying holistic rangeland management before returning home to his grandfather's ranch. He and my husband had been best friends since childhood. Although they'd shared the emotional reticence typical of prairie countrymen — Al Zalenski excepted — they couldn't have been more different in other respects. Frank worked hard, avoided debt, paid his taxes on time, and followed conventional farming practices while Stan forged a radical path through the insular world of Saskatchewan ranchers. I hadn't paid much attention to him until the year I hit grade ten. Then I became infatuated with the rangy, brown-eyed cowboy.

I pulled my hand away from Derek and turned to greet my one-time high school sweetheart. "Hi, Stan. Here for supper?"

He eyed us curiously as he joined Al and Joyce at their table. "You two on a hot date?"

Since I don't usually wear heels and make-up on a summer afternoon, it wasn't an unreasonable assumption. "We're on our way back from a funeral. Staff Sergeant Massey here is helping with the inquiry into his ex-wife's murder."

Derek raised an eyebrow at the Staff Sergeant Massey bit. "She's the woman who borrowed Jeannie's car and was killed when it ran off the road."

"Yeah, I heard about that." Stan looked at me. "Didn't know the two of you were friends."

"Apparently I was the intended victim," I said, silently cursing the genes that turned my cheeks pink. "Derek's trying to keep me from becoming the next casualty."

"Any suspects?"

"There are a couple people of interest," Derek said.

"There've been a few strangers hanging around lately," Al said. "The other day I was fishing from my boat in front of your place, Jeannie. Saw a young fellow skulking around in your garden. When I called out, the bugger took off like the hounds of hell were after him."

"Can you describe this man?" Derek asked.

"Wasn't close enough to see details, but he looked as if a strong wind would blow him away."

"Zayden," I said. "I don't know if he was casing the joint or revisiting the scene of his crime."

"Saw someone else last night around sunset," Al said. "Wearing black, and with a cap pulled over their head. Too dark to know if it was a woman or a man; either way, the person was probably up to no good. The police ought to keep an eye on your place."

"We are," Derek said.

"Too many layabouts with nothing to do but cause trouble," Al continued. "It's a wonder there aren't more break-ins at all those cottages around the lake. Empty most of the year, and some of the locks wouldn't deter a one-armed ten-year-old. I keep telling you, Stan — one of these days someone's gonna trash your hunting shack. You don't even lock the damn door. Nothing worth stealing there, but they'd make one hell of a mess."

Joyce rolled her eyes. "Al, it's time to change the record."

"Anything else, folks?" Nancy asked as she emerged from the kitchen.

"I left bread rising," Joyce said. "So, unless my husband's got more good advice for Stan, we're on our way."

Al got up and placed a handful of loonies on the table. "A man can't be too careful."

As exit lines go, it wasn't original, but that was okay — no one expected originality from Al.

Although the Zalenskis weren't my favourite neighbours, I missed them once they were gone. Al's chatter filled in empty spaces. Nancy had returned to the kitchen to help Dan make supper, and I was left alone with the two men. Normally that would have been fine, but after the events of the past few days, I was feeling fragile. I didn't want to navigate the shoals of relationships with the opposite sex. Not that I was romantically involved with Stan . . . although we did have a history together. He was my first boyfriend, a regular visitor at our house when Frank was alive, and a

member of my community. After Frank died, I'd idly speculated about our friendship developing into something more
intense. It hadn't.

Derek broke the silence. "Want to join us, dude?"

Stan looked at me quizzically. I smiled, and he moved over
to the chair next to mine. "Thanks."

If there's one topic of enduring interest to countryfolk
everywhere, it's the weather. Stan and I commiserated with
each other about the drought and its impact on crops, gardens, pastures, and hayfields. Then the conversation turned
to rotational grazing. While Derek engaged with Stan in a
lively discussion, my eyes glazed over from fatigue and social
stress. By the time they moved on to the shortage of local
abattoirs, I was ready to crash.

"If we head out now," I said, "I'll be able to help Mandi
put dinner on the table."

Stan cocked an eyebrow in my direction. "My mobile says
you called yesterday morning. Any particular reason or did
you just want to chat?"

My heart sank at the thought of asking about my husband's
accident, but delaying questions wouldn't make them easier
to ask. I took a deep breath and plunged right in. "The cop
investigating Monica's death told me that a witness saw Frank
talking to a woman in the bar the night he died. They were in
the hallway outside the washrooms, and they were arguing.
Did Frank say anything about her before he left for home?"

Stan's face went blank. "I didn't see any woman."

"Did he mention her?"

"Wasn't anything to mention."

The tic in his eye was a dead giveaway. "Who was she?"

"For God's sake, I don't remember everything that happened six months ago."

"It was the night your best friend died," I said.

Stan pulled out his wallet, removed a couple bills, and placed them on the table. "The coroner found no evidence of foul play. Let's leave it at that, eh?"

"Maybe the coroner missed something."

"Jeez, woman, give it a rest." He stood up, nodded to Derek, and frowned at me. "See you later, Jeannie."

I watched as he retreated out the door and to the safety of his pickup truck. Then I turned to Derek. "He was lying."

"Might not have anything to do with the accident."

"What else would he mislead me about?"

Derek shrugged. "Maybe your husband was having an affair."

"No way," I said. "Not Frank." I got up from the table and tucked a five-dollar bill under the cream pitcher. "If he'd been seeing anyone else, Al Zalenski would have heard about it. And the next day, everyone in the community would have known the story."

Derek grinned as he walked to the door and held it open for me. "Ready to boogie?"

"Boogie?" I reached the parking lot and started to giggle. By the time we were seated in Derek's van, I was laughing hysterically.

"You okay?"

I nodded. "It's been a long time since I've heard anyone use that word," I said when I could talk.

"Glad I could lighten the mood." He signalled and turned left onto the gravelled municipal road. "I take it you and Stan have a history?"

"He was Frank's best friend."

"Not yours?"

"We dated the year I was in grade eleven."

"Then what happened?"

"We had a fight, and I ended the relationship."

"Oh?"

"Five years later he married a gorgeous extrovert from Montreal. She went to law school and ran off with one of her professors."

"That's life, eh?" Derek reached over and took my hand. "So, I won't get stabbed in the back by a jealous boyfriend?"

"Not by Stan, anyway," I said.

Derek laughed. "The cowboy seems to be a nice guy. Your husband chose his buddy well."

Mandi was tossing a green salad when I entered her kitchen. The late afternoon sunshine streamed through the bay window and spot-lit a table set with the colourful Melmac dishes my sister uses when the grandkids visit. Birdsong and the scent of roses drifted in from the garden and mingled with the aroma of freshly brewed coffee. Without the building blocks scattered across the floor, the room would have provided a perfect refuge for a woman hiding from a killer.

My sister and her husband, John, have shared their Sunday dinner with me ever since Frank died. Although Mandi's nine years younger, the age difference hasn't kept us from being close friends. She's a petite, sociable woman with a freckled face and sandy-coloured hair. That afternoon she wore red shorts and a white T-shirt that made her look like a mature twelve-year-old. Most people like her on sight.

Mandi returned my hug. "It's good to be home again."

"Yeah," I said, "I know what you mean. And with the precocious grandkids no less."

She made a funny face. "Do I detect a note of jealousy?"

Before I could answer, the back door opened, and two small children barrelled inside. They were followed by a broad-chested man in a drab green work shirt and jeans whose retirement was overdue. John was a patient man, but he looked ready for a stiff drink.

"Time to wash your hands," Mandi said, herding the kids into the bathroom. "Jeannie, if you'll set out the food, we can eat in two minutes."

I placed a bowl of Swedish meatballs on the table, along with new potatoes, cooked carrots, and the tossed salad. My sister wasn't into haute cuisine, but she's a generous woman and her meals are always good. I was grateful to be sitting at her table.

Dinner, however, was a disaster. Melissa and Ty were picky eaters. They both whined for hot dogs until Mandi heated up wieners and buns in the microwave. I tried to distract their attention from the lack of ketchup by asking about their day-care friends. No luck there. Finally, when Melissa knocked a glass of orange juice onto my lap while wrestling with her brother, I stood up and grabbed my great-niece by the arm.

"Time out, kid," I said, steering her toward the hallway. Mandi tried to smooth things over, but for once John took my side. Melissa was sentenced to spend the rest of the meal in the bedroom we were about to share.

By the time we'd finished the homemade apple pie, I was torn between self-righteous anger and guilt. The grandkids were young; chances are they'd grow up to become reasonable human beings. On the other hand, should they be allowed to ride roughshod over their elders? I was leaning toward forbearance until Mandi went to call Melissa.

"Oh no . . ."

I jumped up from the table and rushed to the bedroom. The contents of my overnight bag were spread over the log cabin quilt Mandi had made for her guest room. What prompted my sister's dismay, however, was the open bottle of Gucci's

Moonlight Serenade. It was lying on top of the jeans that I'd packed, and it was empty.

"I was going to put some on my wrists," Melissa said. "The way Mummy does. But the bottle slipped out of my hands."

Frank had given me the perfume for my birthday a few weeks before he died. I'd gently chided him for his extravagance, but secretly I was pleased with the luxurious gift. Now, all that was left of it was the overwhelming scent of lavender.

I stared at the empty bottle. "Melissa, how *could* you?"

She started to cry. "I didn't mean to —"

"I know, sweetheart," Mandi said. "But Aunt Jeannie is sad. Maybe we should buy her some nice new perfume."

The last few days had been gruelling. Not meaning to sound like the heroine of a trashy romance, but I craved the comfort of Frank's embrace. Instead, I was stuck with two spoiled kids and the need to dodge the bullets of a crazed shooter. Life wasn't fair. I wanted to scream my outrage. Instead, I pocketed my phone and went outside.

Mandi and John's farmstead would have made a good picture for the cover of *Country Guide* or *Small Farm Canada*. Their house overlooked grain bins, cows grazing in the pasture, and fields of canola and wheat. After Monica's funeral, the pastoral landscape was soothing. Trusting that the killer had no reason to haunt my sister's property, I set off across the pasture toward the Thickwood Hills.

What if the murderer was never found? I couldn't continue to live on other people's charity. Maybe I'd have to sell out and move to the city. It wasn't a completely horrifying prospect. I'd enjoyed my five years going to university in Saskatoon. And while I loved my farm, I hated the thought of spending the coming winter alone. Could Monica have been right when she'd suggested I'd be happier experiencing the joys of urban life?

What if my resistance was not so much principled opposition to the loss of farmland as it was sentimental attachment to the place where I'd lived, girl and woman, for sixty years? I didn't know the answer to that question, but I did know one thing — I couldn't afford to antagonize either family or neighbours if I was going to continue living on the farm. Life in the country is hard. I'd need all the support I could get — and so would they.

The house was peaceful when I returned an hour later. The dishes were done, the kids in bed, and the toys tidied away. John was sitting in his armchair, reading *The Western Producer*; across the room, Mandi hand-quilted a sunflower-design table runner pieced in green, bronze, and gold. It was a scene of domestic tranquility, and I felt a stab of envy.

"Sorry to skip out on the dishes," I said. "Today was tough, but that's no excuse."

Mandi brushed aside my apology. "Don't worry about the kids. They'll settle down tomorrow."

While John made us tea and poured himself a shot of whiskey, I joined Mandi on the sofa. Perhaps it was the funeral that evoked the memories. Or seeing the grandkids replaying a sibling bond that we'd shared. Either way, our talk turned to childhood.

"Kids today feel so entitled," I said, spouting a refrain common to my generation. "Can you imagine asking Mom for a hotdog when she'd prepared Swedish meatballs . . . not that Mom ever did, because meat sauce was less work."

"To hear you talk," Mandi said, "anyone would think we'd been raised on bread and water. Our meals were just fine."

"Because I did most of the cooking. Mom was either away at an anti-war march or so preoccupied with organizing one that she didn't have time for mundane tasks like feeding her kids. And Dad was no better."

Mandi snipped a length of quilting cotton and rethreaded her needle. "We had a better childhood than a lot of people. Our parents loved us."

"They had an odd way of showing it. Remember the year we spent with Nana and Gramps —"

Mandi groaned. "Not that story again."

"Our parents spent ten months building a school in Ethiopia."

"It was for *children*."

I took a sip. "They neglected us."

"Listen to you," Mandi said. "You're talking like a . . . a right-wing reactionary. The community they helped was so poor they could barely feed themselves, let alone give their kids an education. We had wealthy grandparents who were happy to look after us."

"If they were so delighted, why did they hire a full-time nanny? And why did they spend so little time at home?" I knew I was digging myself into a hole, but our conversation had released years of buried resentment. Having got started, I couldn't stop myself.

The year I began grade nine, Mom and Dad had volunteered for an Oxfam project building an elementary school in rural Ethiopia. Mandi and I were packed off to a luxury high-rise in Regina to stay with maternal grandparents we barely knew. Nana and Gramps were senior partners in a prestigious law firm and worked a sixty-hour week. They usually left for the office before we got up in the morning and sometimes didn't get home until after we'd gone to bed.

My sister took a gingersnap from the plate on the coffee table and then passed the cookies to me. "Vilma looked after us well."

"Because you were little and sweet. I was an awkward fourteen-year-old who wanted to go home. Chances are Vilma did too. Imagine having to look after us when she had family of her own in the Philippines."

"It wasn't our fault she needed the money." Mandi let out her breath in a long, slow sigh. "Mom thought you'd like staying at Nana's."

"When did she tell you that?"

"A couple of years before she died. She figured that anyone as obsessed with beauty as you were would have been thrilled to live in their apartment."

"We were imposters," I said. "Country kids aping their upper-middle-class urban counterparts. Nana's Joe Fafard sculptures and Allen Sapp paintings merely illustrated the divide between us."

Mandi took a bite of her cookie and chewed it slowly. "You've always been hard to please."

"It was no fun for a shy farm kid to start high school in an unfamiliar city where she didn't know a soul. If it hadn't been for you, I would have slit my wrists."

"You wouldn't —"

"No, but I felt like it. At least, until I discovered painting."

In the second semester, I'd taken an art class from Mrs. Gregson. Suddenly, my social deficiencies had no longer mattered. While I never became part of the in-group, my work had earned me the respect of fellow artists. And I'd loved painting with the brilliantly coloured oils and acrylics that later became my trademark.

"Every cloud has a silver lining," Mandi said.

I smiled at my sister's earnestness. "Let's just say that art class provided some compensation in an otherwise wretched year. We couldn't even go home for Christmas."

"The Ethiopian kids got their school," Mandi said. "I've always been thankful for that."

"Parents should put their own children first," I said, aware of how priggish I sounded. Aware, too, of my daughter's voice complaining that I was always too busy painting or gardening to spend time with her. What a hypocrite I was becoming.

"Some of our schoolmates would have given a lot to be in our position." Mandi put down her cup and looked at me. "Remember Rachel? Wasn't she in your grade?"

"A grade below me. She failed her first year."

"Mom used to give her mother your outgrown hand-me-downs."

"Don't you wonder how she felt about wearing them? We always wore our cousins' old clothes, but they didn't go to our school so we could pretend Mom had bought them for us." I took a sip of tea and thought about Rachel. She'd been a rail-thin kid with acne and a bad haircut. One day when I was in grade eight, Mom had given her the black leather jacket I'd acquired from my cousin Donna. It had made me feel like a biker chick, and I'd worn it to school every day until I had to suck in my breath to zip it up. The next day, it appeared on Rachel.

"There was no disgrace in wearing cast-offs," Mandi said. "A lot of those folks were poor. Some of the kids didn't get enough to eat. Tammy and Anna DuBois always looked . . . hungry."

"Their mother made rabbit stew," I said. "Chris and Robert used to go trapping."

Mandi nodded. "I felt sorry for the rabbits. But even more sorry for the kids."

I wanted to protest that it was their parents' fault if the kids went hungry, but I knew that was untrue. Local unemployment had been high and wages low. Tammy and her twin sister were the youngest children in a big family. Their dad had worked seasonally for a local farmer. Even if their mom had been a good manager, it would have been hard to keep everyone fed.

"In winter, Tammy used to ask me for the soup Mom sent for lunch," I said. "That was one thing about our community — you might have been teased because you couldn't run fast, but nobody made fun of you for the privations of poverty. Anyplace else, and I'd have been mortified to bring soup to school in a jar cocooned inside a tin honey pail lined with crushed newspaper."

"I didn't know you'd operated a mobile soup kitchen," Mandi said. "How sweet."

"It wasn't by choice," I said. "Tammy was fierce. I had to stay on her good side."

"There's a school lunch program where my Donna teaches." Mandi looked thoughtful. "A lot of her students don't get breakfast. That never happened to us."

She was right. Our parents might have rejected the affluence of their upper-middle-class families and the privileges conferred by a university education, but we'd never gone without food or books or any of the other things they considered important. Nor had we ever lived on social assistance. Compared to a lot of the kids I'd grown up with, we'd had it easy.

Most of our former classmates had moved away in search of better jobs or better marriage prospects. Occasionally I'd see some of them at funerals, and we'd get caught up on family news. But it had been a long time since I'd seen either Anna or her twin.

"Liz told me Chris moved back here from Saskatoon," I said.

Mandi frowned. "Pity he had to leave in the first place. He wanted to farm, but of course buying land was out of the question. Now he's working as one of Al's hired men."

"Any word about Tammy?"

"I heard rumours she had health problems," Mandi said. "Not surprising, really, considering her childhood. I mean, spending your twelfth birthday in the hospital because your brother pushed you off the top of their bunkbed —"

"He didn't push her," I said. "It was an accident."

"Maybe you're right," Mandi said. "Anyway, I did hear recent news of her cousin Rachel. You knew she married an oilfield worker from Kindersley, didn't you? I ran into Joe at the post office. Rachel's oldest granddaughter just had a baby, and she's tickled pink."

The evening passed quickly in the kind of chit-chat you can have with someone you've known all your life. By the time I joined Melissa in bed, I was feeling mellow. Whatever lay ahead tomorrow, I could deal with it.

My positive attitude didn't help me get to sleep. Instead, I lay awake wondering about the woman in pink. Who was she, and where had I seen her before? And what on earth was she doing at Monica's funeral? I was sorting through memories of women I'd known when my cell phone pinged. I opened my text. It was from Derek.

Looking forward to spending the day with you tomorrow.

I smiled and gently hugged my sleeping great-niece.

FRIDAY, AUGUST 3

I awoke to the sound of a small voice beside me. "Aunt Jeannie, are you still mad at me?"

What else could I say? "Of course not, sweetheart. Didn't your mummy ever tell you that bad feelings disappear overnight?" I pulled Melissa close and gave her a hug. "Now, let's get up and help Gramma make pancakes."

Breakfast was a cheerful affair. Melissa and Ty loved pancakes and eagerly devoured a stack of them smothered in Mandi's sour cherry sauce. The decaf coffee was good. And my sister was in high spirits — nothing makes her happier than having the grandkids visit.

Even the weather cooperated. Blue sky, no wind or clouds, and nineteen above by eight in the morning. It was too hot for my taste, but the kids would happily spend the day outside. I'd work in my garden — picking early beans, deadheading flowers, and weeding the perennials west of the house. Derek had promised to mow the grass. I didn't have a lawn, but there was native fescue behind the house and along the driveway. It always looked better after a good trim.

Derek was picking me up at nine. I'd hoped to get away undetected, but no such luck. My hospitable sister forestalled my escape and invited him to join us for a last cup of coffee before we set off for my farm. I wasn't sure why, but the prospect of their meeting made me uncomfortable. After all, Frank had been dead for more than six months.

Like me, Mandi is curious — or nosy, as my kids call it. Since John had gone to town for a tractor part and taken the grandkids with him, she felt free to ask personal questions. He good-naturedly told her about his work, but when she started in on his marriage to Monica, I put an end to the conversation.

"Derek, it's time to go. Thanks for breakfast, Mandi. I'll see you when I get back around eight."

"Why don't the two of you come for a late supper?" she said. "I'll put the kids to bed early so we can have a civilized evening."

I was about to accept the invitation when Jade called. Her dad had promised to come for dinner that night, and she was cooking a "fancy" meal in his honour.

"Ava and Thor won't let me invite Zayden, but they okayed you and Derek. Please come, Jeannie. This is the first time I've organized a dinner party, and I'm scared."

The embarrassment of a family dinner would be nothing compared to sharing a culinary disaster with a disgruntled gourmet. But Jade needed me. When Mandi offered us a rain check, I told my young tenant we'd be there.

Diesel was happy to see me when we arrived at the farm and showed his enthusiasm by winding around my ankles as I watered hanging baskets.

"He looks well fed," I said to Derek. "Thanks for looking after him."

"No problem. Want me to get started on the grass?"

While Derek mowed the perimeter of my gardens, I weeded a mixed bed of daylilies, sedum, and ornamental grass. Then it was time to pick vegetables for lunch.

One of my favourite summer meals is a huge green salad topped with tomatoes, diced cheddar, and sizzling new potatoes garnished with green onions and dill. Derek, however, didn't appear to share my enjoyment of this feast. He was unusually quiet over lunch.

"A penny for your thoughts," I said. It was a useful cliché. How else do you ask a man what he's thinking without sounding unbearably intrusive?

"Don't get me wrong, Jeannie," he said. "This would be a great place for a cottage — I mean, it's beautiful and peaceful, but . . . don't you get tired of the isolation? Not seeing another soul from one day to the next —"

"I visit Liz and Mandi."

Derek picked up a forkful of salad. "It must be hell in winter."

That was a problem. I dreaded the onset of icy winds and snowstorms. Frank had done most of the driving. He'd also provided companionship on the long, dark winter nights. What was I going to do when the first of November rolled around?

"I'll cope." Maybe if I said that often enough, I'd come to believe it.

"Could you move to Saskatoon for a few months?"

I shrugged. My house was part of me. It gave me comfort and a sense of security. How could I leave it behind? The painted landscapes on my walls, scarlet geraniums on my windowsills, beautiful studio with its skylight and view of my flower garden and the lake . . . the thought was unbearable. "Don't worry about it," I said. "It's not your problem."

"Do you always shut down difficult conversations?"

"You're a fine one to talk," I said. "Remember the woman who phoned you the day after you arrived here? When I asked you about her —"

"Okay, point taken."

I toyed with a cherry tomato on my plate. "I'm not going to bare my soul to someone who's not honest with me."

"And you see yourself as a model of transparency?"

I finished my salad and contemplated Derek's question. It didn't take psychoanalysis for me to recognize my guardedness. When I'd married Frank, I'd counted on having someone around for the rest of my life. His unexpected death had put an end to that notion. Knowing that he hadn't intentionally left me didn't help. I was angry, lonely, and scared. Much as I craved intimacy, I wasn't ready to risk going through that loss again.

"What happens when Monica's killer is caught and you go back to Saskatoon?"

"Jeez, lady, it's only a two-hour drive."

Diesel jumped onto my lap and snuggled against me. "It can be a wretched trip in winter."

"You don't become a cop if you're afraid of icy roads. I could come up on weekends."

I resorted to the one excuse available to every recent widow. "I haven't been on my own for long, and — damn it, I'm not used to . . . close friendships with men."

"Does that reluctance apply to your buddy Stan?"

"Of course." I wasn't sure if that was true, but Derek didn't need to know that. "This past week has been . . . overwhelming."

He stood up and stretched his arms above his head. "So, we get back to work, right?"

I nodded. "There are beans to pick and flowers to weed —"

"Never let it be said that Derek Massey can't take a hint."

Our short conversation had left me discombobulated. I had been irritated with Derek for his unwillingness to talk about our relationship; now that he had raised the issue, I'd gone all coy on him. Talk about being inconsistent! And wasn't I being unfair to the man who fed my cat, checked on my house, and provided me with transportation — all while protecting me from a crazy killer? Derek had become important to me. But was that what I wanted? And how much emotional honesty did we owe each other, anyway?

The bigger problem was being honest with myself. My go-to response to vexing issues was to duck and cover. Maybe it was time to change that pattern. Only — did I have to do so now? Telling myself I'd think about our relationship later, I picked up a hoe and attacked the sow thistle that threatened to overrun a bed of lilies.

By five thirty, the grass was cut, the flowers weeded, and the tomatoes watered. Derek and I had showered and changed into clean clothes. I grabbed a pail of green beans, and we set off for Jade's dinner party.

When we pulled up in front of the house, there was a gleaming black BMW parked beside two bikes and the farm's old half-ton. A man with an athlete's body and the face of an American movie star sat in one of the wicker chairs on the verandah. His boyish good looks and skinny Amiri jeans made me feel like an elderly frump. I was prepared to dislike him on sight.

The man stood up. "I'm Ben. You must be Derek and Jeannie." He smiled at me, revealing dazzlingly white teeth. "I've been looking forward to meeting Jade's mentor. She tells me you're quite a gardener."

"Thanks. I enjoy it."

"God knows these kids need good role models."

The arrival of Ava and Thor with a tray of goblets and a bottle of white wine spared me the necessity of a reply.

"Jade wanted us out of the kitchen," Ava said, frowning. "She's into some serious cooking."

I'd been afraid of that. "Maybe I should go in and help."

"She said she can make dinner by herself."

I was about to ask about the bikes in the driveway when the back door opened and Liz emerged carrying a pitcher of iced tea. Following behind her, a bowl of popcorn in his hands, was my son.

"Jordan," I said. "This is a pleasant surprise."

Liz responded to my unasked question. "Jade said to bring a friend, so I did."

I'm biased, of course, but most people would agree that my son is a good-looking man. Tall, blond, and slender like my dad, his farm attire is usually old blue jeans and ratty T-shirts. That evening he looked smart in black cargo pants and a peacock-blue polo shirt.

"Hi, Mom," Jordan said, smiling. "I didn't have anything planned for tonight, so I jumped at Liz's invitation."

"You could have come to visit me." I realized as soon as I'd said them that the words were churlish, as if I were accusing him of failure to do his filial duty. "Sorry, I didn't mean — anyway, it's lovely to see you."

Liz laughed. "Lucky for you, I'm willing to share."

After I'd introduced him to the new man in my life, Jordan joined Derek and Ben in an animated discussion about the prospects of the Saskatchewan Roughriders. Otherwise, the conversation was desultory. The warm weather was making us sluggish, and most of us had been working all day. As I tipped and tailed the beans, I worried about Jade. She wasn't a great cook at the best of times. I hoped she was making something simple.

When the beans were ready, I picked up the pail and marched into the house.

The smell of burnt pastry hit me as I entered the kitchen. Jade was holding a pan of something blackened beyond recognition. Tears rolled down her cheeks.

"The recipe said to bake the strudel for twenty to thirty minutes," she said, "and I took it out after twenty."

Heat poured from the cookstove. I briefly stuck my hand in the oven. It was hot enough to bake pita.

"It's hard to control the temperature when you're cooking with wood," I said gently. "Were you planning to serve the strudel for dessert?"

Jade blew her nose on a cotton handkerchief. "It's the main course, and it's filled with chicken, mushrooms, and wild rice. I made a fancy cake for dessert."

The cake in question listed heavily to one side and its whipped cream frosting was starting to deflate, but at least it looked edible. The same couldn't be said of Jade's entrée.

"How can I face my dad?" she asked, collapsing on a chair. "He'll be so disappointed in me."

"We could start again and make a new dinner if we asked for help."

"Is that what you'd do?"

"Yes," I said. That was a lie, but it was for a good cause. "Now, let's make a plan."

Derek came in as we were taking an inventory of our resources. "Is there a problem?"

"Nothing we can't solve." I handed him a list. "You and Jordan go and pick up a few things at my place while the rest of us start cooking. We are about to prepare a feast."

Once Jade and I had handed out assignments, we dispersed to our tasks. Liz and Thor picked raspberries and vegetables, while Ava tidied the kitchen and prepared salad greens. Jade scrubbed new potatoes and set up a table on the deck. Ben appointed himself sommelier and polished the streaky wine glasses until they glistened. I put green beans on to cook and made a garlicky vinaigrette. By the time Derek and Jordan returned, all we had to do was heat up the focaccia from my freezer.

Dinner, served picnic-style on the deck, was splendid: Greek salad made with freshly picked vegetables, green beans crusted with parmesan, new potatoes sautéed in lots of butter and sprinkled with scallions and dill, and warm slabs of herbed focaccia with brie. Even Ben was generous in his approval.

We were helping ourselves to thin slices of Jade's cake topped with vanilla ice cream and raspberries still warm from the garden when Derek's mobile rang. He looked at the call display and then moved away from us to the opposite end of the verandah. Trying to look casual, I picked up my iced tea and followed him.

"Hey, dude, what's up? . . . You're sure? . . . Thanks. Talk to you later."

He looked at me, half-smiling, as he ended the call. "In case you're wondering, not all my conversations have to do with Monica's murder."

"But this one did, right?"

Derek nodded. "Tony remembered the name of Monica's friend — it's Hunter."

"Does this man have a surname?"

"He said she referred to him only by his first name."

"That doesn't help much," I said.

"It jogged my memory. Hunter's the name of the fellow I saw her with at Prairie Ink."

"Then it must also be the name of the big guy who attended her funeral," I said. "Since all three of them are the same person."

He nodded. "It would be too much of a coincidence to assume that Monica had more than one lover named Hunter."

"So where does that get us?" I asked.

Derek raised an eyebrow. "Us?"

I finished my iced tea and considered the situation. "This man could be connected to the murder. He and Zayden are the only people with a motive for wanting me dead."

"So, Hunter wants to buy your farm, but you won't sell," Derek said. "I still don't see why he'd want to kill you. Why not buy some other farm?"

"That's what I'm wondering. We're obviously missing something. Aside from the fact that he was Monica's boyfriend, what do we know about Hunter?"

"He earned a small fortune in Bitcoin, moved to Saskatoon from Calgary, and got entangled with Monica when he was looking for rural real estate. It's not a hell of a lot to go on."

"Did he work as a salesperson for her?"

Derek shook his head. "The guy was wealthy. Monica's always had an eye for good-looking younger men. And if they have money, so much the better."

"It would help if I could remember where I met the woman he was talking to at the funeral."

"Maybe you knew her when you were going to university in Saskatoon?"

I was about to tell him that I was clueless when Liz came over and took me by the arm. "Come on, you two, join the party."

The rest of the evening went smoothly. Derek, Jordan, and Liz were affable guests, and Ava and Thor generously supported their younger housemate. Jade was giddy with relief at her escape from disaster, while I was pleased at having redeemed myself. Even Ben was an asset to the gathering. Although he knew that she had not done most of the dinner preparation, he praised his daughter's culinary skill. Jade glowed with happiness.

It was well past ten when Liz touched Jordan's arm and suggested they head back to her place.

I looked at my son. "I hope you're not planning to drive back to Saskatoon tonight. Mandi will give you a bed if you don't mind sharing with Ty. Or you can snuggle with Diesel in your old room on the farm."

"Liz invited me to stay with her," he said, his voice hesitant. "Her house is awfully small —"

Derek laughed. "I expect it has a double bed."

I was about to brush off his comment when I glanced at Jordan. His cheeks had turned pink. Call me naïve, but I hadn't considered the possibility that he would become romantically involved with another woman so soon after breaking up with Brandy.

"I can change my plans," he said. "I mean, if you need me —"

"No worry," I said, hoping I didn't look as foolish as I felt. "Mandi and John have my back."

Liz gave me the thumbs up. "See you soon, Jeannie."

Then she and Jordan waved goodbye and walked out the door.

I was standing at the kitchen window watching their taillights disappear down the driveway when Derek came up behind me and put his arms around my waist.

"You did good tonight, love."

"Thanks."

"Tired?"

"Why didn't Jordan tell me about him and Liz?"

Derek shrugged. "You can be prickly at times. Maybe he thought you'd disapprove."

"I'm not prickly —"

"Isn't that why you're staying with your sister rather than here?"

Ava hung up the towel she'd used to dry dishes and walked over to join us. "There was fault on both sides." She cleared her throat. "I'd really like it if you'd spend tonight with us, Jeannie."

"Why?"

Thor rushed to her aid. "We need help picking vegetables for tomorrow's CSA order."

"I know it's awful cheek asking you," Ava said, "but we're desperate."

"No problem," I said. "I'll phone Mandi and tell her not to expect me."

Ava avoided my eyes. "Thanks."

"Jeannie ought to be safe with Ben around," Derek said, smiling. "He looks like a man who could pack a mean punch."

Ben grinned. "I was high school wrestling champ the year I graduated."

"That makes me feel better about my plans for tomorrow," Derek said. "I'm going to Saskatoon to find Hunter."

I raised an eyebrow. "Even though your boss told you to stay off the case?"

"Surely Monica's ex-husband can offer condolences to his replacement."

Ava and Thor wished him luck, and then headed upstairs to bed. After Derek had said goodbye to Jade and Ben, I walked him out to the parking area in front of the house.

The warm summer night was made for romance. Stars shone through a velvety darkness perfumed by evening-scented stalks. An owl called to its mate from a nearby tree, and on the beach across the lake a bonfire burned invitingly. I wanted to jump into Derek's van and drive off with him to my farm where we'd lie in the grass with our arms around each other—

"I'll check up on Diesel on my way back to town," he said, giving me a hug.

"Call if you find out anything about Hunter, okay?"

"Of course."

Our goodnight kiss was long and sweet. Finally, Derek stepped into his van and drove away, and I returned to a silent house.

Later, back in my old room upstairs, I lay awake wondering about Jordan and Liz. How serious was their relationship, and why hadn't I seen it coming? At least on the surface, they appeared to be an unlikely couple — but then, so did Derek and I. Did that mean we should remain "just friends"? And what the heck was wrong with friendship anyway?

While my conscious mind was rational, my subconscious was a greedy child who longed for love but feared abandonment. When I finally fell asleep, I dreamt that Monica and I were sitting together at a dance. I was wearing jeans with grass stains on the knees and a John Deere T-shirt. Monica looked stunning in a sleeveless red linen sheath. As the band played "Blue Eyes Crying in the Rain," Derek appeared and crossed the floor toward us. Then he held out a hand to Monica and, as the fiddles wailed, swept her onto the dancefloor.

SATURDAY, AUGUST 4

I awoke disgruntled with myself. Who did I think I was, a jealous teenager? If Derek wanted to dance with his ex-wife . . . but Monica was dead, and he was in pursuit of her killer. It was time for me to get real and help my house-mates prepare for the weekly CSA delivery.

Thanks to Ava's marketing skills and a little horticultural advice from me, the three of them had established a modestly successful Community Supported Agriculture business. Every Saturday from May to October, they rose early to prepare vegetables for delivery to customers in North Battleford. Local people picked up their own orders, usually mid-week.

"Chris DuBois was out last Tuesday," Jade said as we headed toward the garden. "He told me to say hi to you."

I looked at her in surprise. "Chris DuBois buys your vegetables?"

"Any reason he shouldn't?"

"No, of course not."

I'd assumed that most CSA customers were reasonably affluent. Maybe that was changing — or maybe I was just plain wrong. My old schoolmate lived in Bunchgrass and earned a modest income working for a local grain farmer. I was glad to hear that he managed to buy vegetables from Thickwood Farm.

Since gardens — even weedy ones — are especially productive in mid-summer, there was a lot to do. I picked the last of the peas and the early beans, Thor dug carrots and potatoes, Jade cut herbs and salad greens, and Ava picked the rest of the vegetables. Ben had volunteered to make brunch.

Jade's dad was swearing at the stove when we trooped into the kitchen at ten.

"How the hell can you cook on this blasted antique?"

Smoke poured from the cracks around the stove lids. I opened the dampers. The kindling ignited into tiny flames. "Sorry," I said. "One of us should have shown you how to use the stove."

My parents had cooked with wood, and my renters had been charmed with the idea of doing the same. While it's not great when the weather's hot, you can't beat a fire on a cold day. The food doesn't really taste better than it would if cooked on natural gas, but it satisfies some primal need for warmth and security.

Ben was not a fan of our rustic ways and loudly questioned the intelligence of luddites who failed to take advantage of modern conveniences. While he cooked porridge and made currant scones, I comforted Jade, who'd borne the brunt of his displeasure. A good breakfast, however, restored peace in the kitchen. The porridge, served with raspberries and yogurt, was creamy and smooth, and the scones were flawless. Temper notwithstanding, I was glad Ben hadn't returned to Saskatoon the previous night.

When Ava and Thor left to make the CSA deliveries, the rest of us had the afternoon to ourselves. I had intended to go down to the beach to capture seagulls in flight on my sketchpad. Ben and Jade had packed iced tea and sandwiches for an afternoon of fishing. Then Zayden showed up at the door and hijacked our plans.

"What are you doing here?" I asked.

"Giving you a second chance," he said. "All I need is five acres of lakeshore. Your farm has plenty of room for both of us."

I stared at him, gobsmacked. "What makes you think I want to share it with you?"

"The centre isn't about me," he said. "I'm just the conduit who transmits the healing power of the universe."

I didn't know if Zayden was a conman or a woolly headed idealist. Either way, I wasn't interested. "Lots of places to rent in the city. Transmit your healing from one of them."

"Your land is a sacred space. It has good energy."

"Zayden's right," Jade said.

Ben snorted.

The crazy thing was, I agreed with Zayden. But you can't harness good energy and sell it to the purchasers of New Age healing retreats. At least, that's what I told myself.

"The discussion is over," I said. "I want you to go."

That's when Zayden lost it. He accused me of being a right-wing capitalist, an insensitive settler, and a selfish pig. Fighting back hysterical laughter, I grabbed him by the arm and started to march him toward the door. The next thing I knew Jade was screaming and I was sprawled out on the linoleum with Zayden towering above me.

The battle was short-lived. Jade's dad wasn't just a clothes horse — it didn't take him long to pin Zayden to the floor beside me.

Fists clenched and heart beating in overdrive, I got to my feet. "Thanks, Ben."

"What do you want me to do with him?" he asked.

Jade was crouched beside Zayden, stroking his hair.

"I don't mean to be harsh," I said to her. "But I'm fed up with people viewing agricultural land as so much real estate. This is a farm, dammit. It's neither an acreage development nor a healing centre. It's a place where people grow food."

"Why can't it be more than one thing?" she asked.

"Because it's *my* land and I don't want it used for anything but a farm. Besides, I don't have the energy to rush off madly in all directions."

"We could help," she said.

Ben was still standing next to Zayden with one foot resting lightly on his back. "You kids can barely manage your garden."

Jade started to snivel. I wanted to go home and hole up in my studio, but that wasn't an option. My parents would have welcomed Zayden into the fold. Although I didn't share their altruism, I could at least refrain from making the situation worse. I looked at Ben. "Let him go."

Zayden didn't leave quietly, but finally Jade persuaded him that his situation required a dignified retreat. I sighed with relief as I watched his motorbike disappear around a crook in the road. A tearful Jade had reluctantly agreed to accompany Ben on their delayed fishing expedition. I had the next few hours to myself.

Sketching no longer appealed to me; instead, I would find out more about Zayden. A search of Monica's real estate website revealed that he was employed as an administrative assistant and that his last name was Jones. Bingo! I googled Zayden Jones and hit paydirt. According to a recent news report, he'd been charged with exerting undue influence on one of the residents in a local care home where he'd been employed. I didn't recognize the name of the resident, but I did know someone who worked at the care home. Two minutes later I was talking to Frank's niece.

Amber had put herself through four years of university by working part-time as a care aide, and she knew Zayden. I asked her about the extortion charge.

"The media exaggerated," she said. "Zayden cozied up to Mrs. Greene, and when she told her kids she was giving him five hundred thousand to help build a healing centre, they hit every media outlet in the province."

"And the care home buckled under pressure, right?"

"What else could it do? We must protect our residents. Mrs. Greene talked her son out of going to the cops, but she couldn't persuade our CEO to let the matter drop."

"So, Zayden slunk off in disgrace without getting a penny?"

"He didn't slink. When Jason — he's the son — told him never to set foot in his mother's room again, Zayden went ballistic and started throwing things. There would have been war if Mrs. Greene hadn't intervened." Amber sighed. "Mrs. G spent her career working in child custody. She told me it was a miracle if anyone survived his sort of background unscathed."

"Let me guess," I said. "Too many kids, not enough money, an alcohol problem, and a single mom who either worked the streets or lived on social assistance."

"You forgot the crystal meth," Amber said. "Zayden's the oldest. He was looking after his brother and sisters by the time he was eight."

I hate when negative stereotypes turn out to be accurate. It makes it hard to blame people for their bad behaviour. And child of my parents that I was, it makes me feel guilty. Here was a needy young man begging for help, and I'd turned him away. But I hadn't screwed up Zayden's childhood; why the hell were his problems my responsibility?

Brushing aside the possibility that my parents had done a better job of child-rearing than I give them credit for, I thanked Amber for her help and ended the call.

I was thinking about walking down to the lake with my sketching supplies when Joan called.

"Sorry about the short notice," she said, "but the afternoon is lovely, and I feel like going for a drive. If you're home this afternoon, can I stop in for a visit?"

"Of course. I'd love to see you."

"Three o'clock okay?"

"Great," I said, and gave her directions to my farm. Then all I had to do was find someone who would meet me there and keep the bad guys at bay.

Liz possessed the courage and protective instincts of a bullmastiff. She agreed to act as my bodyguard. I declined her offer to pick me up at Thickwood, however — even a coward like me has her pride. Besides, the twenty-minute walk would help me unwind.

Despite the heat, Nature performed its calming rituals. Gulls circled overhead in pursuit of fishflies and mosquitoes. Western grebes dived in deep water in search of small fish for lunch. A black swallowtail butterfly flitted among the willows. I arrived at my farm ready to cope with the rest of the day.

Liz was sitting in a wicker armchair on the deck, with Diesel on her lap. Beside them, Goliath snoozed in the shade. He sat up and woofed as I climbed up the steps to greet them.

"Thanks for coming, you two," I said, taking Diesel from Liz. "I promised Derek I wouldn't spend time here alone."

"No problem. After his mishap at the height of land, Goliath's itching to meet whoever shot at him."

We checked the perimeter of the garden for signs of disturbance but found nothing amiss. The interior of the house was equally free of intruders. Confident of safety, I took butter tarts out from the freezer and set out mugs and napkins for tea.

Once back outside and settled in comfortable chairs on the deck, Liz asked about Derek. "What's happening with this guy? And why isn't he here doing guard duty?"

"He's tracking down Monica's mystery client," I said. "A man called Hunter."

"I recently met someone around here who has a son with that name." Liz scratched Goliath behind the ears, and he wiggled with pleasure. "Can't remember who it was . . ."

"It can't be the same person," I said. "Derek's quarry is from Calgary. He was also Monica's boyfriend."

Liz whistled. "Love is in the air."

I could feel my cheeks turning pink. "Meaning?"

"Mandi says your relationship with Derek is getting hot and heavy."

I silently cursed my propensity for blushing. "Mandi's a romantic."

"So, there's nothing happening between you and your cop friend?"

"Derek's been a real gentleman."

I didn't blame Liz for looking sceptical. But while I hadn't been completely honest with her, my own confusion made it difficult for me to describe how I felt about the new man in my life. Figuring that the best defence is a good offence, I asked her about her own changed relationship with my son.

"How long have you and Jordan been seeing each other?"

"*Seeing* each other?" Liz laughed. "We've been friends for years. But sleeping together? Only a few days. And before you ask, no, I'm not the reason he broke up with his ex. She was a wimp. Jordan didn't need me to help him see that."

"So he started dating you." I hesitated, uneasy on what was, for me, shaky ground. "Is the relationship serious?"

She shrugged. "Jordan would have to speak for himself, but I'm enjoying it."

"I mean, if it isn't —"

"Jeannie, we're single, consenting adults. Sex doesn't require a lifetime commitment."

"It still seems . . . strange. Unless you're sure you want to be together."

Liz laughed. "Join the twenty-first century."

I had more questions, but there wasn't time for a longer conversation. Goliath was barking, which meant Joan had arrived.

The two women liked each other on sight. They were happily chatting about photography when I went inside to make tea. When I returned bearing butter tarts and a pot of Earl Grey, the subject had changed to the joys of raising poultry.

"I keep telling Jeannie she should get half a dozen hens," Liz said. "Composted chicken shit makes wonderful fertilizer."

"Who would buy your eggs if all your customers followed that advice?" I asked.

Joan poured herself a cup of tea. "You grow your own tomatoes instead of buying them from Thickwood Farm."

"Tomatoes don't need to be fed and watered three hundred and sixty-five days of the year," I said. "And they don't bleed when you pick them."

The conversation continued in that vein. Although I played devil's advocate, I agreed with my friends. Raising food is at the heart of farming. It's one reason I stay here, even though Frank is gone.

Talking about food had made me eager to show off my gardens. After we finished tea, I led a guided tour of my vegetable patch, orchard, and landscaped grounds. Joan was generous in her praise, but what she really wanted to see were my paintings.

"I read about your show at the Kenderdine Art Gallery," she said. "The reviewer praised your technical skill and accessible subject matter."

"It's accessible because I paint what I see around me," I said, rubbing Diesel's tummy. "Anyone with 'technical skill' could do the same. I wish people liked my work because it's brilliant rather than merely beautiful."

The kids jokingly called my house Jeannie's Art Gallery. Oils, acrylics, and watercolours — both mine and the work of fellow artists — adorned every room from top to bottom. While their styles ranged from abstract to photo realism, they all portrayed Saskatchewan's varied landscape. Scenes of shortgrass prairie, parkland lakes, and northern forests rubbed shoulders with flower gardens and wheat fields.

As we ambled from room to room, I consciously breathed slowly and deeply. Although most visitors admired my "pretty pictures," Joan's vision of our shared landscape was at odds with mine.

"I love their bold style and exuberant colours," she said as we stood in my studio, looking at a final group of paintings. "But where are the people? Where are the farmers and ranchers and townsfolk who live in these beautiful landscapes?"

I stared at the picture in front of me. Gulls flew overhead and two stately pelicans glided through the blue water of a tranquil lake fringed with green-leafed poplars.

"I don't need people to make the picture come alive," I said. "The birds provide focal points and add motion."

"Birds don't keep rural communities alive," Joan retorted. "I couldn't stay alone on the farm after my husband died, but if I'd had the option, I'd have moved to Baljennie rather than

North Battleford. Only, it's almost a ghost town. There's not even a grocery store left."

Liz had joined us a few minutes earlier. "Sounds like Prince and Vawn," she said, referring to tiny hamlets northwest of town.

"And dozens of other prairie communities." Joan brushed a hand over her face as if she were weary. "But I shouldn't preach to my hostess. You have a fine collection of paintings, Jeannie, and every right to be proud."

"Thanks," I said, savouring her praise. There'd be time to think about rural depopulation later.

When we completed the grand tour, Joan asked to buy a small painting. "Perhaps a picture of your flower garden."

I beamed at her. "My pleasure."

The door of the studio cupboard where I stored finished work was slightly ajar. I opened it further and reached inside. Carefully, I lifted out the first canvas and turned it to face me. Liz gasped, and I covered my mouth to prevent a scream. The picture showed a grassy slope near the height of land. I'd painted it last July when the hills were covered with orange prairie lilies, but the flowers were no longer visible. Someone had covered most of the canvas with a wash of black paint.

My guts clenched, as if the intruder had punched me in the stomach. I breathed deeply, trying to focus on the painting. It quivered in front of me. Liz grabbed my arm and steered me to the nearest chair.

"Sit down and put your head between your legs," she said as she lowered me onto the seat. "You're hyperventilating."

Somehow, we stumbled through the next few hours. I left a message for Derek when my call went to voice mail and then phoned the RCMP. While we waited for Semchuk and Pierce to arrive, I brewed a pot of mint tea and carried it out to the deck.

"How the hell did this person get in the house?" Liz asked. "Both doors were locked, the windows were closed, and there was no sign of a forced entry."

"Must have picked one of the locks," I said. "I don't know how that's done, but I've read about it."

"Bobby pins," Joan said. "Although I'm thinking of fifty years ago."

Liz scowled. "This person is clever. Knew there was no one home and took the time to ferret out the most hurtful way to send their message."

"Patient too," I added. "This is their fourth warning."

"Fifth," Liz said. "If you count Monica's 'accident.'"

"That was the first." I counted them off on my fingers. "Next, they lured us to the height of land and shot at Jade —"

"The scumbag hurt Goliath," Liz said, leaning over to scratch his head.

"Then there was a second email, followed by the dead coyote."

"And now there's this vandalized painting," she said. "Zayden has a motive. Did you tell the cops about his recent visit to Thickwood Farm?"

I told Joan about the meltdown. She didn't think it made Zayden a suspect.

"That young man confronted you face to face. He didn't send anonymous messages or sneak into your studio while you were away. The person who's harassing you is sly and secretive. Probably someone older."

Liz disagreed, and we debated the subject until Pierce and Semchuk arrived. They were accompanied by an officer from the Forensic Identification Unit.

"O'Toole's good," Semchuk said. "If the perp left prints behind, she'll find 'em."

After the officers had inspected the locks and window fastenings, I took them upstairs to my studio.

"This is the only room they've touched," I said.

Semchuk stared at the obliterated painting. "Someone hates you."

Although it was warm in the house, my blood ran cold. The crime was personal. Whoever had done the deed knew I painted and knew I valued art. The vandalism was their way of rubbing my nose in the dirt.

I told the cops about my recent encounter with Zayden.

"Never a dull moment, eh?" Semchuk said, as O'Toole dusted the painting for fingerprints.

"They weren't wearing gloves," she said. "There are several clear prints on the frame, and one on the brush they used to apply the black paint."

"If Zayden's your man, we'll nab him," Semchuk said. "But if his prints don't match, we're back where we started. And unless the culprit's prints are in our database, we're up the creek without a paddle."

"Did you find out how they entered?" I asked.

"Back door," he said. "A neat job of lock picking. They're either a pro or a gifted amateur. If I were you, I'd change both locks. Tell Massey to find you something state of the art."

I assured him I could do my own research — which was true in a way. I'd enjoyed delving into arcane sources of art history when I was at university, but the ins and outs of mechanical gadgets were beyond me. Frank had taken care of such mundane matters. And I'd paid the cost in dependency.

"We'll let you know the results of our investigation," Pierce said. "In the meantime, I'm glad you're staying with your sister."

"Me too," I said.

After walking through the rest of the house and touring the grounds, the police left. By then, all three of us were ready to crash.

"How about supper at the café?" Liz said. "I'm too wiped to cook."

Joan had arranged to play Scrabble with a neighbour; after hugs all around, she headed back to town. I called Mandi and told her our plans.

"There's lots of food here — tell her to join us."

Dinner back at my sister's was a noisy, rambunctious affair. Liz loved kids, and the feeling was mutual. I'd soon had my fill of knock-knock jokes, but Melissa and Ty were insatiable. While she entertained the kids, I chatted with Mandi and concentrated on the macaroni casserole.

Dessert was raspberries and ice cream. After we emptied our bowls, Liz joined her new buddies in a raucous game of Snakes and Ladders. Mandi and I did the dishes. As I dried plates and cutlery, I told her about our adventures.

"Your day's been more eventful than mine," she said. "The most exciting thing I did was go to the post office, and that was a bust. Nothing but flyers."

"Typical," I said. "No one writes letters anymore."

"Someone wrote one to you. I picked up your mail, and there was a letter in your box. Now, what did I do with it . . ."

"Try the hall table," I said.

It wasn't there. Nor was it on the floor, on the kitchen counter, or in any of the other places that are magnets to the flotsam and jetsam of domestic life.

"I'm sorry, Jeannie," Mandi said. "The darn thing has simply disappeared."

"It probably isn't important," I said. "Was there a return address?"

"Just *Jeannie Wolfert, Bunchgrass* printed with a pencil in block letters. I didn't notice the postmark."

Alarm bells went off inside my head. In its crudeness and simplicity, the missing envelope resembled my anonymous emails.

Mandi scraped out the salad bowl and plunged it into the sink. "The post office was a zoo. Must have been six or seven people passed through while I was talking to Candace."

I nodded. Candace runs the post office, and she's as chatty as my sister.

"Tammy DuBois was just leaving as I got there," Mandi said. "Then Joyce Zalenski arrived — she and Tammy's brother Chris were both picking up parcels. And no sooner had they gone than the people who bought the house next to the tennis court came in to ask about getting a post office box."

"I thought Tammy moved to Saskatoon."

"Must be here visiting. We didn't say more than hi, but, my God, Jeannie, she looked as if she'd been through the wars."

"Too bad you didn't get to talk to her."

Mandi drained the dishwater and hung up the dishcloth. "That's what I thought too. But I did get to visit with Stan. We met in the parking lot. He said to say hi to you."

"Good," I said, placing the last of the dried dishes in the cupboard.

"I've always thought you and he would have made a fine couple — I mean, if you hadn't been married to Frank."

I grabbed the back of a chair to steady myself as Melissa barreled into the kitchen.

"Aunt Jeannie, come and play with us."

"Your gramma and I are talking, sweetie."

"Go ahead," Mandi said. "I've got to put Ty to bed."

Two games of Snakes and Ladders later, I was ready to call it a day. Liz and Goliath went home to shut in her chickens. Mandi dragged Melissa off for a bath. I changed into pyjamas and wandered around the kitchen and living room looking for my letter. It was nowhere in sight.

"Try the mudroom," Mandi said. "And the hall closet."

It wasn't in either place.

I was about to give up and crawl into bed with Melissa when Derek called.

"Just phoning to say good night," he said. "I'll be back tomorrow morning."

"Great. Can you pick up some high-tech locks before you leave the city?"

"That sounds ominous. What happened?"

I told him about the vandalized painting and the visit from Semchuk and Pierce.

"It's a damn good thing you weren't at the house earlier," he said. "Promise me you won't go there alone."

"Not without a bodyguard," I said.

Derek assured me he'd be at the Co-op Hardware by nine. "And I'll get a cat door for Diesel as well as the locks."

"Thanks," I said. "You're a sweetheart."

"That should be my line," he said. "Goodnight, Jeannie. I'll see you tomorrow."

In bed that night, my thoughts circled round and round the missing letter. Maybe my anonymous correspondent had ditched email for snail mail. Maybe they'd had something important to say — perhaps another warning. Maybe they planned to break into the house and kill me in my bed . . .

Turned out, I was wrong about the latter. My stalker was unconventional. They had devised a more ingenious way to commit murder.

SUNDAY, AUGUST 5

I was still in bed when Derek called. "I've got the locks and the cat door. How about I pick you up from Mandi's in a couple hours and we spend the rest of the day at your place?"

"Sounds good," I said. "Did you track down Hunter? In all the confusion, I forgot to ask last night."

"He wasn't home, but I talked to some of Monica's friends. Several of them were happy to tell me that she and Hunter were lovers. Word is he's rich, and that she seduced him with the promise of a mansion on Crystal Lake."

"Did they give any reason for that particular lake?" I asked.

"No one knew exactly, but one friend thinks he has family in this neck of the woods."

I cocked an eyebrow. "Did you learn his surname?"

"No, damn it. You'd think at least one of Monica's friends would know it."

"Surely his name appears somewhere in her papers."

"If it does, Semchuk hasn't informed me of the fact."

I picked up my jeans and wiggled into them with the aid of one hand. "It looks to me as if Hunter's a prodigal son who wants to return 'home' to show off his wealth."

"Or maybe he wants to care for his aging mother," Derek said.

"Yeah, right!" I rummaged in my backpack, looking for a clean shirt. "I assume your ex-wife met him professionally."

"That's what her friends said. Rumour has it that he made a million in bitcoin before moving to Saskatoon. I expect that's why Monica was attracted to him."

"I wonder what he saw in her."

Derek groaned. "Maybe the same thing that I did."

A routine had developed over the course of our working visits to the farm. This time, however, Derek didn't just check the house and grounds for signs of an intruder. He installed the locks and cat door he'd bought in Saskatoon, while I tended pots of flowers on the deck.

I was weeding the begonias when pain shot through the palm of my right hand.

"Damn, that hurts!"

Derek looked up from the cat door. "You okay?"

"Serves me right for not wearing gloves," I said, showing him my injury.

The duct tape I'd wrapped around the handle of my Vietnamese hand hoe had come loose. The result was a gigantic sliver lodged between thumb and index finger.

Derek lifted my hand to his lips and kissed it. "The splinter isn't deep; if you hold still, I'll pull it out."

"Thanks," I said. After forty-one summers of heavy use,

the handle of my hoe was cracked and splintered. "Guess I need a fresh layer of tape."

"Or a new hoe."

"They're not available in town," I said. "This one will have to do for the rest of the summer."

Derek didn't look convinced, but I didn't have time to argue. Instead, I thanked him again for the first aid and headed down to the garden to pick vegetables for lunch.

Red-winged blackbirds sang from a poplar branch over-hanging a nearby slough, and a pair of mallards quacked lazily. Otherwise, the garden was silent and still. Even the sound of highway traffic from across the lake was muted. Lulled by birdsong and half-stupefied by the heat, I mindlessly picked beans — until a faint stirring in the trees roused me. I stood up and glimpsed a tall, sturdy man standing in the underbrush bordering the slough. The ubiquitous jeans and blue denim shirt were no help, but the long hair tied back with a leather cord was a dead giveaway. The last time I'd seen him had been at Monica's funeral.

"Looking for someone?" I asked, pitching my voice so that it carried across the garden.

The man hesitated for a moment and then disappeared into the trees.

I put down my bucket and started for the spot where I'd seen him. "Hey, I just want to talk to you."

But he had vanished. There was no point in charging through dense underbrush in pursuit of a man twenty years younger than me. Instead, I called Derek on my mobile.

Two minutes later he was standing by my side.

"You're sure it was Hunter?" he asked.

"Of course I'm sure. But I don't understand why he didn't stop when I called out to him. Unless he's the person who's been stalking me."

"I'll check to see if he left any traces."

He hadn't. "The land's too hard and dry to show foot-prints, and he didn't leave behind cigarette butts or soft drink cans. There's nothing to show that Hunter was here."

"So, what do we do now?"

"I'll talk to Semchuk. He'll probably send someone out to question your neighbours. If you're lucky, one of them will have seen or talked to him."

"Couldn't you ask the cops to check his fingerprints against the ones on the frame of my vandalized painting?" I asked.

"They'd have to haul him into the station first," Derek said. "Which hasn't happened yet because he's disappeared."

Over a late lunch of bean salad and a cheesy potatoes au gratin, we speculated about the significance of Hunter's unannounced presence on my farm.

"If he wanted to kill me," I said, "why didn't he do so when he had the chance?"

"Maybe he didn't expect to see you and wasn't carrying his rifle."

"Or could be he's an innocent man who was simply cast-ing a nostalgic eye over the land that he'd hoped to own." That story might have made me feel better if I had believed it was true.

"Then he wouldn't have run off when he saw you." Derek got up and took our dessert from the toaster oven. "Anyone with nothing to hide would have stopped and said hi."

We were finishing bowls of rhubarb crisp when Semchuk called.

"We haven't got hold of Hunter yet," he said over speakerphone, "but I've got a couple constables knocking on doors. So far, no one's seen the bugger."

"It would help if we had a last name," Derek said.

"Everyone we talked to knows him only as Hunter."

"Monica's records —"

"A couple references to someone she calls H, but that's it." Semchuk sighed. "If we had evidence against him, we could bring out the big guns, but so far he's just a person of interest."

Derek frowned as they ended the conversation. "If Hunter wants your land, chances are he knows someone around here. All we've got to do is find that person."

"Maybe I can help."

"Not if it means you getting hurt." Derek picked up the pail I'd brought in from the garden. "Want me to give you a hand tipping the rest of those beans?"

I watched as he expertly cut tips and tails and then sliced each bean into three pieces. "You've done that before, haven't you? Before you came here, I mean."

"Mom had a lot of mouths to feed," he said. "In our house, food prep required all hands on deck."

"Is that why you and Monica didn't have children, too much experience living in a big family?"

"Monica didn't cook, unless she was preparing amuse-bouches for a dinner party. Any kid of hers would have gone hungry."

"Didn't that bother you?"

He laughed. "Jeez, woman, what does it matter now?"

"Just curious." Frank had been close-mouthed about personal matters too. He could talk for hours about the inner workings of the tractor and combine but ask him about his feelings and he'd shut down faster than a speeding bullet threatening Lois Lane. Were all men born with a propensity for emotional reserve?

I was about to boil water to blanch the prepared beans when Mandi phoned. Melissa had found my missing letter on the car floor when she and Ty were on their way home from swimming lessons.

"You might want Derek to look at it," she said. "Melissa put her wet bathing suit on it, so the envelope came open."

"And, of course, you couldn't resist reading it," I said. "What does the letter say?"

"Final warning."

A familiar sense of dread flooded my body. "That's it?"

"The writer was concise. And there is no signature."

My sister was trying to persuade me to take refuge at Jordan's place in Saskatoon when Derek interrupted us.

"If Mandi's found the letter, we'd better pick it up before Melissa uses it as drawing paper," he said. "Can you freeze beans at her house?"

The grandkids were playing hopscotch on the sidewalk when we reached the farm.

Their voices mingled with the sound of a tractor hauling hay bales in a nearby field. The scene promised sanctuary. But my stalker had invaded it.

Derek pulled on a pair of the gloves he always carried in his van. "Not that there's much point in trying to protect the writer's fingerprints," he said when Mandi gave him the damp envelope.

My name and that of the post office were written on the front in smudged block letters. Inside was a single sheet of lined white paper that had been torn from a coil-bound scribbler. *Final warning.*

My blood froze. Seeing the words in the writer's hand was scarier than hearing Mandi read them aloud over the phone. "Whoever printed this wrote the other notes as well," I said. "Same writing style."

"I'll drop it off at the detachment," Derek said, placing the envelope and its contents in a clear plastic evidence bag. "Sure you're going to be okay if I leave you here, Jeannie?"

I nodded. "Liz and I are having dinner at the café. Nancy and Dan will keep me safe."

"There's cold chicken and potato salad for supper," Mandi said, her brow furrowed. "If you change your mind, the two of you are welcome to join us."

"Thanks, but I've got to get this evidence to town." Derek wrapped his arms around me in a close embrace. "Want me to come back later and spend the night on Mandi's sofa?"

I shook my head. "Mandi and John are here, and we lock the doors at night. Best way you can help is by talking to Hunter."

"I'll try." Perhaps due to my sister's presence, our good-night kiss was brief. "See you in the morning."

When he left, I ignored Mandi's raised eyebrow and turned my attention to the beans. Not only would freezing vegetables provide a welcome distraction while I waited for Liz to pick me up for dinner, but it would also give me an excuse for avoiding Mandi's inevitable questions about my relationship with Derek.

Cold air blasted us when Liz and I entered the café. Stan sat at his usual table, a mug and empty plate in front of him. Across the room, Joyce and Al Zalenski ate hamburgers and fries while he carried on a running monologue. On the radio, George Jones sang about love, loss, and faithless women.

Nancy greeted us as we sat at the table next to Stan's. We both ordered the day's special: chili and cornbread. It wasn't what I'd have served on a hot summer evening, but what the heck — I wasn't the cook.

"Won't go wrong with the chili," Stan said.

Liz rolled her eyes. "I can't remember the last time I stopped in and you weren't here. Don't you ever eat at home?"

"Dan cooks better. And I like the company."

"Then join us," I said.

"Thanks." Stan smiled at me as he grabbed his mug and moved to our table. "You still at Mandi's?"

"She's stuck with me until the killer's apprehended," I said.

"That cop friend of yours been hanging around a long time," Al said. "Good excuse for enjoying the company of an attractive widow, eh?"

"Don't pay any attention to him," Nancy said, depositing bowls of chili and cornbread in front of Liz and me. "Stan, you want your pie now?"

Heat flooded my cheeks, and I changed the subject. "Mandi met Tammy DuBois in the post office the other day. You remember her, Stan —"

"Crazy as a bedbug," Al said. "Last time I saw her, she was walking barefoot across the field north of your garden."

"When was that?" I asked.

"Couple months ago. She always stays with her brother Chris. They say his wife counts the days until she leaves."

"Tammy's not the only one who's been out walking on Jeannie's farm," Liz said. "Anyone see a big long-haired guy around here?"

"You mean Hunter?" Stan said.

My jaw dropped. "You know him?"

"He's stopped by a few times. Seems to me at least one of his folks is from around here."

"Stan, this could be important," I said. "Who are his parents? Do they still live here? Are they in the village or on the farm? And if they have moved away —"

"Hang on, lady," he said, holding his palms out to stop my flow of words. "He and I aren't best buds."

"But you said you talked to him."

"First time we met I was fixing fence along the old RM road. He'd driven by in a half-ton —"

"Why was he on that road? It's just an overgrown trail that local ranchers use to check their cows."

"I didn't ask. Maybe he was out enjoying the scenery." Stan dug his fork into a piece of Dan's homemade apple pie. "Anyway, he had a breakdown just over the top of the next hill. The engine quit, and he walked back to ask me for help."

"Dude doesn't carry a cell phone?" Liz asked.

"Too far from the tower for a signal," Stan said. "I gave him a ride back to his truck. The ground strap on his battery was corroded, so I helped clean it up."

"Did he ask about me?"

He frowned. "Why should he?"

I poured a second cup of tea from the pot Liz and I shared. "He didn't tell you he wanted to buy a piece of lakeshore land around here?"

"Said something about this would be a good place t' live, but I didn't pay much attention. Lots of city folks dream about a place in the country."

"How do you know he was from the city?" Liz asked.

Stan swallowed a mouthful of pie. "Why the hell are you so interested in Hunter?"

"He's involved in the murder inquiry and the police are looking for him," I said.

"Didn't act like a murderer. When I told him I herded my livestock on horseback, he said he liked to ride. So I invited him to go riding with me. I've met cowhands who couldn't handle a horse as well as he did."

"Do you know anything about his background?" I asked.

"Nope. Next time I see him, I'll send him up to your place, and you can give him the third degree."

"Any idea where he stays when he's here?" I said, ignoring his flippancy.

"Could be he makes a day trip," Stan said.

Although further questions got me nowhere, he'd confirmed my suspicion that Hunter had a connection to the Bunchgrass area. That information alone was worth the price of dinner. And I enjoyed the rare treat of being out in the community on a summer evening. Especially since it meant sharing a table with Stan. He wasn't as chatty or dynamic as Derek, but — like Frank — he was as reliable as they come. That counts for something when you're my age.

Joyce and Al finished their pie and paid for dinner. As they passed our table on the way out, Al leaned over and patted my hand. "You and Liz look after yourselves, eh?"

It's great to be part of a small community where people are aware of your troubles, but I was getting tired of useless advice. "This blasted killer is like a ghost," I said to Liz and Stan. "Sneaks around without anyone seeing them but leaves evidence of their presence behind. How do you deal with someone like that?"

"We got to talk to Hunter," Liz said.

"I'll tell him that if I see him," Stan said, and this time he was serious. Then he turned to me. "But you don't have much to worry about, not with your cop friend acting as bodyguard."

Was it mere wishful thinking to hear a note of jealousy in his voice?

We were on our way back to Mandi's when I remembered that I wanted to pick up a head of cauliflower for curried vegetables the next day. Flea beetles had destroyed my sister's cole crop, but I'd covered mine with mesh cages and had a bumper harvest. It was still broad daylight, and Liz was with me. There couldn't be any harm in a quick trip to the garden.

The farmstead looked deserted when we pulled up in front of my house. Liz ran inside to use the washroom. I should have waited for her, but pride got the better of caution. Humming softly to myself, I set off down the path to the vegetable garden.

Although the air was still warm, the leafy shade felt cool, and I broke out in goosebumps. An odd stillness enveloped the trees. The robins had cancelled their nightly concert, and even the gulls overhead were silent. A whiff of rotting vegetation hinted at Nature's ever-present shadow of death and decay. Crossing my fingers that the heatwave was about to end, I'd almost reached the row of lettuce at the bottom of the hill when something hard reached out from a clump of poplars and knocked me to the ground.

The pain that seared my shoulder was nothing compared to my chagrin. And terror. A heavy log lay across one ankle. Nearby, just off the path, lay a smaller log and a large flat stone. My stalker had set a deadfall trap, and I'd walked right into it. Although I'd never seen one before, I recognized it from pictures on a wilderness survival website. The intended victims were coyotes and other predators. This one was meant for me.

My body wanted to freeze, but my brain said to get out of there. Fast. With the help of a heavy stick, I inched myself into a sitting position. Then I tried to move my leg. The log pinned my ankle to the ground. If I didn't show up back at the house in a few minutes, Liz would come looking for me. But what if the stalker was lying in wait? How could I warn her of their possible presence without drawing attention to myself? I tried to stand, hoping to shift the log enough to free my foot. The log didn't budge. I surveyed the ground around me, looking for a stout branch to use as a crowbar. Then I heard the soft rustle of movement in the trees. Senses alert, I looked up. A shadow fell across my line of sight, blocking the dappled sunlight. Staring down at me was a man with long dark hair.

"Hunter," I said, and for the first time in my life, I fainted.

—W—

When I regained consciousness, Liz was cradling my head in her hands.

"Jeannie, what happened? When you didn't come back to the house, I headed for the garden and found you lying here unconscious."

"Where's Hunter?" I asked.

"Hunter? What does he have to do with anything?"

"He set the deadfall trap," I said.

"What deadfall trap? Are you okay? I mean, you're not hallucinating or anything, are you?"

"I was on my way to the garden when I triggered something that caused a log to fall on me. It knocked me down and pinned my ankle to the ground. Next thing I knew Hunter was looking at me, and I fainted."

Liz gently smoothed my forehead. "There is no log on your ankle."

"But —" Moving carefully, I sat up. Liz was right. I rotated my foot and slowly drew a circle in the air. My ankle throbbed like fury, but it was free to move unimpeded. "What happened to the log? And how did it get off my foot?"

"Did you hit your head?" she asked. "Maybe you have a concussion."

I couldn't see my foot because it was covered by my high-top boot. The boot's padded collar would have cushioned the log's impact. With any luck, I wouldn't have to contend with anything worse than a sore ankle. "I don't think anything's broken. Can you help me to my feet? I want to find the pieces of the trap."

Liz looked at me as if I were crazy, but with her help, I managed to stand on one foot. The other hurt the moment it touched the ground. I grabbed a nearby poplar for support and stood peering into the undergrowth. There was no sign of either the flat rock or the two logs. Surely, I hadn't imagined the dead-fall trap and the vision of Hunter looming over me. But why remove the evidence rather than finish his attempt on my life?

I pointed to the heavy stick I'd used to help me sit up. It was the right length and diameter for use as a cane. Liz picked it up and handed it to me.

"Thanks. I need to get to your truck so I can call Derek on my cell phone."

"Use mine."

I took the proffered mobile. "I'll call when we reach the house, and I can sit. My ankle feels like it's been stepped on by an elephant."

"Want me to give you a hand?"

I shook my head and started to inch my way up the path. When we reached the deck, I clambered awkwardly onto a reclining lounge chair and called Derek.

"Give me five minutes, and I'll call you back. I'm just leaving the cop shop —"

"There's been another attack," I said. "Can you put your phone on speaker and ask Semchuk and Pierce to join you? They'll want to hear this."

I told the three of them about my experience with the deadfall trap and Hunter's appearance at the scene. "Stan's talked to him and thinks he has family in the area, but he doesn't know the man's last name."

Semchuk groaned. "We'll keep digging."

"He also thinks that Hunter's a good guy," I said. "Which doesn't make sense. No one else was around when I triggered the trap, and no one else could have removed the evidence."

"Maybe he's trying to protect someone," Pierce said.

"Who do you suspect, his elderly mother?" Semchuk sighed theatrically. "Don't go anywhere, Ms. Wolfert-Lang. We're on our way."

I rolled my eyes as I handed Liz her phone. "Any chance of tea before the cavalry arrives?"

While it was steeping, she unlaced my boot.

"This might hurt," she said, easing it off my foot.

The flesh under my sock was turning purple, but I could wiggle my toes and flex my ankle. "Let's look on the bright side. At least I won't need an amputation."

Liz had brought me a basin of ice water, and I was sitting at the patio table soaking my bruised foot when two shots in rapid succession rang out from the parking lot.

My friend sprang to her feet. "Get inside. Now." Then, before I could stop her, she raced down the steps and toward her half-ton.

"Liz, get back here," I yelled. But she had disappeared around the corner of the house.

"Idiot," I muttered, opening the back door and hobbling into the living room.

Diesel was napping peacefully, oblivious to the kerfuffle outside. I perched beside him on the edge of the sofa, straining my ears to catch a sound of the shooter. Then a truck engine roared to life. It faded away in the distance as footsteps sounded on the deck. The outside door opened.

"Jeannie?"

"In the living room," I yelled.

Liz appeared in the doorway. "Whoever put a bullet through my front tires better have liability insurance. I'm billing the scumbag for replacements."

—\\\\//—

Derek and Semchuk arrived while we were finishing the pot of mint tea in the kitchen.

"Jeannie, are you okay?" Derek asked as he picked up my injured foot and cradled it in his hands. "Want me to take you to Emergency?"

"It looks worse than it is," I said. "My ankle's bruised, not broken."

"If it was a deadfall trap," Semchuk said, "you're damn lucky to be alive."

"Yeah, well . . ."

"Want me to show you where I found her?" Liz asked.

Derek nodded. "As long as Jeannie stays put while we're gone."

Liz helped me into an armchair in the living room and handed me a back issue of *The Walrus* magazine. "And don't even think about leaving that chair while we're gone."

When they left, I wrapped myself in a lap quilt, but the throbbing in my ankle made it impossible to get comfortable. Despite the heat outside, I shivered. "Probably delayed shock," I told myself, thinking longingly of a hot bath. The prospect of hobbling to the bathroom, undressing, and running water into the tub, however, was too much, so I leafed through the magazine until Liz returned.

"They found evidence that supports your story," she said. "When I left, they were talking about disturbed vegetation and a flat stone that had recently been moved."

"What did they find out about the damage to your truck?"

"They couldn't find any tracks in the gravel," she said, "but someone had been hiding in the shelterbelt. And they found the bullets that destroyed my tires. They're from the same gun as the one used against Goliath and the dead coyote."

"So, whoever set the deadfall trap isn't a boy scout working on his woodcraft badge," I said. "It had to have been Hunter."

When Derek and Semchuk returned, they confirmed my theory.

"We found the trap," Semchuk said. "Someone scattered its pieces in the trees just off the path. Probably our long-haired friend."

Derek nodded. "There's no one else in the picture."

"I'll put out an alert for the bugger," Semchuk said. "He'll be picked up by tomorrow night."

"In the meantime, can't you find out who he is and do a background check?" I asked. "If he's from around here, he might be working with someone."

"We're on it," Semchuk said. "And we're still trying to find the rifle that shot those bullets." He yawned. "Got to get this case wrapped up so I can catch up on sleep."

When Semchuk had gone, Derek pulled up a chair beside mine. "We had an understanding that you wouldn't go to the farm alone."

"I wasn't alone. Liz was with me."

"She was in the house. And with all due respect to your friend, Goliath would have been more useful. Why didn't you take him with you?"

"We planned to go straight to Mandi's, but I needed a cauliflower for tomorrow's supper."

"Next time, stick to your plan," Derek said. "I'm not trying to control you, but for God's sake, don't take unnecessary chances."

Mandi said much the same thing when Derek deposited me at her place a short time later.

"There are lots of vegetables in my garden. You didn't need to risk your life chasing after more. Honestly, Jeannie, for a smart woman you can be awfully stupid."

Derek grinned. "I couldn't have said it better myself."

I threw a quilted cushion at him. "Don't go on about it. My ankle hurts —"

Mandi immediately changed tack and started to fuss over me. "John can look after the kids. I'll run you into town —"

"All I need is a good night's rest." I shifted my foot into a more comfortable position. "And some peace and quiet."

"Hint taken," Derek said, getting up to leave. He leaned over my chair and kissed me. "I'll call you tomorrow. And let Mandi take care of you, okay?"

Derek's departure left me alone with my sister. John was watching TV in the basement family room, and the grandkids were in bed. I steeled myself for further scolding, but she'd either exhausted her reserves or given up on me.

"I swear I've aged two years since that real estate woman's accident," she said. "You'd think the police would have found her killer by now."

"There aren't any obvious suspects. The cops took Zayden's prints last time they interviewed him; they don't match the ones on my vandalized painting. And why would Hunter remove the log from my ankle if he'd put it there in the first place?"

Mandi picked up her knitting and resumed work on the sock she was making for Melissa. "Maybe to throw the police off his trail."

"With his wealth, he could buy any one of several hundred farms," I said. "It doesn't make sense that he'd kill to purchase mine. But there isn't anyone else the killer could be."

"Haven't they left clues behind?"

"Just that fingerprint on my painting, and it's no help. Whoever left it doesn't have a criminal record. No one has reported suspicious behaviour, and the police can't search for a person when they don't know who he or she is. Their only hope is that Hunter will talk — if they find him."

Mandi sighed. "This person's got to be crazy — but that's not much information to go on, is it?"

I was contemplating bed a short time later when my mobile rang.

"Jeannie, I'm so excited," Jade said. "Gramma is on her way to Lloyd tomorrow, and she's stopping here for brunch."

I stifled a yawn. "That's wonderful."

"Zayden's joining us. He wants to meet her."

The "wonderful" news became problematic. "It might be best to wait until Monica's killer is found."

"The police don't consider him a suspect," she said.

Jade was right, although I still had serious reservations about her new boyfriend. But what could I say? My rental agreement with Thickwood Farm didn't give me the right to vet romantic relationships.

"Do you want to come for coffee afterward? You'll like Gramma."

"I'd love to meet her," I said, "but I had an unfortunate encounter with a deadfall trap earlier this evening."

Jade's usual response would have been to pour on sympathy, but that night her focus was elsewhere. "Zayden was here with me. He had nothing to do with it."

Although I wasn't convinced, I gave her a condensed version of my story. "I'm going to spend tomorrow on the sofa with my feet up."

Truth be told, I was looking forward to escaping my troubles by joining Lacey McCrae in the third book of J.E. Barnard's Falls mysteries. Fate, however, had something less pleasant in mind.

MONDAY, AUGUST 6

I was peacefully reading on the sofa when Jade called. "Jeannie?" She sounded on the verge of hysteria. "Zayden didn't show up for brunch. He was supposed to be here an hour ago."

"Maybe he had motorbike trouble," I said. "Have you tried his cell?"

"All I got was his voice mail. And he's not answering my texts."

I put down my novel. "His phone battery could be dead. Or he could have lost his signal."

"He said he'd arrive by eleven, and it's almost noon."

"I'll talk to Derek and get back to you." If Zayden hadn't been involved with Monica, I would have made an excuse and gone back to my book. But he was part of the web in which I'd become entangled. Like it or not, I'd have to help.

Derek swore under his breath when I told him about Zayden's absence. "He's been hanging around your place, right?"

"I saw him once, and Al spotted him another time."

"The shooter may have mistaken him for you."

"That's what I'm afraid of." Slowly I breathed in and out, trying to calm my racing heartbeat. "Is there anything we can do?"

"Check your messages in case they've contacted you."

There was no word from my stalker.

"I'll do a tour of your yard and the gardens," he said. "Keep checking your phone and let me know immediately if there's a text or an email. If Zayden hasn't shown up by the time I'm back at the house, I'll call Semchuk."

Mandi made up a plate of sandwiches and put out a bowl of hummus with cucumber slices and carrot sticks.

"I'm taking Melissa and Ty to their swimming lessons this afternoon," she said, "but John will be around if you need anything."

"And Derek's here," I said. "I'll be fine."

Once we'd finished lunch and they'd gone, I locked the doors and called Jade. She still hadn't heard from Zayden. A call to Derek was equally unproductive. He'd seen no sign of the missing man anywhere in my gardens.

Too restless to read, I limped around the living room, pausing in front of every window to check for intruders. Nothing. Then my mobile pinged. The number was unfamiliar and the text unsigned, but there was no mistaking the sender. They had keyed in five words: *I thought he was you.*

Heart pounding, I phoned Derek. He was checking the woodland north of my vegetable garden. "Not much chance of tracing the stalker's text," he said. "They're probably using a disposable burner phone. But I'll ring the local detachment. We need to organize a search."

Then I called Jade. She took the news more philosophically than I'd expected.

"I knew something bad had happened. Gramma was delayed. She won't get here until tomorrow, but Zayden didn't know that. He was looking forward to meeting her and wouldn't have stood me up."

"The police will find him," I said with more confidence than I felt. "Derek's talking to them right now."

"Ava and Thor will help me search Thickwood Farm," she said. "Zayden will be okay. The spirits will protect him."

The optimism of New Age thinkers never failed to astonish me. "Let's hope you're right."

Derek called as soon as I'd finished talking to Jade. "Semchuk's getting a crew together. He'll be here in an hour. Okay to use your place as the search headquarters?"

"I'd be honoured," I said, and told him that Jade and company would scour their home quarter for traces of the missing man. "If Zayden's injured, we need all the help we can get. I'll phone Liz and Stan."

"Tell them to report here for an assigned area," Derek said. "We don't want volunteers tripping over each other."

"My ankle's still wobbly, but it's a lot better than it was yesterday. If John can give me a ride to the house, I'll make sandwiches and muffins for the searchers. With all those people around, my farm will be safe as churches."

"Can you sit on a stool while you work?" he asked.

"Yes, I can."

"Then make damn sure you do," he said.

I was putting a pan of spicy apple muffins in the oven when Liz and Goliath walked through the door.

"Any word about Zayden?"

I shook my head. "Haven't heard anything."

"The poor kid's probably lying dead in a poplar bluff."

"Unless the stalker intends to prolong their reign of terror. If he or she wanted me dead, I wouldn't stand a chance."

"Don't even think that." Liz plugged in my thirty-cup coffee percolator and filled it with water. "Stan's here. He's riding Prince."

I joined her at the window and watched as he dismounted and dropped Prince's reins to the ground. In cowboy boots, Stetson, and snug jeans, Stan had set more than one heart aflutter. Frank had been good-looking, but his work boots, overalls, and John Deere baseball cap had lacked cachet. Could it be the difference in dress that makes farmers the salt of the earth and cowboys a rural sex symbol? Riding horseback helps. Where's the romance in driving a tractor?

While Stan and Liz chatted about the upcoming search, half a dozen police officers drifted into the house. I was kept busy making more coffee and muffins, refilling the cream pitcher, and pointing people in the direction of the washroom. Pierce hauled in a folding table and set up search headquarters in the living room. Semchuk taped a blown-up picture of Zayden to a portable easel. Next to it he placed a large-scale map of the area between my house and Thickwood Farm. He'd divided it into wedge-shaped sections and assigned one to each of the searchers.

"The young man's been staying at the lodge in Battlefords Provincial Park," Semchuk said. "He left there around ten thirty. The desk clerk says he was wearing baggy white shorts and a pale blue embroidered tunic. The folks at Thickwood Farm expected him for brunch at eleven, but he may have taken a detour to check out the lakeshore in front of Jeannie's house. Unless he was injured or abducted, he should be sitting down to scrambled eggs and bacon round about now. You all know the drill. Report back the moment you see signs of a shooting or a struggle, or anything else that could cause a man to go missing."

When the officers had gone, I told Semchuk that my three tenants were searching the area around their house.

"Give Pierce their contact information," Semchuk said, "and she'll call them with instructions." He turned to Liz, Stan, and John. "You three registered with my constable, right? I want you to comb every inch of the wooded area north of Jeannie's garden, and that includes the borders of both sloughs. Keep your mobiles on and call if you see anything — and I mean anything — that shouldn't be there. A piece of clothing, gum wrapper, cigarette package, Kleenex . . . and take that mutt with you. If he gets hold of the person who injured him, the bastard won't get away."

"Sorry my ankle won't let me help with the search," I said.

Semchuk snorted. "Don't even think about it. You'd be a sitting duck. No crazy sniper's gonna pick you off on my watch."

When Semchuk left, I returned to the kitchen. If the search continued all afternoon, the searchers would need supper. I'd make myself useful by baking bread.

Breadmaking has always been one of my favourite activities. On a winter day, I like mixing the dough and kneading it until smooth and elastic, then watching it rise until ready to bake to a rich golden brown. It is less appealing on a hot summer afternoon, when I often resort to cooking flatbread in a frying pan or on the barbecue. That afternoon, however, I needed loaves — three or four of them. Thankful for my well-stocked pantry, I set out to perform culinary magic.

The afternoon passed slowly, interrupted only by the arrival of Joyce Zalenski with a pecan coffee cake and a pan of cinnamon buns.

"For the searchers," she said. "My old man wanted to help, but he's gone to Lloyd to pick up a combine part. I keep telling him we need to downsize, but you know Al — stubborn as a two-year-old at nap time."

"Thanks," I said. "Can you stay for coffee?"

She shook her head. "The kids are coming for supper, and I need to put a roast in the oven. But I hope you find the young man. Dirty shame when trekking around the countryside means taking your life in your hands. What's the world coming to, eh?"

When she left, I hard-cooked eggs for sandwiches, made two kinds of dip, and washed the vegetables that Pierce picked for me in the garden. As soon as the bread was out of the oven, I popped in a double batch of raspberry jam squares while Pierce made more coffee. Whether or not they found Zayden, the searchers wouldn't go hungry in my house.

Derek and Semchuk were the first to return. While Semchuk exchanged notes with his constable, Derek wandered into the kitchen and helped himself to a sandwich.

"Typical search," he said. "You spend an afternoon peering at every inch of ground you cover, and at the end have sweet bugger-all to show for it."

I passed him a plate and the tray of raw vegetables. "You're not saying it's a waste of effort?"

"Got no choice. There's a real person out there. He could die if we don't reach him in time." He selected a carrot stick and reached for the dip. "Thanks for feeding us."

"Glad to help."

Pierce had called the searchers and told them to return to base for supper at six. When Liz and Goliath arrived a few minutes later, followed by a couple of police constables, we put out the food and piled cotton napkins next to the dishes. Then I joined Liz.

"No trace of Zayden," she said. "I hope that doesn't mean he's dead. What if your stalker buried him or dumped his body in the lake? He might never turn up."

"That's what I'm afraid of," I said. "Are you going out again after supper?"

"I told Pierce I have to be home by dark to shut in the chickens, but I'm good until then."

Jade, Ava, and Thor entered the kitchen looking like weekend warriors returning from battle. Unlike the other searchers, they had worn shorts and T-shirts that gave no protection from tree branches and prickly vegetation. While the gently rolling hayfield and pasture would have been easy to search, part of the quarter is heavily wooded with scrub poplars and a dense undergrowth. Saskatoons, wild gooseberries, rose bushes, and other shrubs had torn at their clothes and covered them with scratches. Jade was bleeding from a cut on her arm. I hastily covered the injury with a bandage from the bathroom cabinet and resisted the urge to suggest she wear a long-sleeved shirt and pants the next time.

The meal was a hasty — and solemn — affair. If Zayden wasn't found in the next three hours, it would be too dark to continue searching until the next morning. Warm nights meant no risk of death from exposure, but that wouldn't help if he was lying somewhere injured and bleeding.

Pierce and I were washing dishes when Stan came over to thank me for supper.

"Going back to the search?" I asked.

He nodded. "Heck of a note to get shot just because you're wandering around someone else's property."

"That's what Joyce said too." I smiled at my old boyfriend. "It was good of you to join us, especially since you've never even met Zayden."

Derek walked over and put an arm around my waist. "That's what I like about these rural communities — people take their responsibilities seriously." He gave me a quick hug. "Need a ride back to Mandi's? I'll be out searching until dark."

"No problem," I said, wondering if the comment on rural people was meant sardonically. "I'll get a ride with John."

When he'd gone, Stan looked at me inquiringly. "Doesn't that cop have a job back in Saskatoon?"

"He's on holiday," I said. "And it's been handy having him around."

"As a cross between security advisor and general dogsbody?"

"Something like that." I finished my jam square and wiped my hands on a napkin. "It's nice having a chauffeur."

"Don't get used to it," Stan said. "You pay a price for dependence."

I stared after his retreating back. Was that a warning or an expression of bitter experience? Stan didn't strike me as the dependent sort, but I hadn't seen much of him around the time his marriage broke up. How could I know what emptiness and heartache his ex-wife had left behind?

Pierce was on the phone talking to the local media, and everyone else had gone back to the search. I gathered up the remaining dirty dishes and carried them to the sink. The coffeecake and cinnamon buns were gone, and there were only a few muffins and jam squares left. But I was getting tired. It was time to put my feet up.

I was relaxing on the sofa when Liz called. "Remember you said you'd lend me your chain saw? I'm still climbing over some of the trees that got knocked down by the storm. Can I pick it up on my way back to the house?"

"It's in the old wooden grain bin that Frank used for storage," I said. "But there's no light in there. You'll never find it without a flashlight."

"Damn! I left mine at home."

I stood up and reached for the walking stick John had made me. "I need to get outside for a bit. Send Goliath to meet me, and I'll be there in five minutes."

"Going somewhere?" Pierce asked when I'd ended the call.

I told her I wanted to get something for Liz. "Goliath will provide escort service, and the place is crawling with cops. They'll keep me safe."

Liz's dog was waiting for me by the door. I gave him a hug, and we set out for the grain bin.

The cooler air and evening birdsong should have lifted my spirits; instead, I worried about Zayden. A light breeze from the north would make the outdoors increasingly inhospitable to an injured man. How ironic it would be to die from a chill during one of the hottest summers on record.

A short walk brought us to the row of round steel bins where my husband had stored grain. At one end stood a square wooden bin. Ever since Frank had stopped growing canola, it provided storage for a mishmash of out-of-season tools and small equipment.

As we approached, Goliath lifted his head, sniffed the air, and growled.

"What's up, buddy?"

There were police officers all over the place — surely my stalker wouldn't be out looking for me. I turned on my flashlight and shone its beam in a wide circle. Voices sounded in the distance, but there was no one near the wooden bin.

"Zayden?"

When there was no answer, I pushed open the door. Inside, it was dark. The air was warm and smelled of musty grain. Goliath rushed past me. I followed, cursing as I stumbled over an empty pail. Then a derelict hand tiller blocked my path. By the time I'd climbed over it, Goliath had reached the old seed bags piled in one corner. He stopped. Grabbed a bag with his mouth. And pulled. A sandal-clad foot appeared.

Breathing hard, I joined Goliath. Together we removed the surrounding bags. Zayden was lying motionless on the ground. His pale tunic and white shorts had turned a dark rusty-red.

First aid training forty years earlier hadn't prepared me for the sight of so much blood. Or for its heavy, metallic smell. But there wasn't time to indulge in squeamishness. The young man was in trouble. Trying to ignore my heaving stomach, I knelt at his head.

"Zayden, it's Jeannie. Can you hear me?"

He didn't answer, but I could feel a pulse when I put my fingers on his wrist. I sent Goliath to wait for me outside. Then I called for back-up.

"He's unconscious, but still breathing," I told Pierce.

"Can you provide directions for air ambulance?"

I described the location of the bins and told her the pilot could land in the field behind them.

"Stay where you are until Semchuk arrives," she said. "And unless you can help the victim, don't touch anything."

Liz arrived as I ended the conversation. She took one look at Zayden and dropped to the ground beside him. "Ho-lee! This is bad."

I nodded. "How are your first aid skills?"

She took his hand in hers. "He needs a lot more than first aid."

"I wonder how long he's been lying there. Surely someone's searched this area."

"Probably saw a pile of bags surrounded by snow shovels and empty oil pails," Liz said, "and didn't come inside."

Outside, Goliath barked, and a man's voice called my name.

"In here," I said.

Derek and Semchuk entered.

"How is he?" Derek asked.

"Not good. Constable Pierce called the STARS air ambulance. There's a helicopter on its way."

I trained my flashlight on Zayden as Derek knelt beside him and made a quick inventory of his condition. "Looks like a penetrating abdominal injury. If the bullet didn't exit, he's out of luck."

"Should be some blood on the ground if the kid was shot here," Semchuk said.

"Did the shooter drag him to the grain bin," I asked, "or did he crawl in here to hide from them?"

"No drag marks," Semchuk said. "He came in using his own steam."

While Derek stripped off his shirt and pressed it against the gunshot wound, Semchuk phoned the forensic techs. Liz and I went outside to wait for the ambulance.

"How are you doing?" she asked, putting an arm around me.

I swallowed hard, proud that I'd managed to keep my act together. "Better than Zayden, that's for sure."

"Do you need to go back to the house?"

"I'm fine." My answer wasn't entirely true, but it was close enough.

Beside us, Goliath pricked up his ears and barked.

Liz pointed toward the south. "There it is."

The helicopter flew toward us. When it reached the small field behind the grain bins, it hovered for a moment before landing on the grass. Two paramedics carrying a stretcher climbed out. I guided them to the open door of the wooden bin, and they disappeared inside.

Hands over my ears, I returned to where Liz was standing.

"Want to stay here until they're gone?" I asked, straining my voice to be heard above the roar of motor and whirling blades.

She nodded. We waited until the men reappeared, with Zayden strapped to the stretcher. Semchuk followed close behind.

"He's going to St. Paul's," one of the paramedics said as they loaded him into the waiting helicopter. "We'll call when we get there."

Over the course of the next twenty minutes, the rest of the searchers drifted in. Semchuk interviewed me and Liz and tore a strip off the hapless constable responsible for searching the grain bins. Then, with the aid of powerful flashlights, Derek and the Mounties tramped the surrounding area, looking for evidence of where the shooting had taken place.

When the crime scene techs arrived, Liz, Goliath, Stan, John, and I were huddled together in front of the wooden grain bin, high on adrenaline and the camaraderie of the search.

Liz was the first to move. "Goliath and I better get home before the coyotes eat all the chickens. Jeannie, I'll pick up that chainsaw later."

"Thanks for coming," I said. "You, too, Stan. And John."

Stan was about to walk Liz to her truck when Pierce called to say Zayden had arrived at the hospital in Saskatoon.

"He's in surgery," she said. "The emergency room doctor says there's a good chance of recovery if he survives the next twenty-four hours."

Mouthing a silent prayer, I returned to the house to say good-bye. Diesel was purring contentedly on Constable Pierce's lap. I wished them both goodnight and limped back to where John had parked his truck. It was time to get home to Mandi and the grandkids.

During our short drive, I thought about Zayden. He had been an annoying young man, but his injury replaced my anger with sympathy. Would his dysfunctional mother and younger siblings visit him in the hospital? Mandi would be waiting for John and me with hot tea and hugs. We were lucky. Not for the first time, I counted my blessings.

TUESDAY, AUGUST 7

D erek planned to spend the day helping Semchuk with his investigation. After our frantic search for Zayden, I was glad to spend a quiet morning at home. Mandi and I played hide and seek with the grandkids, helped them build a bird feeder, and organized a scavenger hunt. Although I could have come up with a list of activities I'd have preferred, the kids and Mandi were happy — and that made me happy too.

After lunch, we took Melissa and Ty to their swimming lessons at the beach in Bunchgrass. It was deserted most of the year, but on a warm summer afternoon it overflowed with both cottagers and local folks. Gulls flew overhead, their cries competing with children's voices and the distant hum of highway traffic. Kids swam and played tag while parents and grandparents read paperbacks, touched up their tans, and relaxed in the sunshine. Melissa and Ty joined six other youngsters by the water's edge, where a lean young woman in a navy swimsuit would teach them how to dogpaddle. I spread my towel on the sand and stretched out beside Mandi.

She was telling me about Melissa's upcoming birthday party when I noticed a shaggy-haired older man in well-worn denim standing near the playground. He was smoking a cigarette and watching two little kids going up and down the slide.

I nudged Mandi and pointed in his direction. "Isn't that Chris DuBois?"

"Yes, it is. Want to go over and say hi to him?"

We walked over to the playground.

"Hello, Chris," I said. "Nice to see you."

He turned and nodded to us. "Jeannie. Mandi. How you girls doing?"

"We're here with my grandkids," Mandi said. "Melissa and Ty are taking swimming lessons."

"Them two are mine," he said, pointing to the two kids. "They're Clem's youngest."

Chris had been a good-looking boy when we'd been at school together, but age and hard physical work had taken its toll. He was a ghost of the broad-chested star of our schoolyard games. The only things about him that hadn't changed were his sparkling brown eyes and lazy grin.

"Is Clem still in Bunchgrass?" I asked. Chris's son and Jordan had been classmates in elementary school. Although they hadn't been close friends, they'd been in Scouts together and had both played on the local softball team.

"He and the family moved to town," Chris said. "Got a job at the Co-op service station. Your boy still in Saskatoon?"

In typical small-town fashion, we exchanged news about our offspring. Then I asked about his sister Tammy.

"I heard she's here visiting," I said. "Mandi met her at the post office."

"Don't know nothing about that."

"She was only one grade ahead of me in school, so we knew each other well as kids. It would be good to see her again."

"Tammy's in Saskatoon," Chris said.

I adjusted my sunglasses. "How's she doing?"

"No worse than most people."

"Married?"

He took a drag on his cigarette. "Son of a bitch left her just before Christmas."

"Sorry to hear that," I said.

Surreptitiously, I studied his face. Chris reminded me of someone I'd seen recently. While Mandi carried on the conversation, I played a virtual slideshow in my head. Then it hit me. I'd met another man who had the same deep-set eyes and heavy jaw.

Mandi was asking about Tammy's twin sister, Anna, when I interrupted. "Chris, do you know a big fellow named Hunter? Long dark hair —"

"Couple guys around here with that name." He finished his cigarette and ground the butt underfoot. "Now if you'll excuse me, ladies, I gotta corral the kids. Get them home in time for supper."

"What was that about?" Mandi asked as we watched him herd his grandchildren toward an old grey half-ton parked near the playground.

"Chris clammed up when I mentioned Hunter," I said.

"So?"

"And he was evasive when I asked about Tammy."

"I'm not sure how that is significant."

"She was his favourite sister."

Mandi turned away from me and used one sandaled foot to draw a circle on the grass. "Did Frank know Tammy?"

I looked at her, surprised by the question. "Of course. They were in school together."

"I mean, were they friends?"

"Not really. No more friends than she and I were." I frowned. "Why do you ask?"

"No good reason."

I hate it when people taunt me with innuendo. "Come on, Mandi, give."

"Seeing Chris reminded me of the last time I saw him and Frank together," she said. "It was at the fall supper, just a couple months before his accident. They were standing next to each other in the buffet line. Tammy came along and started flirting."

"With Frank?"

She nodded. "The poor man was embarrassed. He muttered something unintelligible and walked away. Toward the washrooms. She followed him. I didn't see her again after that."

Suddenly, I was shaking. According to Semchuk, someone had seen Frank talking to a woman outside the washrooms at the Beaver the night he died. There couldn't be a connection between his story and Mandi's, but even so . . .

"I didn't see Tammy at the supper," I said.

Mandi put a hand on my shoulder. "The incident didn't mean anything. I thought it was odd, that's all."

"He never had anything to do with her."

"I know." Mandi smiled apologetically and briskly changed the subject. "Fortunately, the DuBois family is none of our business. Let's talk about my precocious grandkids instead."

I pasted an answering smile on my face. "That's fine with me."

I was convinced, however, that Chris was hiding something. Was there an innocent explanation for his secretiveness? Or had he been protecting a skeleton in the family closet?

When swimming lessons were over, we packed up the kids and set out for home.

"Gramma," Melissa said, "can we stop and visit Liz? I want to see the pigs and chickens."

"Me too," Ty said. "Last time you were too busy."

Mandi turned to me. "What do you think, Jeannie?"

"Good idea. I haven't been there for several weeks. Want me to call and check with Liz?"

My friend was taking a break and amenable to a visit. A few minutes later, we pulled up in front of her tiny house.

Although it looks like the homestead of a 1970s back-to-the-lander, Liz's farm reflects the best practices of modern regenerative agriculture. It's a diversified smallholding that includes pastured pigs and chickens, an orchard that showcases Saskatchewan-bred fruit, several large vegetable gardens, and half a dozen hives of honeybees. Kids love both the animals and her ramshackle collection of handmade buildings. Chief among them is the house she built the year she moved to the farm. A cross between an Edwardian dollhouse and a Romani caravan, it always enchants Mandi's grandkids.

Liz met us at the door, wearing olive-green cargo pants, a long-sleeved cotton shirt, and an aged Tilley hat.

"You kids want to help gather eggs?" she asked, handing Melissa a willow basket.

I'd already seen the pigs and chickens more times than I care to remember. While Liz took Mandi and the grandkids on a livestock tour, I slowly walked down to the lakeshore. Unlike the public beach in Bunchgrass, it was quiet, occupied only by sandpipers strutting along the water's edge in search of food. I sprawled out on the sand, glad for the silence after a day spent with two noisy kids. Bathed in the sun's warmth, I was wondering if I had time for a nap when a solitary canoeist rounded a bend in the shoreline.

I got to my feet and waved at him. "Hi, Stan. Catch anything?"

He headed the canoe toward shore. "Half a dozen pickerel."

"Lucky you," I said. Frank had done the fishing in our family. His death had left me dependent on my neighbours' generosity.

"I'll drop off a couple filets next time I'm out your way."

"Great. I'll give you supper."

Stan jumped out of the canoe and pulled it up on the beach. "How's your ankle?"

"Almost good as new."

He frowned. "I hope you don't blame Hunter. He didn't set that trap."

"How do you know?"

"I don't think he's your stalker."

"There are no other suspects," I said.

"Maybe the cops haven't looked hard enough."

"Or maybe Hunter's guilty." I ran a hand through my wind-tangled hair. "Have you seen him lately?"

"Nope."

"Would you tell me if you had?"

He smiled, brown eyes dancing. "Maybe not."

"At least you're honest," I said.

People lie during murder investigations. At least, some people do. Only, you can't tell who's lying and who isn't. And since that same problem plagues other areas of life, things get difficult. Especially when it comes to relationships.

My conversation with Mandi had made me wonder about Frank. And Tammy. I wanted to ask Stan if he'd seen them together, but the question was too absurd. My husband was a conventional man who liked order. Tammy was wild and erratic. Whoever coined the phrase "opposites attract" wasn't thinking about either of them.

I was searching for a subtle way to frame the query when my mobile rang. It was Mandi. "Jeannie, where are you?"

"At the beach. With Stan. He was out fishing."

"I was afraid you'd fallen down and hurt yourself."

"Hey, I'm tough."

"Good, because I don't have time to cope with another bruised ankle," Mandi said, her voice acidic. "In case you've forgotten, we're expecting Derek for a barbecue tonight."

I said goodbye to Stan. He clasped my hands in his for a moment. "Don't worry about the rumours around Frank's accident, eh?" he said, as if he'd been reading my mind. "You're the only woman he ever loved. Whatever happens, remember that."

Stan returned to his canoe. I watched him paddle away, baffled by the subtext of his parting words. Of course there'd never been another woman in my husband's life. What made him assume I'd thought there had been?

When we got back to the house, Derek and John were sitting on the patio, sharing a pitcher of shandy. While Melissa and Ty told their grampa about the afternoon's adventures, I had a few quiet words with Derek.

"Mandi and I met Chris DuBois on the beach. He's an old schoolmate. I think he knows something about Hunter."

Derek raised an eyebrow. "Yeah?"

I told him about the resemblance between the two men. "Hunter could be Chris's illegitimate son. In which case, Chris might know where to find him."

"You can't make assumptions based on vague similarities."

"They're not vague," I said. "We artists have an eye for detail. Your old buddy should talk to him."

He laughed. "Thanks, Sherlock. I'll pass that on to Semchuk."

"Even if Hunter had nothing to do with Monica's murder," I said stiffly, "he might have useful information about who did."

The conversation was getting heated, so I wasn't sorry when Mandi asked me to help with supper. I made Caesar salad and a jug of icy sangria while she marinated Black Angus steaks and prepared garlic bread. Then we went out to the garden and picked the season's first corn.

Dinner on the patio was almost a celebratory affair. Although someone was out there stalking me, there was a sense of relief because Zayden was still alive. Derek reported that the bullet had been removed and that it had missed his liver and other vital organs. Once the danger of infection passed, he'd be transferred to rehab at City Hospital. Then all we'd have to worry about is ensuring that the shooter couldn't harm him or anyone else again.

Robins chirped and the resident Baltimore orioles serenaded us from a treetop as we lingered over sour cherry cheesecake and decaf coffee. Then my mobile rang. I looked at the caller ID and groaned. What did Jade want now?

"Can you come over for ice cream? Gramma got here this afternoon. I'd like you to meet her."

In all the kerfuffle, I'd forgotten about the proposed visit. "We're just finishing supper —"

"Please, Jeannie. Derek could join us."

"He's meeting Semchuk for coffee at Shady Nook. And I need to help Mandi with the dishes."

"Don't stay home on my account," Mandi said. "I promised to play board games with the kids tonight, so you'd be on your own."

I sighed. After sharing accommodation with other people for the past ten days, the prospect of solitude was enticing.

As befits my parents' child, however, I take my social responsibilities seriously.

"Okay," I said. "I'll be there in half an hour."

—\\\\//—

A handsome older woman was sitting at the patio table. I smiled at her and then did a double take.

"Anna!" I said, blurting out the first words that came to mind. "What are you doing at Thickwood Farm?"

"My God," she said. "It's Jeannie."

The woman before me was tall, with a kind of statuesque beauty. She wore a floral print dress, and her grey hair was swept into an elegant chignon. When I'd last seen her forty-five years ago, she'd been a skinny girl in ill-fitting hand-me-downs.

"Your granddaughter didn't tell me you'd grown up in Bunchgrass," I said, sitting in the chair next to her.

Jade shook her head. "Gramma Rose spent her entire life in Saskatoon."

"We went to school together," I said. "Only, I knew her as Anna."

The woman beside me blushed dusky red. "I was christened Anna Rose. But I dropped the Anna when I left home."

"I don't understand," Jade said. "Mom said you were born at City Hospital. When I moved to Thickwood Farm, why didn't she tell me I was moving to your old neighbourhood?"

"She didn't know." Rose's eyes filled with tears. "I was ashamed of my family. So I lied."

I was about to point out that their poverty hadn't been her fault, when an old grey half-ton pulled up beside the house. A man got out and walked over to where we were sitting.

"Hi Chris," Jade said. "Are you here to pick up the potatoes? Ava left a bag for you behind the house."

"Thanks." He nodded at me. "Hello, Jeannie."

Then he turned to Rose. His eyes widened and, for a moment, I thought he was going to faint. "Anna!"

Rose got up from the table and held out her hands to him. "Chris, I'm so happy to see you."

I couldn't read the conflicting emotions that washed over his face. All I knew for certain was that powerful feelings fueled him when he pulled her to him in a long, close hug.

Jade turned to me in bewilderment. "How does Gramma know Chris DuBois?"

"They grew up together," I said. "Chris is her brother."

Between the two of them, Rose and Chris told Jade about their impoverished childhood in Bunchgrass.

"It wasn't all bad," Chris said. "We had way more freedom than kids today. And there was always someone around to hang out with."

Jade looked at Rose, accusation written on her face. "I always wanted relatives, but Mom said you were an only child. You should have told her about your family."

"I made a bad mistake." Fat tears rolled down Rose's cheeks. She dabbed at them with a tissue. "Life at home was hard, but that was no excuse. My sister wasn't well. I shouldn't have left her."

"What was wrong with her?" Jade asked.

"Hit her head falling off the top of a bunk bed," Rose said. "She'd always been wild, but after the accident her behaviour got worse. When Mom couldn't control her, she locked the poor kid in the woodshed. Of course, that didn't help."

"Tammy would scream the place down," Chris said. "One time I let her out. Dad said he'd knock me silly if I tried that again. I should have stood up to him. But I was scared."

Jade stared at them, her eyes like saucers. "That was child abuse. They should have gone to jail."

"Things were different back then," Chris said.

"Not that different." Rose said. "But Mom and Dad weren't bad people. Most of the time they did the best they could. They had too many children and not enough money. Sometimes I ask myself, would I have done better in their situation?"

Dusk had fallen, and a slight chill replaced the day's warmth. Rose shivered.

"Want to go inside?" Jade asked. "I'll make tea."

She nodded. "You're welcome to join us, Jeannie."

I would have liked to stay, but the three members of the DuBois family didn't need me at their reunion.

"Another time," I said. "But thanks for the invite. Now that you've a granddaughter living here, I hope we'll get together again."

Lights shone in the windows as I approached the access road to my house. We'd agreed that Derek would sleep there until the killer was behind bars. Doubtlessly he, and not an intruder, was responsible for the lights. But what if Hunter had picked my locks and gone inside? Unsure if that was the real reason for calling, I picked up my mobile.

"Just checking to see if everything's okay," I said. "I'm on my way back to Mandi's —"

"Are you alone?"

"Why wouldn't I be?"

"Just asking," he said with a laugh I could only describe as lascivious. "I'll put the kettle on."

Two minutes later I was standing in my kitchen watching Derek spoon Earl Grey into my favourite teapot.

We'd spent many hours together at my farm, but that evening I felt strangely self-conscious. Pleased that I was still wearing the embroidered sundress I'd put on for Mandi's barbecue, I took two mugs from the cupboard. "Want to have tea on the deck?"

A moth flitted by as I lit candles and placed them on the table. Diesel jumped up on a chair and stared at them, his eyes glowing in the darkness.

"Don't burn your whiskers, old buddy," I said.

Derek poured the tea. Then he reached across the table and took my hands. "I'm glad you're here."

"Me too. I didn't want to go to Thickwood Farm, but my social diligence has been rewarded. Not just by the pleasure of your company, either. I met Jade's gramma. Turns out we went to school together in Bunchgrass."

"Jade hadn't told you that?"

"Jade didn't know," I said, and told him about our encounter.

"Must have been quite a shock," he said.

I sipped my tea. "Rose left home suddenly. That was back when she was called Anna. The day she turned seventeen, she packed a bag and disappeared in the middle of the night without a word to anyone."

Preoccupied with my own life, I'd almost forgotten the sensation her departure had caused in our small community. Chris had reported her to the police as a missing person. A day or two later, they'd tracked her to Saskatoon.

"I got the rest of the story from Chris's wife," I said. "A few years ago, she went off the road during a heavy rain. While Frank was pulling her out of the ditch with the tractor, I made coffee. She told me Chris went to the city and tried to talk to his sister, but all she said was that she didn't want to see him or anyone else from the family ever again. He was heartbroken."

While Derek returned to the kitchen to add more water to the teapot, I thought about the woman I'd known as Anna.

She had been a quiet girl and a good student. Unlike her twin, she'd never been in trouble at school.

"I can see why she and her sister didn't get along," I said when Derek reappeared. "Anna was conventional and ambitious. It would be hard to imagine anyone more different from Tammy."

"Those women have really got under your skin, haven't they?"

Something was niggling at the back of my head, but I couldn't identify what it was. "Goodness knows why. I barely had anything to do with them when we were schoolmates."

"Forget about them for a while." Eyes sparkling, he grinned at me. "I can think of more interesting ways to spend the rest of the evening."

I smiled back at him. "Yeah, me too."

Derek pulled me to my feet and wrapped his arms tightly around me. Heat flooded my cheeks and electrified my entire body. I pressed against him, feeling his warmth through his T-shirt and jeans. He slid his hands under the straps of my sundress and inched them forward. Then, as I closed my eyes and sought his lips with mine, I suddenly realized why the wrinkled old woman in the pink cotton dress had looked familiar.

"That was Tammy," I said.

He muttered something unintelligible and kissed me on the mouth. I pulled away from him. "Remember the old woman who was talking to Hunter after Monica's funeral? I knew I'd seen her before. Her name's Tammy DuBois. She's Anna Rose's sister."

"Jeez, lady, your timing sucks."

"Sorry," I said. "But her name just came to me. It's no wonder I didn't recognize her earlier. The last time I saw her, she was young and beautiful."

Derek groaned. "Remind me again why this is important."

"I'm sure Tammy and Hunter are related. If we track her down, maybe she can tell us where to find him."

"And how do you propose to find Tammy?"

"We'll ask Chris for her phone number and address. He said she lives in Saskatoon."

"Okay, but can't we do that tomorrow?" He glanced at his phone. "It's almost ten — too late to call people who aren't suspects."

"Tomorrow, then." I pulled out my own phone. "I'd better tell Mandi I'm going to be late."

He winked at me. "Tell her you're having a sleepover and will be home tomorrow."

Having sex is like riding a bicycle — you don't forget how it's done. Six months in a wheelchair and I'd have had to learn to walk again, but making love came easily. It was wonderful to spend the night in my own bed, and even better to share it with Derek. I'd been afraid that Frank's ghost would haunt my dreams, but it didn't. Sleep — when it came — was sweet and peaceful.

WEDNESDAY, AUGUST 8

I awoke to the gentle sound of Derek's breathing. He lay sleeping beside me, hair dark against the white pillowcase. For a moment I watched his chest rise and fall, and then I leaned over and kissed him. He opened his eyes and smiled.

"Morning, love."

I returned his greeting, suddenly conscious of my naked body. Once you reach sixty, a good pair of pyjamas helps conceal some of the indignities of advancing age. I grabbed the edge of the sheet and was about to cover myself when Derek lifted my hand to his lips.

"You look beautiful."

Beauty is in the eye of the beholder, I reminded myself, biting back the adolescent impulse to tell him he needed glasses.

"So do you," I said. Derek was an attractive man despite age spots on the backs of his hands and a slightly rounded belly that had probably been flat ten years earlier.

He held out his arms and pulled me close. The musky smell of his body mingled with the scent of mignonette drifting in from outside my open window. I touched his face, the skin bristly beneath my fingers. It felt the way Frank's had when he'd needed a shave. Surprisingly, the thought caused me no distress.

Later, lying in bed sweaty and relaxed, we heard the soft pad of velvety feet on the stairway. Diesel entered the bedroom and meowed.

"He wants breakfast," I said.

Derek glanced at the clock on the bedside table. "Or lunch."

"Thanks for letting us sleep in, buddy," I said as he jumped onto the bed.

While Derek fed Diesel and put the coffee on, I made saskatoon-lemon muffins and put them in the toaster oven to bake. Then I phoned Chris.

"Tammy moves around a lot," he said when I asked for contact information. "Her phone ain't working, and I don't have no address."

"I need to talk to her," I said, "about the man named Hunter. She was talking to him after a recent funeral —"

"What business is that of yours?"

Chris had a point — but no way was I going to tell him that the person in question was a murder suspect. Unfortunately, I couldn't think of another way of getting the information I needed.

"No luck," I said after we'd ended the call. "Chris claims ignorance of Tammy's whereabouts."

"Think he's telling the truth?"

"No," I said. "And there's no point talking to Anna Rose. She's not in contact with her sister."

We threw ideas around until the muffins were ready but

didn't come up with a plan. The sun was already hot, with no prospect of cooler temperatures until evening. By judiciously opening windows at night and closing them in the morning, I usually managed to keep my house comfortable on the warmest summer days. This day was an exception.

"Let's have breakfast in the treehouse," Derek said. "It should be cooler up there."

"My thoughts exactly," I said.

He filled a Thermos with coffee while I packed the muffins in a paper bag.

Diesel came running to meet us when we stepped outside. He purred contentedly as I picked him up and kissed him on his nose.

"Want to climb up to the treehouse with us, buddy?" I asked with a sly glance at Derek. "There's a comfortable chaise lounge up there, and we might need a chaperone."

With Diesel in the lead and Derek bringing up the rear, we climbed until we reached the sturdy wooden cabin. I followed my cat through the open doorway and onto the cabin floor, Derek right behind us.

"Ready for breakfast?" I asked.

"Unless there's something else you'd rather do first."

"We can do that later," I said with a smile. "I'm starved."

Diesel was nibbling some of the cat treats I keep in the treehouse, and Derek and I were finishing the muffins, when I noticed a sprinkling of crumbs under the child-size table.

"Someone's been up here since our last visit," I said, pointing at the offending particles.

Derek knelt on the floor and sifted them through his fingers. "Potato chips. They could have been here for months."

"They weren't here eight days ago," I said. "I would have noticed them."

"Hunter?"

I nodded. "Maybe he's used it as a lookout point. The treehouse provides a good view of the house and grounds. If we could catch him up here, he couldn't easily get away. Then he'd have to talk to us."

"I'll tell Semchuk," Derek said. "Maybe he'll assign a constable to hang around here. But it's a long shot. It could be hours or days before Hunter — or someone else — returns."

"Before you call in the cops, I want to try my hand at surveillance."

"Many hours of boredom for five minutes of excitement," Derek said. "And no guarantees."

"Just for a couple hours. I'll never get another chance."

"I fervently hope you don't," Derek said.

Despite his insistence that a short surveillance was unlikely to yield results, we finally agreed that I would hole-up in my studio for the next two hours. Its south-facing window provided a superb view of the treehouse. If anyone approached it, I'd text Derek, who'd be hidden in a dense thicket of shrubs.

Once he'd locked his van in the garage, we took up our respective positions.

The first fifteen minutes passed quickly. Senses alert, I peered through the window with unblinking intensity. Then the adrenaline rush subsided. Although I never tired of the view, I usually admired it in short snatches. Two solid hours devoted entirely to watching for an intruder suddenly felt like a very long time. Unable to read for fear of missing Hunter, I replayed the previous night in my mind. It was every bit as wonderful in retrospect as it had been at the time.

Then my mobile rang. Welcoming the distraction, I glanced at the unfamiliar number. Could the caller be Hunter?

"Hello," I said.

The woman's voice was seductive. "Ask Derek where he was Saturday night."

I stared stupidly at the phone before answering. "What business is it of yours?"

She laughed. "I hope you don't think you're the only woman in his life."

"Who are you? And how did you get my number?" My heart was thumping so hard I was afraid she could hear it.

"A friend of Derek's," she said. Then the line went dead.

Mind racing, I called the number that had appeared on call display. A mechanical voice informed me that the customer was away from her phone.

Damn! Now what?

I was debating the wisdom of asking Derek about his movements on Saturday night when I caught a glimpse of a man. He was creeping through the shelterbelt toward the stand of poplars at the south end of my garden. Putting aside questions about the anonymous caller, I punched in Derek's number.

"Hunter's on his way."

"I'll be ready for him," he said. "Meet us on the deck in ten minutes?"

I watched as our man climbed the ladder to the treehouse and disappeared inside. Two minutes later, Derek followed him. I put down my binoculars and went downstairs to make coffee.

As I spooned decaf into my espresso maker, I considered the woman's call. Derek had spent the night in Saskatoon. Had he met her for a romantic rendezvous? And who the hell was she, anyway? Fortunately, I didn't have time to dwell on these questions. Voices outside suggested that the two men had arrived. I picked up mugs and the freshly brewed decaf and carried them out to the deck.

Derek, poker-faced, sat across the table from his quarry. Hunter's eyes were alert and his shoulders tense beneath a faded denim shirt. He moved his lips in the parody of a smile.

"Hello, Jeannie."

I plopped down the mugs and shook his extended hand. Aside from size, Hunter didn't look scary. In well-worn jeans and Stetson, he easily could have passed for a local rancher. I had to remind myself that he may have been Monica's killer.

"We've been looking for you," I said. "Thanks for lifting the log off my leg —"

"Don't mention it."

"Do you know who set the trap?"

He shrugged. "It wasn't me."

I pulled out a chair and sat beside him. "Then who was it?"

Hunter remained silent, eyes fixed on the table.

"Why have you been spying on me? Any why run away every time I see you?"

Across from us, Derek grinned.

"What are you smiling at?" I snapped. Diplomacy wasn't my strong suit at the best of times, and the anonymous phone call had made me cranky.

"You need to refine your interview technique. Maybe start with small talk."

I ignored his advice and turned back to Hunter. "You know who killed Monica, don't you?"

He fiddled with a poplar leaf that had landed on the table in front of him. "I could use a cup of that coffee."

"Who was it, Hunter?" I asked, picking up the pot of decaf.

"I had nothing to do with what happened."

"The police think differently. They want to talk to you."

Hunter watched my hand as I filled his mug. "I'm sorry about the . . . accidents, but I've nothing to tell them. Or you."

I studied his face as I handed him the coffee. Then, my vague suspicions coalesced into certainty. "Your surname is DuBois, isn't it?"

He nodded.

"And you're related to Chris. And Tammy. She's your mother!"

Hunter's face was impassive.

"Do you know that you have an aunt named Anna Rose?"

His eyes widened and his breathing quickened, but he remained silent.

"She's Tammy's twin."

"Sorry, I can't help you."

Sweat was trickling down his face and his hands were shaking. I might have backed away if my own life hadn't been at stake.

"Anna Rose is staying with her granddaughter at Thickwood Farm," I said. "Do you know where that is?"

Hunter nodded.

"The police want to talk to you. We can stop at the farm on our way to the station."

"Do I have a choice in the matter?" he asked.

"The cops haven't charged you with anything," Derek said.

"They just want me to help with their inquiries, right?" Hunter's voice dripped with sarcasm.

Derek finished his coffee and set down the cup. "Sorry, dude, but that's the way it is. Want me to bring you back here afterward?"

He nodded and got to his feet. "My car's parked close by. May as well head out now and get the interview over with."

I gave Diesel a parting hug. Then I followed the two men to Derek's van.

Although Johnny Cash is not my favourite singer, I was grateful for his rich baritone on our short trip to Thickwood Farm. I called Jade to let her know we were coming. Otherwise, the three of us remained quiet. Much as I wanted information about the anonymous caller, I wasn't going to ask Derek about her when Hunter was present.

When we pulled up beside the house, Derek broke the silence. "Okay if I sit in on the meeting?"

I looked at Hunter, who shook his head. "No cops."

"Okay," Derek said. "But I'm not leaving you alone with these women. I'll stay in the van. The four of you sit outside where I can see you."

Hunter's footsteps lagged as we approached the two women drinking tea on the verandah. Rose got up and met us at the top of the steps. She looked cool and elegant in a short-sleeved lavender dress.

"Meet Hunter," I said. "He's Tammy's son."

If Rose was surprised, she didn't show it. She smiled at her nephew. "You're a younger version of my brother Chris."

Hunter collapsed onto the nearest chair. He stared at the tea leaves in the bottom of Jade's cup for a long time before he finally spoke. "That's what Mom says — I remind her of Uncle Chris." He paused for a moment before continuing. "She doesn't talk much about her past, but she did mention a sister named Anna."

"I never thought I'd meet Tammy's son," Rose said. "You're a fine-looking man. Your mother must be proud of you."

"Why didn't you keep in touch with her?" Hunter asked.

"When I left home, I was done with the past," Rose said, twisting a linen napkin in her hands. "Started a new life in Saskatoon and never looked back."

"Didn't you visit your parents?"

She shook her head. "Life at home had been so damned hard. And once I'd married Jade's grandad, I didn't want to tell him that his father-in-law was an alcoholic and a ne'er-do-well who could barely feed his family. So I told him my parents were dead. My husband wasn't a curious man."

Hunter's eyes were bright with unshed tears. "Mom said her mother cried for weeks after you'd gone."

"I didn't want to end up a drudge like her," Rose said. "Now I'm wondering if I should have stayed for the sake of Tammy and Chris." She looked straight at Hunter. "I hope Tammy has told you more about your family than I've told my daughter."

"She kept in touch with Chris. He was always good to us." Hunter picked up the cup of tea Jade had poured for him. "Did you know Mom lived in Saskatoon for the last five years?"

Rose sighed. "Yes, I did. But it had been so long since I'd seen her that I didn't know how to reconnect. I was afraid she'd slam the door in my face, and I wouldn't have blamed her if she had."

"Mom's . . . not like other people," Hunter said.

"Never has been." Rose tried to take his hands in hers, but he pulled them away. "There was a devil in that girl. Even as a little kid."

"She's gotten worse since my stepfather left," Hunter said. "Mom was upset."

I thought about the Tammy I used to know. I wouldn't have described her as possessed by the devil. A better term might have been daring. And impulsive. "Has she seen a doctor?" I asked.

"No," Hunter said, almost reluctantly. "She hasn't."

An ugly idea thrust its way into my head. "You've been trying to protect me from her, haven't you? And now you're searching for your mom so you can watch over her."

Rose eyed me sharply. "Something bad has happened. What aren't you telling me?"

The sun shone from a clear blue sky, goldfinches twittered in the trees, and the sweet scent of canola wafted in from a nearby field. On cold winter nights, I dreamt about such halcyon days. It would be cruel to destroy the tranquil scene with my nasty suspicions. Yet Rose and Hunter needed an honest answer.

"Hunter wants my farm," I said slowly. "A realtor named Monica tried to buy it for him. The last time she came out here, a storm disabled her car. I lent her mine. Unknown to me, someone had cut the brake line. She died when my car went off the road a couple kilometres from here."

It was a bald telling of a complex tale, but Rose easily filled in the blanks. "Why would Tammy want to kill you?"

Hunter groaned and covered his face with his hands.

"I don't know," I said.

"Do you have evidence against either of them?" she asked.

"Nothing concrete." I told Rose about the anonymous messages, the shooting at the height of land, the dead coyote and vandalized picture, and the potentially lethal deadfall trap. "If Hunter hadn't rescued me, she would have come along and finished me off — that is, unless he was the person who set the trap. There's no direct evidence against her, but the cops have eliminated most of the other suspects. And Tammy certainly has the necessary woodcraft skills."

"You forgot to mention the attack on Zayden," Jade said. Wide-eyed, she turned to Rose. "Oh God . . . Does this mean *my great-aunt* shot him?"

Rose was silent for a long time. When she finally spoke, her voice was weary. "My sister didn't do well in school, but she had other talents. Chris said she was a cross between Annie Oakley and a backwoods Tool Time Tim."

"That's why we have to find her," I said. "But it doesn't explain why she wants me dead."

"It's my fault," Hunter said. "If I hadn't coveted your land . . ."

"I don't understand," I said, surprised by his biblical choice of verb. "There's lots of land for sale around here. There's a quarter section across the lake that's been on the market for months."

He sighed. "Once I found out that Mom was trying to . . . persuade you to sell to me, I told her I'd changed my mind. But I was too late. She'd already cut your brake line, and Monica was dead."

"Why did you 'covet' my land?" I asked.

Hunter shook his head and looked down at his feet.

"I should have been there for both of you," Rose said. "Tammy's life was hard. And the fact that she was her own worst enemy can't have made it any easier."

"Blame your parents," I said. "That's what I've done."

Rose and Tammy's folks had raised seven kids in a log shack half the size of the house I'd grown up in. Although local reputation said he was a good worker, picking roots and hauling bales for area farmers, it was common knowledge that George DuBois was a drunk. Monday evenings after art class, I'd see him weaving across the churchyard on his way home from the bar. Even if their mother had done the best she could with the hand she'd been dealt, her good intentions would have been small comfort to kids who went to bed hungry.

"Blaming your parents doesn't help," Hunter said. "Nothing else does either."

I reached out and touched his hand. "Derek said you and Monica were close. I'm sorry for your loss."

"Biggest mistake I ever made," Hunter said. "We were supposed to have coffee the night she died. I was going to tell her that our relationship was over."

"Why?" I asked, curiosity getting the better of good manners.

"I'd just found out about her high-pressure sales tactics," he said. "The woman I was dating was no better than a crook."

I thought of the glow on her cheeks as she told me about needing my car so she could meet a friend in Saskatoon. "Did Monica know that you had planned to break up with her?"

He shrugged. "She wouldn't have believed that a man like me could resist her charms."

"I think she honestly liked you," I said, but decided not to tell him that she had borrowed my car because she was desperate to have coffee with him. The poor guy was already plagued with guilt.

"The DuBois men have a way with women," Rose said, smiling sadly. "My aunts told me that Dad was a real charmer when he was young."

I looked at Rose. "What are you going to do now?"

"Find Tammy," she said as she pulled a cell phone from her purse and left us for the solitude of the house.

Jade was trying to comfort Hunter when Rose returned. "Chris doesn't know where she is, and I can't think of anyone else to call. He's the only one in the family who's kept in touch with her."

"Mom isn't good with people," Hunter said.

"That's not the only problem." Rose perched on the edge of her chair and looked at him. "Chris said Tammy *borrowed* his truck. Without telling him."

"Damn — I was afraid of that. Mom shouldn't be driving. If Derek drops me off near my car, I'll cruise the backroads and look for her."

"It's too late for that," Rose said. "We've got to call the cops."

Hunter shook his head. "No. They'll lock her up."

"She needs help," Rose said. "And we can't leave her free to kill again."

"Mom has to have space. Put her in jail or a treatment centre, and she'll panic. I need to find her and keep her safe." He stood up and looked at Jade. "May I use the washroom?"

"Second door on the left," she said. "You can't miss it."

In retrospect, we realized that we shouldn't have let him go into the house alone. Rose and I were wondering how we could persuade Hunter to tell the police about Tammy when we heard the front door open and close. Moments later two engines started up, and we saw Frank's old truck disappearing around a bend in the driveway with Derek's van in hot pursuit.

We all sat dumbfounded until I jumped to my feet.

"Tell me that wasn't Hunter driving."

"He's so much like Chris," Rose said. "Warm-hearted and impulsive, but not always sensible. Tammy was an outdoorsy kid. She knows every hiding place in a ten-mile radius. No way he's going to find her if she wants to stay hidden."

"That was the Thickwood Farm truck he drove off in," I said. "How the heck did he know where to find the key?"

"It was on a nail by the back door," Jade said. "And he didn't steal it. Hunter's one of us now."

I grimaced. "Derek's not going to see it like that. He's going to be royally pissed off with us for letting Hunter get away."

"This is partly my fault," Rose said. "If I'd stayed in contact with Tammy, I could have gotten her help. Maybe she wouldn't have gone off the rails like that."

"You aren't responsible for her," I said, wondering for the umpteenth time exactly how much responsibility we do have to our family. Women have traditionally sacrificed their own interests for those of their parents and kids, and look where that altruism's got them.

We were arguing about whether to call the police when Derek returned from his unsuccessful attempt to head off Hunter.

"Why the hell did you let him get away?"

"If it comes to that," I said, "why the hell didn't *you* intercept him?"

Derek sighed. "Semchuk wants to see him at the station."

"Then Semchuk should have got his act together and come out here," I said. "Hunter knows that his mom murdered Monica. He's searching the backroads looking for her."

"So, you handed him the keys to your husband's old truck —"

"He asked to use the washroom," Rose said. "It didn't occur to any of us that he'd find the keys and use them."

I introduced Derek to Tammy's twin.

"I'm sorry my sister is causing trouble," Rose said. "As a kid, she never figured out how to cope with life. Guess she hasn't changed much since then, eh?"

Derek frowned. "There's no more evidence against Tammy than there is against Hunter. He still could be the killer. Instead of looking for his mom, he could be heading for a hideaway up north."

"He seemed genuinely concerned about her," I said.

"There's been more than one murderer who's cried at their victim's funeral."

"Have you talked to the police?" Rose asked.

He nodded. "They're putting out an APB for both Tammy and Hunter. Semchuk's also sending officers to search the area. I've left a message on Hunter's mobile asking him to contact the RCMP, but I won't hold my breath waiting for that to happen." He handed Rose his card. "I'm sorry to involve you in this. Even if your sister is innocent, we need to find her. And Hunter. Let me know if either of them shows up, okay?"

—\\//—

We were both silent on our way back to my place. Derek looked tired, and I was still distracted by the anonymous call from the sexy-voiced woman. Who was she, and why had she contacted me? Maybe a jealous ex-girlfriend, or — worse still — a current girlfriend . . .

"You're unusually quiet," Derek said as we reached the turnoff. "I'm sorry I yelled at you for letting Hunter get away. Even experienced cops have been fooled by clever conmen."

"I don't see Hunter as a conman," I said. "But that's not the problem."

"Then what is?"

I hesitated, afraid of what he might tell me.

"Spit it out, Jeannie."

"I got a phone call this morning. . ." I stopped and took a deep breath.

"Go on."

Tears prickled against my eyelids. "The caller said to ask where you were Saturday night. When I inquired what business it was of hers, she laughed . . . and said she hoped I didn't think I was the only woman in your life."

Derek frowned. "Did she identify herself?"

"Just said she was a friend of yours — and then hung up."

"Damn!"

We pulled up in front of the garage, but neither of us got out of the van.

"So, where *were* you Saturday night?"

"In Saskatoon. I was trying to find Hunter, remember?"

What I really wanted to know is if he'd shared a bed with someone, but how do you ask that question to a man you've known less than two weeks? "Who's the woman, and why did she call me?" I asked instead.

"I don't know why she called you —"

"Take a guess," I said. "The woman knows who I am and how to contact me."

Derek sighed. "I ran into an acquaintance last time I was in Saskatoon. We went for a drink. Maybe she was the caller."

"Why would this 'acquaintance' assume proprietary rights over you?"

"You don't know when to stop, do you?" he said, opening the van door. "My private life is none of your concern."

He must have heard my sudden intake of breath. "Sorry, Jeannie, I didn't mean exactly that —"

"Then what did you mean?"

"I don't like being cross-examined," he said.

"And I don't like being lied to."

"I didn't —"

"Sins of omission," I said. "You might not have lied, but you've failed to tell me some important truths."

Derek sighed again. "It's been a tough morning. The day's only half over, and we still have two possible killers on the loose. Can we continue this discussion later?"

"You want to help Semchuk with the search, right?"

"That would be a hell of a lot more useful than wrangling with you."

Recent events had left me depleted. And I was still scared. I reached out and offered Derek my hand. "Let's have tea first, and then you go track down the bad guys."

While I was heating water, Semchuk called. Derek put his phone on speaker.

"Chris DuBois says he hasn't seen Tammy recently. I may not believe the bugger, but I did learn something interesting from his wife. Tammy's husband wanted her to see a therapist. When she refused, he called it quits."

"So that's the reason," I said. "I'd wondered why he'd left."

"Apparently, he's the one who kept her on the straight and narrow. Since then, her behaviour's been erratic and she's been talking about righting past wrongs. The wife wasn't clear about when these wrongs were committed or who committed them, but she thinks they involve Hunter."

"Can you get information from someone in the healthcare system?" Derek asked.

"I tracked down her doctor," he said. "She hasn't seen Tammy for fourteen years."

"Go figure," Derek said. "Want a hand with the search?"

"Anytime, old man."

"I'll call you when I'm ready to leave Jeannie's."

We drank our tea on the deck. The spicy scent of pinks wafted in from the garden. Goldfinches twittered at the feeder, and butterflies sipped nectar from a pot of purple salvia. A young phoebe watched for insects from its branch on a nearby tree. Beside me, Diesel purred contentedly. I thought about Tammy experiencing her own version of paradise while exploring the Thickwood Hills as a child. Being locked up would just about kill her.

Derek was about to ring Semchuk when he received an incoming call. He looked at the display screen and groaned.

"Massey here . . . five-thirty, eh? Yeah, I'll be there." He swore under his breath as he holstered his phone.

"Problems?" I asked.

"That was a colleague in Saskatoon. They've finally picked up the suspect in an assault I witnessed a couple weeks ago. I need to be at the station for an identity parade at five-thirty."

"This afternoon?"

"The other witness is leaving on a business trip tonight."

"But you're on holiday," I said inanely.

"Can't be helped," he said. "I'm an important witness."

While Derek called Semchuk to explain his delay, I checked the time on my cell phone. He didn't have to be in Saskatoon for another three hours. It was only a two-hour drive. That left an hour before he had to leave. I weighed the benefits of skimming across Crystal Lake in a canoe versus engaging in angry debate. The latter would leave me wrung-out and wretched. It would be better to resolve our differences when we both had more energy. At least, that's what I told myself.

I smiled at Derek. "Want to join me in a quick canoe trip before you go?"

Nature has a way of putting petty injuries in perspective. By the time we returned to the house, I was *almost* ready to forgive whatever sins Derek had committed. While he checked the doors and windows, I threw some clean clothes into a suitcase. Then we were on the road for the return trip to my sister's place.

"I'll join the search for Tammy and Hunter if I get back to Bunchgrass before dark," Derek said as we turned onto the RM road. "Want me to call when I reach North Battleford?"

"Thanks, but there's no need," I said. The day had been draining, and I was already thinking longingly about bed.

"Pick me up early tomorrow, and I'll give you breakfast at my place."

"Make it blueberry scones," he said, "and it's a deal."

We pulled up in front of Mandi's house. I was about to open the van door when Derek reached over and took my hands in his.

"Don't think badly of me."

"Is there any reason I should?"

He laughed and kissed me on the forehead.

"Goodnight, Jeannie."

Mandi greeted me at the door, wearing a pale blue eyelet sundress.

"Nice," I said. "What's the occasion?"

"John and I need to go to town. His mom fell and broke her wrist this morning. Will you stay with Melissa and Ty so we can go to the hospital to visit her? We'll be back by eleven."

"Of course," I said. "Sorry to hear about her accident. Anything else I can do to help?"

"No. Just make sure to invite Liz and Goliath to spend the evening here. Derek would have my hide if we left you alone."

"Right," I said, forgetting that Liz goes salsa dancing on Wednesdays.

"There's canned salmon for sandwiches —"

"Mandi," I said, "I can handle supper. And the kids. You don't have to worry about a thing."

My sister didn't look convinced, but after further instructions she and John left for North Battleford. I mixed mayonnaise and fresh dill with the salmon, spread the mixture on thinly sliced bread, and added lettuce. Then the three of us sat down at the table.

The first part of the evening went well. Melissa and Ty ate sandwiches and carrot sticks without a murmur of protest. Afterward, Melissa helped me do the dishes. Then, after four games of Go Fish and five Beatrix Potter books, the kids went quietly to bed. Either their behaviour had improved, or mine had.

Once the kids were asleep, however, I started to fret. I needed distraction from thoughts of my mystery caller almost as much as I needed protection from the stalker. Liz was in town, and there was no answer when I called the folks at Thickwood Farm. No doubt Stan was home, but the easy camaraderie we'd shared when my husband was alive had vanished. No way was I asking him to come over and sit with me. My sister's windows and doors were locked, and the nearest neighbour only five minutes away. I'd be okay until Mandi and John returned.

In the meantime, I'd freeze the beans Mandi had left cooling in the cellar.

The first batch was chilling when I heard a vehicle on the driveway. Heart racing, I looked out the kitchen window. Headlights illuminated the garage. Then, three things happened in rapid succession. A shot rang out, the dusk-to-dawn yard light went black, and a rock flew through the living room window.

Panic-stricken, I looked for my mobile. I thought I'd put in on the table. But it wasn't there. As I looked around, a skeletal figure battered away jagged glass shards and crawled through the hole in the window. I swept my gaze around the kitchen. The phone was on the counter next to the fridge. I picked it up and started to dial nine-one-one. Before I could finish, the pale moonlight revealed a long-haired woman holding a rifle. It was pointed directly at me.

"Gimme that phone," she said. "And don't scream. We don't want t' wake them kids."

I handed her the mobile, trying to keep my hands from shaking. "Hello, Tammy."

"Let's go," she said, jabbing me with the rifle barrel.

"Where? I can't leave my sister's grandkids —"

"Mandi will be back soon."

"She'd like to see you," I said. "I'll make tea —"

"No tea." The tip of the barrel dug into my side. It was cold and hard. And meant business.

"You don't need the gun. I'm unarmed and not dangerous."

Tammy ignored my request. With her rifle prodding from behind, I walked out the front door. The starlit night was sweetly scented by tea roses, but I was so distraught I barely noticed them. Mandi's grandkids were alone in the house, and I was heading for an unknown destination with someone who wanted me dead.

Chris's half-ton, recognizable by the fluorescent bumper sticker proclaiming "No Baby on Board," loomed in front of me. Heart pounding, I climbed into the front passenger seat.

"What do you want with me?" I asked.

Tammy stared straight ahead. "That farm should be mine."

I looked at her, bewildered. "My farm? The one that Frank left me?"

"It should be mine," she repeated, her voice expressionless.

"Why?"

"You had no moral right to it."

The accusation was ludicrous, but I didn't want to debate it with Tammy. Frank and I had been married forty years. If I wasn't entitled to the land, who the hell was?

"I'm sorry you feel that way," I said.

She turned the key in the ignition. "Shut your mouth and let me drive. Any funny business, I shoot."

We headed east on Hillside Road, then turned onto a narrow track that twisted and turned through the dark countryside.

Before long, I'd lost all sense of direction. Tammy drove fast, one hand on the wheel, the other touching the rifle propped up beside her. I sat motionless, terrified by my thoughts and by her grim presence. My captor was mad. Was she taking me to a lonely spot where she could shoot me without fear of discovery? Or did she have something even more sinister in mind?

Derek was in Saskatoon, and Frank was dead. I was on my own.

—W—

An eternity had passed when we finally pulled up beside a tiny shack.

It had been ages — or so it seemed — since we'd seen any sign of human habitation. The shack sat alone on the edge of a poplar bluff surrounded by darkness. Tammy opened the truck door and, rifle under one arm, jumped to the ground. I would have clung to the familiarity of the cab, but she motioned me to follow.

Once inside the tiny building, Tammy lit the propane lantern that hung by the door. "Don't try to escape. We're in the middle of nowhere, and I'm a good shot."

The light revealed a small room sparsely furnished with a wood heater, a table with two chairs, a set of shelves along one wall, and a narrow wooden bed. The shelves contained mismatched dishes, a jug of water, pantry staples, and two rolls of toilet paper. A green canvas backpack lay half-open on the bed. Whatever this place had once been, it was now Tammy's lair.

"Take a look at your new home," she said.

"Why have you brought me here?"

"You set the cops on my trail. Now you're gonna make sure nothing bad happens to me."

"Am I a hostage?"

She laughed bitterly. "They won't do nothing to a crazy woman as long as you're here."

I looked at Tammy. The schoolgirl with a slender body and thick black tresses had turned into a gaunt old woman with scraggly grey hair and haunted eyes. As if aware of my scrutiny, the corners of her mouth turned up in an ugly smile.

"Not very nice, eh, what rough living does to a woman? You've been lucky, pampered by a hard-workin' man."

"He's dead," I said.

"And left you a rich widow."

"Comfortable, not rich."

"They amount to the same where I come from," Tammy said.

This was no time to debate the definition of wealthy. I was in an isolated cabin with a woman who had a gun. Maybe if I turned the conversation to our shared past, she would mellow.

"You were good at hunting and trapping even as a kid," I said. "I used to envy you those skills."

Tammy snorted. "You didn't need to put food on the table if you wanted to eat."

She was right. Although my parents had chosen to be poor, I'd never gone hungry. And my grandparents — two lawyers, an engineer, and a dentist — had provided a safety net. I knew life wasn't fair. But that didn't make me responsible for my old schoolmate's unhappiness.

"I've never done anything to hurt you."

"You took Frank from me," she said.

Could Tammy believe what she was telling me? Unlikely as it sounded, I had to find out what she meant. "Really? When did that happen?"

"The summer he finished high school. In Saskatoon. One morning we ran into each other on the street. He asked me for lunch. After that, we went out together every day."

I did a quick search of my past. That was the summer I'd broken up with Stan and spent most of August at art workshops. Frank had been in Saskatoon for three or four weeks helping his gramma get ready to sell her house and move into a senior's condo. And Tammy had left home for life in the big city. Could they have dated during that time?

"He was still a kid," I said. "Going for lunch with you doesn't mean he made a commitment."

"Wasn't just lunch," she said. "Frank loved me."

Tammy's purple track suit was ragged and dirty, and her long grey hair needed a good wash. But she'd been pretty as a girl. I didn't want to think about the possibility that my husband had been romantically involved with her.

"Frank never said anything to me about you."

"We were screwin' each other," she said. "I had a room in a house on Twenty-Second Street. Afternoons when his gramma was napping, he'd come round to my place. We always ended up in bed."

"I don't believe you."

Her lips twisted into a grin. "Remember the scar on his ass? The one he got from misjudgin' a barbwire fence?"

Frank wasn't there to receive my fury. Tammy was. I wanted to smack the grin off her face. But she had a gun. Slowly I unclenched my fists.

"The two of you had a summer fling. I'm sorry you got hurt."

"It don't matter now. He paid for his sins."

"How?"

Her grin widened. "The bastard ain't ever gonna betray a woman again."

Suspicion niggled at the back of my mind. But I couldn't afford to antagonize Tammy. I needed to defuse the situation.

"Tell me how buying my land would make things better for you," I said.

"Hunter wants it. And you wouldn't sell to him."

"Jeez, Tammy, with the money he offered, he could buy property anywhere."

"He wants his great-grandfather's land," she said.

I vaguely remembered Tammy's grandfather as an old man surrounded by kids. He'd lived with his family in what used to be the teacherage across from the school. Sometimes at recess I'd see him smoking his pipe on the front step or tottering around the tiny fenced-in yard. Nobody had ever told me he was a farmer.

"Are you telling me he once owned the land Frank bought from his parents?"

"Not all of it," she said. "Just the lakeshore piece where your house sits."

Frank had treasured an old RM map from the 1930s, but for the life of me I couldn't remember who had owned the land before his grandfather bought it halfway through the Depression. Maybe Tammy was right.

I tried to keep her talking. "I didn't know it used to belong to your grandfather. Did he ever live there?"

"Raised a family on that land. But Grandad had to sell and move to town. He couldn't make ends meet on sixty acres."

"And now you want me to leave the place I've lived for forty years so his great-grandson can return to a home he's never known," I said.

"I want my boy to be proud of his ancestry. That land's gonna be my gift to him."

"Gift?"

"Once you've agreed to sell, my son can buy your farm. That's my gift: getting the agreement."

"Hunter might not approve of the tactics you're using to get it," I said.

"He don't have t' know." Tammy poured a mug of water

and drank it without pausing for breath. "Not much I can do for my boy except that."

"Hunter's a capable adult who can manage his own affairs. He's going to be upset when he finds out that you've . . . bullied me."

"I don't intend for him to find out."

"He already has," I said. "Your son's been hanging around my place for the last few days. He's trying to protect me."

I told Tammy about Hunter's near-miraculous appearance soon after my encounter with her deadfall trap. "He's a fine man. You can be proud of him."

For a few seconds Tammy's face lost its haunted look. Then pride was replaced by something that looked close to despair. "I didn't do right by him when he was a kid," she said. "My old man was pissed about supporting a bastard son, and I never protected him the way I should."

"That's a tough one," I said, pity fighting for supremacy over anger and fear. "There are lots of things I wish I'd done differently when Tanya and Jordan were young."

"Done differently!" Tammy spat out the words. "I'm not talking about sending my kid to a different school or taking him on a fancier vacation; I'm talkin' about keeping him safe. My Ernie was mostly okay — he didn't hit Hunter or anything. But he was a mean drunk. Called my boy a freeloader or leech when he'd had a few too many. Hunter was proud. Wouldn't eat the old man's food. Got himself a paper route the day he got picked up for shoplifting a bag of cookies. The kid was only nine. After that, he paid for his share of the groceries until he left home."

What could I say to something like that? "I'm sorry your partner hurt him —"

"That's why he needs your farm. A man with land can hold up his head."

"Tammy," I said, "there's land for sale on the other side of the lake. Hunter doesn't need my property."

She shrugged. "You got family land. Why shouldn't he?"

I wasn't about to debate the ethics of capitalism with my kidnapper. "Let's try to figure out something that works for both of us."

"I'm going to bed," Tammy said. "You wanna go outside for a pee?"

My brief hope of escape was dashed when she accompanied me out the door and held her rifle at the ready while I did my business. Once back inside, she directed me to a chair and picked up a coil of rope from the floor. "No point tryin' to get away," she said as she wrapped the rope around my middle and bound me to the chair. "Them knots are tied by an expert."

Having assured herself that I was helpless, my captor pulled from her knapsack what appeared to be an epi-pen. She filled it from a small vial. Then she jabbed it into her arm.

"Insulin," she said. "I'm diabetic."

I tried for empathy. "So was Frank's mom."

"Would have been better for Frank if he'd been diabetic too," she said, her expression unreadable. "He might not have died in that accident."

I took a deep breath, the cord tightening around my chest as it expanded. Because of my mother-in-law's condition, I'd read about diabetes. I knew that giving insulin to non-diabetics could affect their motor skills and judgement. If Tammy had injected my husband with her medication, he would have been disoriented when he stepped into his car for the drive home.

"I needed to punish him," Tammy said. "He wouldn't listen when I asked if Hunter could buy his granddad's home quarter."

"You were at the bar that night," I said quietly.

"When I saw him, I knew it was a sign. But he wouldn't talk to me. I needed to show him I was important too."

The information was too much to digest. Stunned, I gazed mindlessly at the nearest shelf. A rolled-up magazine lay wedged between two saucepans only a few feet away. Tammy had left my hands free. While she climbed into bed, I reached out and grabbed it. The magazine was an old issue of *Field & Stream*. Before the light went out, I looked at the mailing label. It had been addressed to Stan Hanson.

THURSDAY, AUGUST 9

The tiny room was stifling, its window still closed against the day's heat. I tried to undo the knots, but Tammy had been right — they'd been tied by a master hand. She lay a few feet away, tossing about restlessly and occasionally crying out in her sleep. If I wasn't afraid to wake her, I could attempt to inch the chair forward by rocking it back and forth. A bread knife lay out of reach on the top shelf — I could use it to cut the rope. Instead, I sat, sleepless, in a hard wooden chair, brooding about my plight.

When Mandi and John got home, my absence — coupled with the broken window — would have prompted a call to nine-one-one. Derek would have joined the local detachment in an immediate search for me. But what could they do in the dark, especially since they had no idea where to look? Stan's hunting shack was in an isolated spot somewhere on the far edge of his rangeland. It was unlikely either Semchuk or Derek was aware of its existence.

I needed to convince Tammy to give me my freedom. Deprived of light or any sound but her erratic cries, I considered the options. What if I wrote a letter promising to sell her my land? Or, better yet, created a written — if unofficial — bill of sale? Would she realize that a document signed under duress is invalid? My old schoolmate had good judgement when it came to woodcraft, but I doubted her shrewdness extended to legal matters. The alternative, however, was unthinkable. Tammy killed me. Then my kids sell her the land.

Having decided to attempt some real-estate chicanery, I closed my eyes and practised deep breathing. But sleep didn't come.

My horror over Tammy's confession had gone dormant while I wrestled with the problem of how to survive. Now it blossomed into outrage. I tortured myself with images of the wild, dark-haired young woman making love with the man I'd started dating a few months later. Their lips meeting in a long, slow kiss. Naked limbs entangled on the sweaty sheets of a cheap rooming house. These images were replaced by a picture of Tammy in the purple track suit injecting Frank with insulin. Despite the heat, icy shivers ran up and down my body. I gritted my teeth and started to shake.

When I woke from a fitful sleep, grey light illuminated the window. Soon it was replaced by a rosy glow. Morning might bring the arrival of Derek and officers from the local detachment, but I couldn't count on rescue. Besides, Tammy had a gun. She wouldn't sit idly by while the cops released her prey. I needed to find a solution in which no one got hurt.

Before long, the bunk creaked. Tammy sat up and threw back the blankets.

"Morning, sunshine," she said, as if last night's trauma hadn't happened.

"Tammy, I need to pee."

She got up, still wearing yesterday's clothes, and untied the rope. For a moment I considered trying to capture the rifle — I was taller and heavier than she. But Tammy was fast and strong. And knew how to shoot. Discretion prevailed, and I docilely walked out the door.

Without the presence of my escort, it would have been a postcard-beautiful prairie morning. Mallards quacked softly as a white-tailed deer drank from the slough, a hawk flew overhead, and a pair of coyotes eyed us from the top of a nearby hill. The air was still cool, and the field gilded with sunshine. Much as I needed distraction, I couldn't enjoy the Arcadian scene. Not with an armed woman waiting for me.

Business done, we returned to the shack. I made cowboy coffee on the single-burner camp stove, Tammy standing guard with her rifle trained on my back. When it had boiled for a few minutes, I placed a box of crackers and a jar of peanut butter on the table. Breakfast was ready.

Fear had destroyed my appetite, but I forced down a cup of strong, gritty coffee. Tammy tucked into the food as if she hadn't eaten for a week. While she was spreading her fourth cracker with peanut butter, I asked if she had a pen and paper.

"Why?"

"If you let me go, I'll make out a bill of sale for my farm."

Tammy laughed. "Think I was born yesterday? You'll call the cops."

"It'll take me eight or nine hours to walk home," I said. "By that time, you can give the bill of sale to Hunter and go into hiding." It was a crazy scheme, but maybe she'd go for it.

She shook her head. "I gotta think on it. And talk t' Hunter."

"You've got a cell phone — why not call him now?"

"Batteries are dead."

"I'd give you a couple thousand dollars — enough to charter a bush plane and lay in supplies. Go far enough north, and no one will find you."

"How would I see my kids?"

I shrugged. "The cops are going to be looking for you regardless of what you do."

Tammy picked up her cup and flung it across the room. The cup smashed against the wooden floor. Coffee pooled in a widening circle around the broken fragments.

"Don't threaten me."

Now what? Having already killed twice, Tammy didn't have much to lose. Another murder wouldn't significantly increase her prison sentence. I'd have to keep her talking until help arrived.

"Tell me about your kids."

A glow of pride lit Tammy's face. "They done okay."

Listening to the tale of their achievements, I felt a tiny glimmer of admiration for her. Against the odds, all four of them had created decent lives. While Hunter was the star of her story, the other three had jobs and long-term relationships.

"The younger ones didn't get rich like Hunter, but none of them are living on the street. And both the girls are married."

"Any grandkids?"

"Three. The oldest starts at that technical school in Saskatoon this fall. She wants to be a youth care worker." Tammy took a bite of cracker. "I didn't have that kind of chance."

"Life's tough," I said.

"It wasn't for you and Mandi."

I wasn't about to embark on a pissing match to see who'd suffered the most in childhood. If I had, Tammy would have won. Hand-me-down clothes and lumpy porridge couldn't compete with chronic hunger and an alcoholic parent.

"You must have been a good mom," I said.

Tammy got up from the table, rummaged in her backpack, and emerged with a pencil and rumpled sheet of lined paper. "Write out the bill of sale," she said. "I'll give it to Hunter."

I'd never so much as seen a bill of sale, but chances are Tammy hadn't either. All I had to do was make it sound official.

"I, Jeannie Wolfert-Lang, do hereby agree to sell the following property, with all its buildings, to Hunter DuBois."

A legal description of my home quarter followed. I concluded with the price that — according to Monica — Hunter was willing to pay, dated and signed the document, and handed it to Tammy.

"Now you sign it. As the witness."

Five minutes later, document signed, Tammy had made another pot of coffee and was spreading a fifth cracker with peanut butter. I peered out the window. A field of native grassland, its vastness punctuated by clumps of poplars and several tree-ringed sloughs, stretched out to distant hills. As I watched, a tiny figure appeared near the horizon. It grew until the figure became a man on horseback riding toward the shack. He stopped some distance away, dismounted, and tied the reins to the branch of a large poplar. Like the hero of an old-time Western, Hunter had come to the rescue. But who was the damsel in distress — me or his mom?

Tammy must have heard the hoofbeats. After a quick glance out the window, she ordered me to get under the bed and stay there.

"And don't make a sound," she said. "Not 'til I know what direction the wind's blowing."

I wasn't about to argue with a woman holding a gun. Sucking in my stomach, I dropped to the floor and squeezed under the bunk. Dust bunnies clung to my shirt and pants.

The door creaked open. "Mom?"

"You wanna coffee, son? I just made a pot."

"Sure, if you give me that rifle. Chris is worried. You should have asked before you borrowed it, eh?"

"We need protection," she said.

"Let me handle this." Hunter's voice was patient. "That's what a son does — he protects his mother."

"Don't let the cops lock me up."

"I won't," he said. "But I've got to have that rifle."

"Tell Chris thanks."

A metallic sound suggested that he'd taken the gun and was unloading it. "Chris is worried about Jeannie too. You know where she is?"

"Jeannie's not a problem anymore," Tammy said. "She's willing to sell."

I couldn't see what was happening, but the ensuing silence suggested that she'd handed him the bill of sale.

"I need to find her," he said. "Is this her signature on the paper?"

Tammy cleared her throat. "She said it was legal."

My first impulse was to announce my presence. Hunter had appeared to be on my side — surely he'd protect me from his mom. But what if family loyalty overrode his sense of right and wrong? While I might be able to escape from Tammy, a skinny woman older than me, I had no chance against her son. I was still debating the issue when he dropped to his knees and reached out to touch my arm.

"It's okay to come out, Jeannie."

I rolled out from under the bed. "How did you know I was there?"

"Stan needs to sweep his floor. You left tracks in the dust." Hunter helped me to my feet. "Thank God you're alright. Derek said you were missing. Did Mom —"

"She broke into Mandi's house and kidnapped me."

"That land should be yours," Tammy said to him. "I had to make Jeannie sell it."

He put an arm around her shoulders. "It's time to let her go."

Tammy shook her head. "The cops scare me."

His voice was soothing, as if he were talking to a frightened child. "You'll be okay. They won't hurt you."

"Promise?"

"I promise."

"Going to jail would kill me."

"I know," he said.

"Locked up like that — I couldn't breathe." Tammy pulled him to her in a tight embrace. "You're a good boy, Hunter."

"Do you have a cell phone?" I asked him. "I need to tell Mandi I'm okay."

"There's no signal here."

"Of course." I brushed off some dust bunnies and wiped my hands on my jeans. Now what? How do you ask a man if he's about to turn his mom over to the police?

Hunter had his own question. "Can you ride Stan's horse?"

"What happened to the truck you borrowed from Thickwood Farm?"

"Flat tire. And no spare."

I looked out the window. The horse was an enormous brute. The thought of climbing into its saddle sent quivers of fear through my belly. "How did you know where to find me?"

"Last week I rode out with Stan to check the pasture. I saw the shack then. Mom knows this country. I figured she might use it as a hiding place."

I nodded. "How far to Mandi's?"

"About thirty k."

"What if I get lost?"

"Prince would find his way home." Hunter tried to smile. "If you're scared of horses, you can wait here. Stan could come and get you."

Tammy laughed. "I'd be ashamed to be such a coward."

I dreaded the prospect of waiting alone in the shack for rescue. Tammy's taunt settled the matter. "No problem," I said. "I can do it."

"How's your ankle?"

I lied. "As good as new."

While Tammy jammed clothes into her backpack, Hunter and I filled two cardboard boxes with her remaining food supply and carried them out to the truck.

"Where are you taking her?" I asked as I handed him my box.

"Somewhere safe."

"But you will call the police, right?"

He placed the box in the back of the truck. "I'll handle this in my own way."

"Your mother kidnapped me at gunpoint," I said. "She planned to kill me."

"It won't happen again," he said.

"Not if she's locked up, it won't."

Hunter looked me in the eyes for a long time. When he finally spoke, his voice was sad. "My mother has trouble with impulse control. Sometimes that causes her problems."

"Her and lots of other people," I said.

"No one was supposed to die."

"Yeah?"

Hunter sighed. "There are things you don't understand —"

"Tell me about them."

"Mom wants to help me. Forcing you to sell your land at gunpoint is the only way she knows how." He handed me the bill of sale that Tammy had given him. "I'm sorry about the kidnapping."

"Your mother told me I'm living on what used to be your great-grandfather's homestead."

He nodded. "I had this stupid idea that owning it would establish my place in the world, that it would give me . . . roots. I've always been a nomad who drifted from one place to another."

"Not everyone is cut out for farming," I said. "Or did you see yourself as landed gentry?"

Hunter laughed, the sound bitter in the morning air. "No one's going to believe that a kid from across the tracks could have a good reason for wanting to move home. Especially if he made his money in Bitcoin. But I love this place." He leaned against the truck and stared out across the pasture. "Mom and I used to come here when I was little. Back when she was young and still had dreams. Sometimes we'd stay with Chris, but mostly we'd camp out in the hills. She taught me how to hunt and trap and ride horseback. So I could be at home on the land, she said. Then she had the twins. After that, life got . . . more difficult."

I didn't know whether to sympathize or tell him to stop whining. But his childhood had been a lot harder than mine had been. Who was I to pass judgement?

"I used to imagine living here," he said. "But we always had to return to the apartment over the pawn shop on Twentieth Street."

Tammy's arrival put a merciful end to the conversation.

"Can we have lunch with Chris?" she asked.

"We'll see. Hop in the cab, and I'll be with you in a minute." He turned back to me. "I need a few hours."

"Hunter, you can't just let her go."

"Stay here while I get Prince, okay? I'll help you mount."

The thought of riding distracted me from other worries. Prince looked even bigger up close than he had from a distance. Hunter introduced us to each other, boosted me into the saddle, and adjusted the stirrups. I sat there petrified. It was a long way from the animal's back to the ground.

"Relax," Hunter said. "He won't hurt you."

Although our plan was looking increasingly problematic, I figured I could stay on the horse at least as far as the first farmhouse. Then all I had to do was phone Stan to come and get me. He'd ride back to his place, and I'd follow in his pickup. Then he'd drive me to Mandi's, and my sister would serve me hot buttered toast and tea. The prospect was unbelievably appealing.

I gently shook the reins. "Come on, Prince, let's go."

The horse broke into a gentle trot. I'd assumed that Hunter would follow for the first dozen or more kilometres, but he passed me before we'd gone more than a few hundred yards. The truck picked up speed and soon vanished behind a poplar bluff. I was alone on a four-legged beast that I didn't know how to ride.

"Sit still and let Prince do his stuff," I told myself. "He knows what he's doing. Chances are, he wants to get home as much as I do."

For the first twenty minutes or so, all went well. Prince followed the faint track left behind in the grass by Chris's half-ton. Since he appeared to know where he was going, I gave him his head, holding the reins in one hand, and hanging on to the pommel with the other. It was a bumpy ride, but I managed okay until he increased his pace. Then the trouble started. I was alternately thrown up into the air and slammed down onto the seat of the saddle. Several hours of that treatment, and I wouldn't be able to sit for a week.

As it turned out, a sore rear was the least of my problems. We were clipping along, my seat hitting the saddle with hypnotic regularity, when we reached the top of a gentle knoll. A deer dashed across our path. Three coyotes raced behind it, tongues hanging out and bodies low to the ground. Prince abruptly stopped in his tracks. By some miracle, I managed to free my feet from the stirrups before I went flying over his head.

If I had hit one of the giant rocks scattered across the hillside, I might not have survived to tell this tale. As it was, I landed in a dense patch of scrubby rose bushes and wild gooseberries. They didn't provide a soft landing, but at least they cushioned my fall. I lay winded on the ground, scratched by their thorny branches. Although my injured ankle throbbed like fury, I was alive.

It seemed a long time before I felt strong enough to sit up. Prince was peacefully grazing nearby. Maybe I could lead him to a big rock and use it as a stepping block to help me remount.

The fall, however, had exacerbated my earlier injury. When I tried to stand, my ankle twisted under me. I'd have to inch my way to the horse. And then get back in the saddle. Literally. The alternative was to wait for rescue. The surrounding countryside must have been crawling with searchers. Even if Hunter hadn't told Stan I'd set out for home on Prince, someone would find me. Eventually.

Tammy's taunting words came back to me. "I'd be ashamed to be such a coward." No way was I going to play the Victorian heroine tied to the railway track.

The sun was already hot. I had neither hat nor water. Sunstroke was only an hour or two away. There was no choice but to get back on Prince.

I grabbed hold of two saskatoon bushes providentially growing amongst the prickly shrubs and used them to pull myself forward. The horse wasn't far away, but progress was slow. Even with the help of one good foot, my arms quickly tired. Rest stops became more frequent. By the time I reached Prince, my shirt and jeans were filthy and soaked with sweat.

"Good boy," I said. "Now all I need to do is climb up on your back."

The horse regarded me for a moment, and then returned to grazing the shortgrass prairie. I scanned the ground around us. A large, flat stone lay on the other side of Prince. Maybe he would stand still while I crawled onto it and used a stirrup to pull myself upright. Then one foot into that stirrup, the other over the saddle, and I'd be ready to ride.

It seemed like an impossible task, but desperation lent me strength. Somehow, I managed to regain my seat, Prince standing motionless beneath me.

"What a fine horse," I said, stroking his neck. "Think you can get me safely home, old fellow?"

We set off across the grassy field. Prince, as if aware of my limitations, settled into an even trot. I looked up at the sun. It shone like a beacon straight overhead. Twelve noon. It had taken us three hours to get this far. And we still had a long way to go.

We'd been travelling for an eternity when we reached a dirt track. I couldn't tell where we were — the track looked familiar, but I'd lost all sense of direction. Until then, Prince had kept to the open prairie. Now he increased his pace to a gentle canter and set off to follow the road.

I'd been so focused on staying in the saddle that I'd had no energy for anything else. With the prospect of farms and people close at hand, I relaxed and let myself think about Derek. Was he one of the searchers out looking for me? I started to fantasize about his giddy relief at my safe return when the rumble of an oncoming truck broke the stillness. Maybe Hunter had changed his mind about letting me go free.

Heart thudding, I shook the reins and tried to urge Prince off the road and into the adjoining field. He ignored me.

The truck stopped, and two men got out. Blinded by the sun, I couldn't see who they were. Then I heard a familiar voice.

"Mom, thank God you're here. Stan and I were worried. We've been out searching for you since daybreak."

"Jordan," I said, "am I ever glad to see you." Then, to my chagrin, I started to cry.

"Jeez, are you okay?"

My son had rarely seen me in tears. He walked up to Prince and patted me on the leg as gently as if I'd been made of glass.

I wiped my eyes with a grubby hand. "I think I'll live."

"Aunt Mandi phoned and said you'd gone missing. What happened?"

Stan appeared behind Jordan and handed me a clean handkerchief. "Never seen *you* on horseback, Jeannie. You are one tough cookie."

"Tammy kidnapped me. She took me to your hunting shack and held me at gunpoint. Then Hunter arrived. He was riding Prince —"

"So that's how he got here," Stan said.

"You didn't talk to Hunter?" I asked.

"Didn't even see him."

Jordan frowned. "So, this fellow stole your horse —"

"Borrowed it," Stan said. "Jeannie, we need to get you to the hospital."

I shook my head. "My body's bruised, not broken. But Mandi must be worried. Someone needs to phone her."

While Jordan called his aunt and assured her I was okay, Stan offered to help me down from Prince and into his truck.

"Jordan can drive you to Mandi's," he said. "I'll follow behind on my four-legged friend here."

"Thanks," I said, "but he and I set off together. The two of us are going to see it through to the end."

My son had other ideas. He scolded me for getting on a horse when I didn't know how to ride, and then all but ordered me into the truck cab for the rest of the trip.

"Forget it," I said. "Prince and I have taken the measure of each other. I'm sticking on his back until we're home."

Then I touched my heels to his sides, and we set off for Mandi's place.

After riding across rolling grassland punctuated by rocks and gopher holes, the rest of the trip should have been easy. It wasn't. We were only five kilometres from John and Mandi's, but I'd barely slept the night before. I was dirty, tired, hungry, and thirsty. And every bone and muscle in my body ached. Even worse was the realization that Tammy was still out there, Chris's rifle in hand and ready to strike again.

The situation wasn't made easier by the cheering crowd gathered in front of the house when we arrived. I didn't want to talk to anyone. I wanted to bathe, change my clothes, and eat lunch.

Jordan helped Stan support me as I slid down from Prince. Then the two men made a seat with their arms and carried me to a bench beside the front step.

The scene might have been a replay of the one at my farm the day we searched for Zayden. Semchuk and Pierce were there, along with Liz, the folks from Thickwood Farm, and four other neighbours. Only Derek was missing.

Mandi must have sensed my distress. "Thanks for your support, folks," she said, raising her voice so it carried over the crowd. "We'd love to have you visit later, but right now my sister needs rest."

Stan was the first to move. "I'll be off, then."

"Mandi's directive doesn't apply to you," I said. "You're welcome to stay for coffee."

"Another time. You need to be with family." He briefly clasped my hands. "Take care, Jeannie."

Then he mounted Prince and set off at a canter toward home.

Soon the only people left were Mandi, Jordan, Semchuk, and Pierce. Mandi had sent John and the grandkids to a neighbour's place and had unsuccessfully tried to get rid of Semchuk and Pierce. They refused to budge until they talked to me.

"The sooner we hear what happened, the sooner we're out of here," Semchuk said.

"Shower first," Mandi said, cautiously putting an arm around my shoulders. "The explanations can wait."

Semchuk was about to help Jordan carry me into the house when Derek arrived. He jumped down from his van and raced across the parking area toward the bench where I was sitting.

"My God, Jeannie, are you okay?" He plopped down on the bench and wrapped his arms around me. "I just got Mandi's text —"

"Where were you?"

"Searching the backroads east of here. There was no cell signal —"

"Tammy kidnapped me," I said, trying to keep my voice from shaking. "She held me hostage in Stan's hunting shack. God knows what would have happened if Hunter hadn't come looking for me."

"No more talking," Mandi said. "Derek, you'll have to wait for her story, the same as everyone else. Jeannie's getting cleaned up before she says another word."

Before Jordan could move to help him, Derek swept me up into his arms and carried me into the house. With Mandi following close behind, he deposited me on a chair she had set in the bathroom. My sister helped me undress and seated me on a stool she'd placed under the shower. "Call when you're ready to come out," she said. "I'll put water on for tea."

The hot shower revived me. Before long I was comfortably settled in a reclining armchair with a mug of camomile tea and a plate of hot buttered toast. They tasted as good as I'd imagined.

"Now you can talk," Mandi said.

I started with the rock through her living room window and ended with my roadside meeting with Jordan and Stan. When I finished, I looked at Semchuk and Pierce.

"What happens next?"

"We've got officers looking for Hunter and Tammy," Semchuk said. "Neither of them answers their cell phone, and Tammy's brother Chris doesn't know where they are."

"Most likely gone into hiding," Mandi said.

Semchuk nodded. "We've alerted local airports and the train station in Saskatoon, but it's not likely they'll use public transport. Hunter's driving his uncle Chris's half-ton. He stopped at a service station and convenience store five hours ago. According to the owner, he filled both his gas tank and a couple of jerry cans. He also stocked up on enough food and soft drinks to last several weeks. Tammy knows this area, and she's got relatives they can call on for help. Unless they do something stupid like try to cross the border, they can keep out of sight for a long time."

"Couldn't you spot them from a helicopter?" Jordan asked.

"Not if they stay under cover," Semchuk said. "And we can't get warrants to search every building in the vicinity."

"Is Hunter going to be in trouble?" I asked.

He nodded. "The courts don't like people obstructing the course of justice. But he might get off lightly. His mother won't. Not after committing murder."

I suddenly realized that I was the only person who knew that she'd also killed Frank. While I'd have to tell the police, I recoiled from exposing to the public eye that bit of local history. Besides, I was ready to collapse from exhaustion.

Mandi once again took charge. "Enough, already," she said to Pierce and Semchuk. "If you have more questions, come back later. I'm putting Jeannie to bed."

My sister is a force to be reckoned with. Soon the cops were gone, leaving Derek as the only non–family member. He sat down beside me.

"I'm helping with the search for Tammy. Need anything before I leave?"

"Mandi will take care of me." I took a deep breath. "But I haven't forgotten that conversation we were supposed to have yesterday. It hasn't been cancelled — merely postponed."

"I know." He took my hands in his. "I was worried about you."

"Thanks for being here," I said.

He smiled. "It was my pleasure."

Jordan raised an eyebrow as Derek kissed me goodbye. I suspected he'd have questions afterward, and I was right.

"Mom, is this relationship serious?" he asked as soon as we were alone in the living room.

I shrugged. "Derek's a good guy. Most of the time, I like him a lot. But he's not a farmer." No way I was telling my son about the phone call from an anonymous woman.

"People commute," Jordan said, his voice hesitant.

"It's a long drive. Four hours, round trip."

"Yeah." He groaned. "Hell of a way to spend a good part of the day, never mind the economic and environmental cost."

"Derek and I are a long way from having that discussion," I said. "But I assume you're thinking of you and Liz."

He looked down at his hands. "How do you figure out if you want to commit to someone?"

"Wish I knew the answer to that." I took a sip of lukewarm tea. "But aren't you getting ahead of yourself? Two weeks ago, you were dating Brandy —"

"I like independent women better," he said, and grinned. "Women like my mom."

"Didn't look like it, when you wanted me to ride home in the truck instead of on horseback," I said.

Jordan blushed.

I smiled at him. "Independence can be a mixed blessing. Without the support of a lot of people over the past few weeks, I'd be dead."

"You've done your bit supporting them."

"We all do what we can." I patted his hand. "I hope you find what you're looking for."

"I have. But . . . Liz farms. A long way from Saskatoon."

"Can't think of anyone I'd like better as a daughter-in-law."

"I didn't say anything about marriage. We're just . . . friends."

"That's a start."

"It might be as far as we get," he said. "Liz is a lot like you. She needs to control her own space."

"The two of you can still make commitments. But if you're looking for a partner, you'd better find someone who wants roughly the same thing that you do."

"Liz would never leave her farm."

"Would you leave Saskatoon?" I asked.

Jordan sighed. "How can I? My work's in the city."

"You could get a job at the hospital in town. Or change careers."

He frowned. "We'd be the only young people out here. I don't want to spend all my free time playing bridge and old-time dancing."

"How about the folks at Thickwood Farm?"

"They're not going to stay," Jordan said. "Not as long as you're the person who makes all the decisions."

"It's my land, and I pay the taxes. They've got cheap rent —"

"And no security of tenure. Who'd want to plan a future on a farm that could be sold from under them?"

The day was suddenly too much for me. I'd been held at gunpoint, thrown from a horse, and obliged to sign a fake bill of sale. I didn't need to have my son accuse me of being a control freak. For the second time that day, I burst into tears.

"Mom, I didn't mean —"

Mandi appeared out of nowhere and gently took Jordan by the arm. "Sweetie, your mom's tired. Let's give her a chance to rest, eh?"

"Right." He leaned over and kissed me on the cheek. "I told Liz I'd join her for supper before I head back to the city. Are you going to be okay when I'm gone?"

I fished a handkerchief from my pocket and wiped my eyes. "Of course, I will."

"And . . . don't tell Liz about our conversation, okay?"

"Your secret's safe with me," I said, happy in the thought of a relationship between two people I loved. The problem was one of compatibility. I couldn't quite see my oh-so-urban son spending the rest of his life on a prairie farm. Liz would doubtlessly say that being in love didn't mean you had to live together. Perhaps she was right. Perhaps I was hopelessly out of fashion in my correlation of love with marriage.

After Jordan had gone, I slept. When I awoke, the grandkids were running around the kitchen, and Mandi was putting supper on the table. She had made potato salad and prepared a platter of fixings to go with barbecued hamburgers. Normally I would have dug in with gusto, but that evening I toyed with my food.

My son's assessment of the situation at Thickwood Farm disturbed me. I'd taken pride in being a good landholder — financially generous and willing to help my tenants. What if that wasn't enough? Maybe they wanted a level playing field on which they could share decision-making.

"Aunt Jeannie, how come you're not eating?" Melissa asked.

I ate a mouthful of potato salad. "Sweetie, I'm doing my best."

"If you're sad, you can watch *The Lion King* with me."

"Thanks." I smiled at my great-niece. "I'd like that."

When Mandi rejected my offer to help with the dishes, I curled up on the sofa with Melissa and Ty. I don't usually watch Disney movies, but with Jeremy Irons as part of the cast, how bad could it be?

Derek phoned just as the closing credits rolled across the screen.

"We're calling it quits for the day. No sign of Tammy and Hunter, and no guarantee that we'll do better tomorrow. Finding anyone in that maze of dirt trails and dead-end roads would be a bloody miracle."

I repositioned my ankle on the sofa footrest. "Maybe you should ask for help from Stan and his neighbours."

Derek laughed. "Bring on the cowboys, eh? The media would have a field day if we risked the lives of civilians."

"Your life's important too."

"Couldn't be a cop if I wasn't willing to take chances."

"At least be careful," I said. "I don't want your death on my conscience."

He was silent for a moment. "Is that the only reason you're worried about me?"

Loneliness and desire had warred with jealousy until I no longer knew my own mind.

"Goodnight, Derek. Thanks for keeping me safe."

FRIDAY, AUGUST 10

Mandi and I had finished breakfast and were lingering over tea when Stan appeared at the back door.

"Here to visit the invalid?" she asked, flashing a mischievous smile.

"Yep." He pulled up a chair across from me. "How you doing, Jeannie?"

"My legs aren't working as well as they should," I said, "but the rest of me is fine. All I need is Tammy behind bars and life can return to normal."

"After six hours on horseback, I'm surprised you can walk at all," he said.

"Who'd have thought stubbornness had a good side, eh?" Mandi got up from the table. "I'm off to weed the garden. Jeannie, make sure you call if you need anything while I'm gone."

"Better hustle if you want to get the weeding done before it rains," I said. "Or is that wishful thinking?"

The sky had clouded over during the night, and the temperature dropped below fifteen degrees. While I hated the possibility that it would disrupt the search for Tammy, I revelled in the prospect of a downpour. Some of the grain crops might be past saving, but a good soaker would at least replenish groundwater and sloughs.

Stan shared my preoccupation with crops and weather, and over the last of the breakfast tea we exchanged the sort of chitchat rural people engage in everywhere. Then Stan picked up his Stetson. "Anything I can get you before I go?"

I had to think fast. Stan was the only person who could shed light on what had happened the summer before I'd started dating Frank. He might be reluctant to talk, but I needed help. And what kind of cowboy could say no to a lady?

"Did Frank have a relationship with Tammy the summer he finished high school?" I asked.

Stan looked at me as if I'd suddenly sprouted flowers in my ears. "Where the hell did that come from?"

"Tammy said they were lovers."

"My God, woman, that was over forty years ago."

"Was she telling the truth?"

"They were kids. Away from home and lonely. They had a fling. It wasn't important."

"It was to her," I said.

He swatted away a fly that was buzzing around his face. "Did she tell you about Frank when she imprisoned you in my hunting shack?"

I nodded. "I wouldn't sell Hunter the land that used to be her grandfather's. So she convinced herself that having had sex with him gave her a right to take it."

"If that were true, the courts would be overwhelmed with lawsuits."

"Tammy wasn't interested in lawsuits," I said. "She wanted revenge."

He cocked an eyebrow. "Forty-two years later?"

"She said she talked to Frank the night of the stag. When *he* wouldn't sell her the land, she injected him with insulin before he headed home in the fog. At least, that's what she implied."

"And you believed her?"

"Any reason I shouldn't?"

A truck rumbled past on the RM road, the sound of its diesel engine changing as the driver shifted gears.

"Tammy doesn't always tell the truth," he said. "Chris blames it on the head injury she suffered as a kid."

"That doesn't mean her story was a lie."

Stan reached across the table and patted my hand. "Jeannie, the coroner investigated the cause of Frank's death. There were no traces of drugs in his body."

"It would have helped if they'd known what they were looking for. Maybe the police should reopen the case."

"Is that what you want, Frank's personal life opened to public scrutiny? Tammy's already facing charges of murder and kidnapping."

"I want to know what really happened," I said.

"Sometimes that's not possible." His eyes held mine in a steady gaze. "Don't blame Frank. They were both single, consenting adults with no commitments to anyone else."

Stan was right, but that didn't make me feel much better. Relationships between women and men were too darn complicated. Why the hell didn't most of us remain single?

Once Stan had left for home, I hobbled into the living room and stretched out on the sofa. John had gone to the beach with the grandkids. Mandi was in the garden. I was alone, with time to take stock of my situation.

Even if Tammy hadn't caused Frank's death, she had killed Monica. And she'd tried to kill me. If Hunter hadn't intervened, she would have succeeded. How much sympathy did I owe her anyway? Other people had difficult childhoods. They had head injuries. But they didn't usually become murdering lunatics. Even factoring in a background of class discrimination and poverty, why was she hiding from the police when other women her age were at home enjoying their grandkids?

I was contemplating free will versus social determination when Jade called.

"Jeannie, we have a problem," she said, her voice ragged. "We need you at Thickwood Farm —"

"I'll call Derek."

"Not right away. We have to talk to you first."

"Jade, what's going on?"

A loud thud assaulted my ear. Then a woman shrieked, and the line went dead.

I was staring at my mobile when Mandi came in carrying a ripe muskmelon. "Look what I found in the garden —" She broke off when she saw the expression on my face. "Now what?"

"Trouble. Jade asked me not to phone Derek —"

"Ring him anyway," she said.

My call went to voice mail. I left a message while Mandi talked to Semchuk at the RCMP detachment. Then she helped me to my feet.

"Let's go."

"Want me to call John?" I asked as we climbed into her Subaru.

"Jade's a drama queen," she said. "Let's find out what's going on before we drag the kids away from the beach."

Chris's half-ton, which Tammy had been driving when she kidnapped me, was slewed across the driveway. The last time I'd seen it, Hunter had been behind the wheel as he and his mom drove away from Stan's shack. Either she'd escaped from his custody, or the two of them had collectively sought refuge with Jade.

Thunder rumbled as Ava met us on the verandah.

"It's bedlam in there. Tammy showed up a couple hours ago looking for her sister and hurling curses at anyone who approached. When she started throwing things, Thor corralled her in the bathroom. Now he's standing guard over the door."

"Where's Hunter?" I asked.

"We don't know," Ava said. "There was no answer when Jade called his cell. But she did get hold of her Gramma Rose. She's on her way here from Saskatoon."

"Did you talk to the police?" I asked.

Ava looked down at the verandah floor. "Jade insists that Rose or Hunter make that call because they're 'family.'"

"Jade doesn't get to decide," Mandi said. "I've spoken to Semchuk. He'll be here in an hour."

We were about to go in the house when Hunter galloped up on Prince. He dismounted, dropped the reins to the ground, and stumbled over to join us.

"Where is she?"

"Inside," Ava said. "I'm one of Jade's housemates. We've been wondering when you'd get here."

Hunter collapsed in a wicker chair. "I've been trying to keep an eye on her, but she escaped."

"Where were you?" I asked. "And why didn't you get in touch with Derek?"

"I was going to follow you when we left Stan's shack," he said, "but Mom freaked out. She was scared and wanted to hide at Chris's place. So, I drove there, only Chris said his house was the first place the cops would look."

"He was right," I said. "Then what?"

"He phoned a friend who lives on a dirt road a long way from the nearest neighbour. The friend and his wife were leaving for Swift Current, but he said we could use the house while they were gone. Chris gave me directions, and I drove there last night."

"Stopping at a service station on the way for gas and groceries," I said. "What did you plan to do when the owners got home?"

Hunter passed a hand over bloodshot eyes. "I wasn't thinking that far ahead. Mom was asleep, but I didn't know what I'd do when she woke up. I couldn't let the police take her away. She'd be terrified."

Torn between sympathy and outrage, I touched his hand. "How did she escape?"

"I'd barricaded the doors with heavy furniture. Figured I'd hear her if she tried to move it. But I didn't. I'd been awake all night and dozed off on the sofa. She stole the keys from my shirt pocket and climbed over the portable dishwasher. When I woke up, she was gone."

"Why come here?" Ava asked.

"I told her about meeting Aunt Rose," Hunter said. "She wanted to talk to her."

As if his words had been an incantation conjuring up the older woman's presence, a small grey car appeared in the driveway. Rose climbed out of the driver's seat.

"That sister of mine in trouble again?" she asked as she joined us on the verandah.

"She got away from me," Hunter said, his voice breaking. "I tried to keep her safe from the police —"

"Some people need more help than any one human can give." Rose took him by the hand. "Let's go find her and see what can be done."

Mandi, Ava, and I followed them into the house. Inside, it was strangely quiet. Jade crouched on the floor near the bathroom door while Thor, face grim, stood guard.

"Hunter," he said, "thank God you're here."

Tammy started shrieking and banging on the door. "Help! They've taken me prisoner —"

"Let her out," Hunter said. "I'll talk to her."

As soon as she was freed, Tammy rushed to her son. "Help me. Please help me."

"Mom, you were safe. Why did you run away?"

"You said Anna was here. I wanted to talk to her." Tammy looked around the room, her eyes glancing over her sister with no sign of recognition.

Rose stepped toward her. "Hello, Tammy. It's me, Anna."

"Go away. You're not Anna. My sister is young and beautiful. You're an old woman."

"We're both old. It's been over forty years . . ."

Tammy stared at Rose for what seemed like a long time. Finally, recognition flickered across her face. "You went away and left me."

"I know I should have visited —"

Without warning, Tammy lunged at Rose and grabbed her around the neck. "You wanted me dead. That's why you let them lock me in the woodshed."

Hunter's swift response suggested that this wasn't the first time he'd had to restrain her.

"Mom, let go," he said, wrapping his arms around her in a choke hold.

Tammy struggled briefly. Then her hands went limp, and she collapsed on the floor.

254

Jade led Rose to the sofa. "Are you okay, Gramma? You're not hurt, are you?"

"My sister should have had therapy years ago."

Hunter knelt beside Tammy and stroked her hair. "It's okay — you're safe here."

"Not much we can do for her now," Rose said.

"She's afraid," Hunter said. "A therapist would have got her locked up."

"It's too late for that kind of help." Rose looked at me. "You called the cops, right?"

I nodded.

Thor cleared his throat. "An institution may not be the best place for her. If we could find something better —"

"Good intentions don't butter the bread," Rose said. "It's either hospitalization or jail."

Rose was right. If Tammy was "lucky," her lawyer would make a case for diminished responsibility. The judge would rule her unfit to stand trial. Even if she were placed in a psychiatric unit, she would lose her freedom. And end up terrified. Unfortunately, there was no better alternative.

While Rose tried to reach Chris, Jade walked over to her aunt and started to sing. Tammy closed her eyes and swayed from side to side in time to the music. Then Mandi and I dredged up lullabies we'd sung to our babies. The younger folks added harmony or hummed along. Soon we'd wrapped Tammy in a soothing blanket of gentle sounds.

When Pierce and Semchuk arrived, they walked in on a peaceful scene. Rose, Mandi, Ava, Thor, and I were standing in a semicircle around Jade and Hunter, who were quietly singing "All Through the Night." Tammy lay curled up on the sofa. Asleep.

The two cops stared at Tammy. I could imagine how bewildered they must feel. The woman who had evaded capture for fourteen days looked frail and elderly. Dressed in a ragged purple tracksuit and wearing her long grey hair in braids, she could have been a harmless eccentric grandmother. Instead, she was about to be charged with murder.

"Can you leave her until she wakes up?" Hunter asked. "This may be the last good sleep she has for a long time."

Semchuk had started to refuse his request when Derek entered. He took one look at Tammy and groaned.

"It's days like this that make me wonder why I became a cop."

Rose walked over to Tammy and gently shook her. "We're not doing my sister a favour by dragging this out. If you cops are gonna arrest her, get on with it."

Tammy woke up. As soon as she saw them, she started to scream obscenities at the uniformed officers. Pierce handcuffed her, while Semchuk formally arrested her on charges of murder and kidnapping. I couldn't tell how much of what he said registered with Tammy. All I knew for certain was that she was both furious and scared.

Hunter called a lawyer and then announced that he was going with them to the station.

"Tammy's not the only one in trouble," Semchuk said. "You'll be lucky if you escape charges of obstructing the police in their inquiry."

"She's his mother," Jade said. "He had to help her."

Semchuk shrugged. "A man at my pay grade doesn't have to make that call."

"You'll come back here afterward, right?" Jade asked Hunter as she gave him a hug. "I mean, you're family now, and we stick together."

"Thanks," he said. "I'll see you tonight."

Finally, to everyone's relief, the four of them left. As Pierce led her out the door, Tammy turned and looked back at me. For a fleeting moment, her eyes cleared.

"I didn't set out to kill anyone. Just wanted to help my boy come home."

—**—

Although it was well past noon, no one wanted lunch.

"Time for me to go," Mandi said. "Jeannie, I expect you're itching to get home. Do you and Derek want to come for supper tonight? You can pick up your suitcase then."

Derek's two-week vacation leave was almost over. I was about to say that we wouldn't have many more nights together when he made our excuse.

"The chief wants me back in Saskatoon tonight," he said. "I'm going to be selfish and ask to have dinner alone with Jeannie. But I'd like to join you next weekend if that's okay with you and her."

"Tonight?" I said. "I thought you didn't have to work until Monday."

"Couple guys are off sick. I'm covering a shift."

Mandi smiled. "We're always happy to see both of you."

Then she hugged everyone in sight, said goodbye, and headed back to John and the grandkids.

"You go home, Jeannie, and spend time with your man," Rose said. "These three can manage on their own."

"You're returning to the city?" I asked.

"I will tomorrow," she said. "Unless Hunter needs me to stay longer."

I accepted Jade's invitation to join them for brunch the next morning and echoed Mandi in giving everyone a fare-well hug. Then Derek and I climbed in his van and set off for my farm.

We made the short trip in silence. I'd been anticipating another day together and had mentally postponed our "difficult conversation." The realization that it had to happen soon tied my nerves in knots.

A light rain was falling as we pulled up beside the garage. I opened the van door and stepped out into a grey world covered with mist.

"Nice, eh?" Derek said.

We held hands as we walked up the steps to the deck. Diesel was curled up on a lounge chair. He sat up and greeted me with a friendly meow.

I picked him up and gave him a hug. "It's good to be home, buddy."

Derek declined my offer of coffee and muffins.

"If we're going to talk about what's eating you, we'd better get it out in the open before it spoils the rest of the day."

Rain thrummed on the deck's fibreglass roof. I gazed at the line of spruce behind the house, their branches covered in silvery drops of water. Relationships had changed in the almost forty years I'd been married to Frank. And Derek had been single for much of that time. I didn't expect him to live like a monk, but I did expect him to be honest. If he was seeing other women, I wanted to know about them.

"That woman's laugh the other day suggested the two of you did more than chat over coffee. Who is she?"

"Her name is Kat," Derek said, "and she's an administrative assistant for the police services in Saskatoon. Is that enough information?"

"Kat. The woman you talked to the night we had pizza on my deck. You saw her the day you went to Saskatoon to look for Hunter, didn't you?"

He nodded. "We met by accident. Ran into each other on the street."

"Why did she phone me?"

"How the hell should I know?" He picked up the local paper that had been sitting on the table and twisted it between his fingers. "You'd better ask her."

"Her voice had a . . . a proprietary air as if you were her possession —"

"Jeannie," he said. "Nobody owns me."

"Or me either," I said. "But that's no excuse for keeping secrets from each other."

Derek broke the long silence that followed my gentle rebuke. "I'm sorry. I should have told you about Kat, but I was afraid you wouldn't want to see me anymore."

I reached across the table and traced his lips with my finger. "I hadn't intended for you to become such a big part of my life."

The rain continued to fall, splashing off the roof and onto the dogwoods massed against the deck. Celestial music to gardeners and farmers in this drought-stressed land.

"Are you sorry that happened?"

"No," I said.

Without being conscious of it, I'd assumed our relationship would continue to develop in the direction it was heading. I hadn't factored in the presence of another woman. For all I knew, Derek could be a sailor with a "girl" in every port.

"I'm not trying to control your life," I said. "But I need information to make decisions about mine."

"Information such as who I'm sleeping with?"

I flinched at the blunt words. "Yes."

"Why does that matter to you so much?"

How do you tell a man that you've known for only two weeks that you equate physical intimacy with commitment? And that you don't want sex without knowing that you're both in the relationship for the long haul?

Serial monogamy, my daughter used to call it before she and her partner, Dillon, bought a place together. Not necessarily "'til death do us part," but commitment for the life of the relationship. I wasn't a prude — at least, I didn't think so — but I was leery about bed-hopping. I didn't want him alternating between me and another woman — or two.

"Call me greedy, but I don't want to share you with anyone."

Derek got up and walked around the deck. When he returned to the table, his hair was wet with rain. "My parents were physically faithful to each other, but there was no joy in their marriage. I wish they'd both been able to kick up their heels and get more pleasure out of life, even if it wasn't with each other."

"Maybe they should have separated," I said.

"They had eleven kids."

"Yeah, well . . ."

I didn't tell Derek that my hormones were raging, and that I wanted something more than camaraderie. He sat only a metre away from me, close enough that I could touch him. The night we'd spent together had been a balm to a woman coming out of six months' celibacy. All I had to do was take him by the hand and lead him upstairs to my bed . . .

It would have been so easy. I stood up and started to reach for him — and then stopped. Derek was warm and charming and . . . sexy. I wanted to feel his naked body against mine again. But maybe I was simply reacting to Frank's absence. Maybe I'd feel the same desire for any eligible man. And even if I really was in love, did that mean I had to let Derek set the rules for our relationship?

The rain continued to drum its message of salvation.

I looked at the blue-eyed man sitting across the table. "I don't want to deal with anonymous phone calls and women popping up all over the place. I need stability."

"And predictability?"

"I hope I'm not turning into a boring old woman set in her ways."

"God, no." He picked up my hand and pressed it to his lips. "You're prickly and opinionated, but I love being with you."

"And so . . .?"

"Jeannie, I don't like ultimatums."

"Nor do I."

We looked at each other for what felt like a long time. Finally, I broke the silence.

"Don't make me end our relationship."

"Someone has to do the hard stuff. Isn't that why women keep men around?" His voice was light, but I could hear the edge beneath its surface.

I wanted to pretend the anonymous phone call had never happened, to return to the halcyon days when we'd first met. But that wasn't possible. And it was unfair to keep him dangling when I'd already made up my mind.

"Let's keep in touch," I said.

He pulled my house key from his pocket and handed it to me. "I'll get my bag."

When he returned to the deck, bag in hand, I threw my arms around him.

"Goodbye, Derek."

We walked together to his van. I leaned against the driver's side and closed my eyes as he slowly kissed me on the lips.

"Goodbye, love," he said.

Then he opened the van door, hopped inside, and was gone.

I turned my face up to the rain and let it wash away the tears pouring down my cheeks.

Derek's call came at midnight. I'd been lying awake feeling sorry for myself when his name appeared on my mobile screen.

"Hey," I said. "Everything okay?"

"Jeannie, I have bad news."

My momentary pleasure took a nosedive. "Don't tell me Tammy's escaped."

"Not yet, she hasn't. But the lady just swallowed enough diazepam to knock out a horse."

SATURDAY, AUGUST 11

Flashlight in hand, I stumbled through darkness and driving rain to Thickwood Farm. It would have been easier to phone, but my parents had taught me to deliver bad news in person. Whether Tammy's attempt at suicide constituted bad news was, of course, open to debate. Either way, I needed to tell Hunter his mom was in an ambulance on her way to the hospital.

The cross-country trek might have been exciting to an active twenty-year-old. It wasn't to me. What with falling in a muddy pothole and tripping over rocks greasy with rain, I felt every one of my sixty years by the time I arrived at the house.

Fortunately, the door was unlocked. I ran inside, pounded up the stairs, and flung open the door of my old bedroom.

"Hunter, it's Jeannie."

"What's wrong?" he asked, sitting up in bed.

"It's your mom," I said, turning on the light. "She tried to kill herself."

Trying to catch my breath, I gave him Derek's message.

He stepped onto the bedside mat wearing only black boxers. "She was in police custody. How did she get hold of diazepam?"

"The constable who searched her must have missed it," I said. "The doctor's going to pump her stomach."

Hunter pulled on jeans and a T-shirt. "I'm going to the hospital."

I thought about Jordan; what if he were in Hunter's situation? Even though hospitals give me the heebie-jeebies, I had to ask. "Want me to go with you?"

"Thanks," Hunter said. "Can you drive my car?"

I don't know which was worse, riding Prince or driving an unfamiliar Audi on rain-slicked roads through inky darkness. Hunter was no help. He stared silently into space while I peered out the windshield trying to see the elusive white line on the highway's edge.

My nerves didn't improve when we reached the hospital. I remained silent when Hunter informed the duty nurse that I was his aunt, and then followed him through a maze of curtained cubicles until we reached Tammy. She was surrounded by the electronic gadgets of high-tech medicine, hooked to machines that even under the best circumstances would have given me nightmares. The situation was as surreal as a Salvador Dalí painting. Standing beside her son, I looked down at the helpless woman lying motionless on the white-sheeted hospital bed.

Hunter took one of her hands in his. "I'm here, Mom."

She opened her eyes. "Hunter," she said, her voice barely a whisper.

I reached for her other hand. While I wasn't ready to grant absolution, at least I could wish her well on whatever journey lay ahead.

"Godspeed to you," I said, slowly enunciating the archaic word.

Outside in the hallway, footsteps sounded on tiled floors and the crackle of an intercom broke the silence. I was about to tell Hunter that I'd wait for him in the sitting room outside when Tammy spoke again.

"Frank's death wasn't my fault. I didn't do nothing to him."

"What?"

"We can talk about that later," Hunter said.

"He deserved to die," she said. "But I didn't kill him."

I stared at her face, lined by years of hardship and grief. "Why did you lie about the insulin?"

It took a long time for Tammy to answer. When she did, her voice was so quiet I could barely hear her. "You stole my man. I had to make you pay."

I opened my mouth to protest my innocence, and then pressed it shut again. Why debate ethics with a woman who could be dying?

Minutes passed. Tammy seemed to rally, but then she became restless. Her breathing became laboured, and her grip tightened on my hand.

"Hunter?"

Then lights flashed and a siren beeped. Three people wearing hospital garb rushed into the crowded cubicle. I took Hunter by the arm and stepped back from Tammy's bed.

"Let's give them space, okay?"

We stood in the corridor until a plump woman in pale blue scrubs brought us each a plastic chair. And then we waited. Although it couldn't have been more than twenty minutes, it felt like a long time before a woman in a white coat emerged from the cubicle and told us that Tammy was dead.

I stayed in my chair while Hunter returned to her bedside to say goodbye to his mom. Then it was back to the rain-streaked

Audi and the drive home at sunrise as the heavens filled with morning light.

I awoke to sunshine and a clear blue sky. The air was redolent with petrichor — that wonderful earthy smell of rainfall on warm, dry ground. In the garden, robins scratched for earthworms and bees gathered nectar from pots of purple verbena. Marigolds and zinnias glistened, their petals washed clean by the rain.

My mood was no match for Nature's exuberance. I was sitting on the deck listlessly paging through a cooking magazine when Jade called.

"Please come for brunch, Jeannie," she said. "Hunter's upset, and we don't know how to help him."

I'd had it up to my neck with my neighbours at Thickwood Farm. But it wasn't their fault they were young, or that they lacked my years of experience at playing Mom. I sighed and told Jade I'd be there in half an hour.

Rain had rejuvenated plant life. Tammy had ceased to be a threat. And I was grateful to be alive. But all I could think about was Derek. It was all very well to say with Harriet Vane, in Dorothy Sayers's *Have His Carcase*, that the best remedy for heartache is not "repose upon a manly bosom," but "honest work [and] physical activity." I'd always been good at getting things done. Now the prospect of painting and gardening brought no comfort.

I spent the rest of my walk replaying the previous day's scene with Derek. To no good purpose. All it did was make me tired and sad.

When I arrived, the four young people were drinking coffee. The kitchen smelled of cinnamon and fresh baking.

Hunter's eyes were still red, but his tears of the previous night had been replaced by self-recrimination. "Mom wouldn't have killed Monica if I hadn't wanted that land so damn much," he said. "And she wouldn't be dead from an overdose. What a stupid waste — I mean, what the hell would I do with a farm? And I didn't even know my great-grandparents."

"You're no more to blame than Jeannie," Thor said quietly. "Individuals shouldn't have to own land to use it. You're both pawns of the capitalist system."

I rolled my eyes. "That's what my parents used to say. While my prospective in-laws fed the masses, my parents held meetings and organized protests."

"We grow food," Ava said, an edge in her voice. "And damn good food too."

She was right, but I was feeling irritated. Why was everything my responsibility? "If people want new ownership structures, they should create them. Instead of sitting around whining for help."

Thor frowned. "I didn't mean —"

"Don't worry about me," Hunter said. "I'm returning to Saskatoon, and not coming back." He stood up and surveyed the room. "Nice place, this, but I'm out of here."

Jade touched his arm. "How about you move in with us?"

"You're getting ahead of yourself," Ava said. "We haven't reached consensus yet."

"But we could use more folks on the farm," Thor said.

"You three do realize that you barely know this man, right?" I picked up a spoon and fiddled with it. "Hunter, no one blames you for your mom's actions. If you want to move back here, I won't stand in your way. But right now is not a good time to make major decisions."

Hunter nodded. "Thanks. I'll think about what you said."

Then the kitchen timer rang. Jade went to the stove and removed an enormous pan of cinnamon buns. Molten caramel oozed from plump spirals of dough studded with raisins and baked to a rich golden brown.

"Wow!" I said and joined Ava and Thor in a round of applause.

Since Hunter wouldn't stay for brunch, Jade packed him a couple buns for the road — but not before she extracted his promise to return after Tammy's funeral.

"I'll ask the spirits to guide you," she said as all four of us hugged him goodbye.

Brunch was an awkward affair. Although the buns tasted wonderful, Jade's invitation to Hunter was an uninvited guest at our feast. In spite of what I'd told him, I wasn't sure how I felt about having Tammy's son as a neighbour.

"About Hunter," I said. "Even though he's Jade's second cousin, he may not be a good fit. I mean, he's a city kid —"

"So are we," Thor said. "But Hunter likes the farm. And he isn't afraid of work."

"He wants to live here," Jade said. "That's why he wanted to buy your land."

"We talked to Hunter before you got here," Ava said. "He's strong. And he knows about horses. We could get a team of Clydesdales and use them instead of a tractor and fossil fuel."

"But we don't know if he wants to move in with us," Thor said. "Maybe he'll go back to Saskatoon or Calgary."

"Either way," Ava said, "we need to make it easier to attract new people."

"Do you have anything particular in mind?" I asked.

"We like the co-op model, but it won't work if you can overthrow our decisions." Ava picked up her table knife and placed it horizontally across her plate. "Any chance you'd sell us the quarter?"

Instead of answering her question, I hedged. "Buying land's expensive."

"Thor and I can get loans from our folks. And Hunter has money."

"And if he doesn't want to join you?" I asked.

"We could manage without him."

"Zayden would help," Jade said. "He'd love to live here."

Ava and Thor answered almost in unison. "No!"

"Zayden's still confined to bed," I said, hoping to stave off conflict. "It's too soon to make decisions."

"But he's getting better —"

I quickly changed the subject. "Not that money's the big issue."

"Then what is?" Ava asked, her voice needle-sharp.

I silently counted to ten. "You need to back off. Give me time to consider your offer, okay?"

"How soon can you let us know?"

Thor touched Ava's hand. "Sweetie, let's not push our luck."

We left it at that, but I knew I'd have to make a decision soon. There was no good reason to oppose their plan. My tenants lacked experience, but Ava and Thor were bright and learned fast. And the three of them would look after the land, which was more than some prospective owners would do. Even if I sold at a price below market value, protecting the lakeshore from development would be worth the financial sacrifice. The least I could do was consider Ava's offer.

On my walk home, I thought about the last conversation I'd had with Joan. She had been adamant that we needed to find ways to encourage young people to take up farming, even if it meant creating alternatives to private farmland ownership. At the time I'd dismissed her idea as hopelessly utopian, but the last few days had made me wonder. If my land were owned by a co-operative or community trust, there'd be no need for Hunter to buy it or for me to agonize about transferring it to the next generation of farmers.

Mandi had a different idea. She'd been talking to Jade and called as I approached the sidewalk to my house.

"Co-op farms don't work," she said. "Remember what happened to Matador and all those other co-operatives the provincial government helped start for returned vets back in the forties? The last one disbanded at least a dozen years ago."

"They worked for a while," I said.

"People don't stay committed unless they own their land."

I had a sneaking sympathy for Mandi's view but chose to play devil's advocate. "We don't have enough experience with farmland co-ops to pass judgement on them."

"Folks care about what's theirs," she said.

"Maybe Hunter would join them," I said, going out on a limb. "He could help make amends for all the trouble his mother caused."

Mandi snorted. "You're joking, right? If the venture failed, you could lose your property. Are you willing to risk that?"

I hesitated, aware of the price I'd already paid to protect my farm. But times change and people age. I couldn't hang on to my parents' old homestead forever.

"Maybe it's a risk worth taking."

My sister disagreed, but we ended our conversation amicably. I was about to step onto the sidewalk when I glanced down at the ground. Someone had left tire tracks in the mud. Two sets of tracks. One coming and one going. It couldn't have been Tammy. . .

Diesel was sitting in a patch of sunlight on the front step. I ran toward my cat, clutched him to me, and climbed up to the deck.

Sitting on the mat by the back door, exactly where the dead coyote had been, was a brown cardboard box. Taped to it was a white card inscribed in a neat hand. *You won't get a sliver from this one.*

Semchuk's business card poked out from beneath the box. *Tell Massey he owes me one.*

I held my breath as I opened the box. Inside was a shiny Vietnamese hand hoe.

Suddenly, the day brightened. I laughed as I picked up the hoe and ran my hands over its smooth wooden handle. Then, unbidden, my eyes filled with tears.

"What do you think, old buddy — should I sell Thickwood Farm?"

Diesel and I had settled in chairs on the deck, he with a bowl of kibble and me with the inevitable mug of tea. I had to decide what to do with my parents' land, but he was no help. Liz had already given me her blessing. Shortly after they'd moved in, she'd suggested that I sell it to my tenants. Mandi had discounted the idea of a co-operative, but she's an obliging soul and would soon come round. That left only Tanya and Jordan with a stake in the matter.

I was about to ring Jordan when Tanya called my mobile.

"Mom, what's going on out there? Jordan just told me about your accident. And the kidnapping. Why didn't you call me?"

"I didn't want to disturb your holiday."

"We got home a couple hours ago," she said. "I'm at Jordan's now."

"Put your phone on speaker," I said. "I want to talk to both of you."

I could hear Tanya quietly telling her brother about my request. Then Jordan came on the line. "What's up?"

I told my kids about the offer to buy Thickwood Farm.

"Go for it, Mom," Jordan said.

I tried to word my question delicately. Liz had only a quarter section. What if she and Jordan became a couple, and she wanted to expand her holding? "Are you sure you won't need it some day?"

He laughed. My son's always been able to see through my efforts at diplomacy. "If I ever have occasion to want land, you're sitting on more than a thousand acres."

"Why would you want Mom's land?" Tanya asked. "You don't farm."

"Haven't you heard of career changes?"

Tanya didn't rise to the bait. "Dillon and I don't need land. You may as well sell to someone who does."

My daughter is happily ensconced with her partner in their townhouse condo half a block from the river in Saskatoon. And since she enjoys her position as office manager for a major law firm, she's not likely to consider moving to the country anytime soon.

"So, I can go ahead and do what I think best?" I debated about the wisdom of telling the kids that Hunter might be one of the purchasers, then decided they had a right to know. "Tammy's son might be one of the people who'd live there. Jade wants him to join them at Thickwood Farm."

"Jeez, Mom," Tanya said. "I mean, how would you feel living next to a man whose mother had tried to kill you?"

"That wasn't his fault," Jordan said. "Liz thinks he's a

good guy. She phoned to offer condolences after his mom died, and they had a long talk. She says he's serious about becoming a farmer."

"Since when have you been influenced by Liz?" Tanya asked. "But you're right that he's not responsible for her behaviour. If you want to sell, go ahead. Although I can't imagine why a man like him would want to live on Grams and Gramps' old place. If I had his money, I'd buy something close to Saskatoon."

I considered telling Tanya about my short-lived relationship with Derek before she heard about it from Jordan but decided not to have that conversation over the phone. It would be best for both of us if we could look each other in the eye while we talked.

"How about you and Dillon come out to the farm tomorrow? You, too, Jordan. It's been over a month since all four of us were together."

"Mom, we've just got home."

"The two of you can get a ride out with me," Jordan said. "I suspect that Mom wants to tell us about the new man in her life."

So much for my decision to postpone that conversation. "We're no longer together. But he and I parted friends."

"What new man?" Tanya asked. "Dillon and I go away for three weeks —"

"I'll tell you about him tomorrow," I said.

"You'd better. I'd hate to be gone for a month and come back to find you married."

"I liked Derek," Jordan said.

"So did I. Sometimes relationships just don't work out."

"I want to hear all about it," Tanya said. "Dillon and I have to be back in the city by ten, but that gives us plenty of time for the grisly details."

I was smiling when I got off the phone. While I've never played the role of matriarch, I enjoyed the company of my kids. Talking about my relationship with Derek would break new ground — Frank and I had never wanted to burden them with our problems. My husband, however, was dead. I needed to find new ways of relating to my family. Although the process would be challenging, we cared about each other and would get through it okay.

In the meantime, I had a decision to make. Strangely enough, it wasn't as hard as I'd anticipated. *Thickwood Farm Co-op.* The words sounded good. Taking a deep breath, I dialed Ava's number.

My parents would have been proud of me.

ACKNOWLEDGEMENTS

I live and write in Treaty 6 territory, home of the Indigenous peoples of the region and the Métis Nation of Saskatchewan. I acknowledge the people who preceded me on this specific parcel of land in the northwest part of the province:

- my parents Helen (D'Hondt) and Gaston Ternier; my uncle Lucien D'Hondt; and my grandfathers, Frank D'Hondt and Jerome Ternier
- the earlier farmers, both settler and Métis
- the Métis, Cree, and Saulteaux trappers who took part in the fur trade
- the Cree and Saulteaux hunters and gatherers who made this parkland their home

Thanks to the many wonderful people who helped make *Grounds for Murder* a reality:

Friends and family who read earlier drafts of this novel: Irene Ternier Gordon, Jim Ternier, Judy Ternier, Kathryn Green, Jan Coffey, and Vicki Obedkoff. Your comments and support have been invaluable.

Cpl. Kathryn Ternier, who answered my questions about how the RCMP works, and Wanda Drury, who gave me the lovely word "petrichor."

My husband, Doug, who provided essential technical assistance; my friend and fellow writer Liz James, who honed my Facebook skills; Meghan Nickelson, who set up my blog; and Wendy Lockman, who provided my photo for the book cover.

My kids, Jon Daniels and Jocelyn Daniels, because they're important to me, and our cat, Diesel, who appears in the novel.

The Saskatchewan Writers' Guild, which funded virtual writers in residence Gail Bowen and Marie Powell, who critiqued sections of my work, and which subsidized Gail Bowen's evaluation of an early draft of this novel.

Cat London, my substantive editor, and Laura Pastore, copy editor, whose attention to detail made this a better novel.

Jack David, co-publisher and editor; Sammy Chin, managing and production editor; Cassie Smyth, publicist and audiobooks manager; and all the other fine people at ECW Press who made this book happen. My gratitude to you is beyond measure.

Friends, including those on Facebook, who cheered me on.

Entertainment. Writing. Culture. ━━━━━━━━━━

ECW is a proudly independent, Canadian-owned book publisher. We know great writing can improve people's lives, and we're passionate about sharing original, exciting, and insightful writing across genres.

━━━━━━━━━━━━━━━━━━━ **Thanks for reading along!**

We want our books not just to sustain our imaginations, but to help construct a healthier, more just world, and so we've become a certified B Corporation, meaning we meet a high standard of social and environmental responsibility — and we're going to keep aiming higher. We believe books can drive change, but the way we make them can too.

Certified

Corporation

Being a B Corp means that the act of publishing this book should be a force for good – for the planet, for our communities, and for the people that worked to make this book. For example, everyone who worked on this book was paid at least a living wage. You can learn more at the Ontario Living Wage Network.

This book is also available as a Global Certified Accessible™ (GCA) ebook. ECW Press's ebooks are screen reader friendly and are built to meet the needs of those who are unable to read standard print due to blindness, low vision, dyslexia, or a physical disability.

FSC
www.fsc.org
MIX
Paper | Supporting
responsible forestry
FSC® C103567

This book is printed on Sustana EnviroBook™, a recycled paper, and other controlled sources that are certified by the Forest Stewardship Council®.

The National Farmers Union (nfu.ca) works for a just and sustainable food system in Canada and beyond. Some of the proceeds from the sale of this novel are slated to fund a (tentative) project to protect farmland in Saskatchewan.

ECW's office is situated on land that was the traditional territory of many nations including the Wendat, the Anishnaabeg, Haudenosaunee, Chippewa, Métis, and current treaty holders the Mississaugas of the Credit. In the 1880s, the land was developed as part of a growing community around St. Matthew's Anglican and other churches. Starting in the 1950s, our neighbourhood was transformed by immigrants fleeing the Vietnam War and Chinese Canadians dispossessed by the building of Nathan Phillips Square and the subsequent rise in real estate value in other Chinatowns. We are grateful to those who cared for the land before us and are proud to be working amidst this mix of cultures.